The Messenger

By the same Author
LODESTAR
THE GENTLEMEN'S MAFIA
DEATH VALLEY
MALICE

The Messenger

A Novel

L.M. SHAKESPEARE

HOPCYN PRESS

To Dr John Ernest Thomas

Hopcyn Press
42 Russell Rd
London W14 8HT
Tel: +44 (0) 20 7371 6488
Email: info@hopkinpress.com
www.hopkinpress.com

ISBN 978-0-9572977-9-1

Printed in Great Britain by the MPG Books Group, Bodmin and King's Lynn

Somewhere there flies
a small sweet feathered bird
that flickers like fire
in the higher
air.

And in my dreams
I think that once I heard
the song it sings
there.

Chapter One

THERE ONCE WAS A MAN who almost lived in that pigeon loft. If you follow along with your eye to where I'm pointing on the left, you can see it just before the dry stone wall that marks the end of the garden. You can hardly call it a garden, either; a strip. The bottom slope of the mountain lies beneath it, and all it consists of is that spine of land going along for about thirty yards before the point at which the loft is bedded down onto the rock.

The man built the loft himself. Nice grey boards, all well-laid. He learned his carpentry in the pits. Then, having got the loft, he started with two pairs of birds, followed by their nestlings.

Coal miners all over the country love homing pigeons. They race them with fanaticism. Since some of the most famous races start on the continent, these men knew the meteorology and geography of Europe with a knowledge deriving nothing from conventional history but which had everything to do with the needs and preferences of a homing pigeon. To the despair, perhaps, of the local teacher they grew from boys who never could remember who Napoleon was to men who knew France like the backs of their hands, but all according to the railway tracks and the collection points, and in accents made up by themselves with no reference to the French.

If you stood on the back mountain on a Sunday afternoon you would see packs of birds exercising, flying high, low, tipping this way and that way, keeping their formation and their separation, one pack from the other, until each owner called his birds back to their loft.

Like the others in the valley, this man I'm telling you about built up his team, and he was happy. He would come home from the pit, talk to his wife, have something to eat, and then out he'd go along the path to see to his pigeons, smiling to himself, looking up at the sky for other wings, and noticing everything to do with the world above ground.

Sometimes Beth, his wife, would go with him. When she was pregnant she would pick her way along that narrow path, and to a man walking in the street below who looked up, her ripening body was profiled against the rising swell of the mountain in a most beautiful way. I remember it. The wind would blow her dark and glossy hair, and she was the sort of woman who was often smiling. Skin very pale; gentle ways, but with a brightness about her.

But when her time came, she died in childbirth. It is not at all clear exactly what went wrong. The baby was very nearly strangled in the womb, and Beth herself simply died. The next day her husband came out of the house to feed the birds, looking like a man who would never speak or eat a square meal again. His skin was grey and his skull showed through his face. In the succeeding weeks he kept the pigeons alive, although he gave them food with a hand so starved of happiness it could have choked them. And behind him somewhere in the house his sister Betty looked after the child. They called her Bethan, after her mother.

As if unwilling to enter the world fully under the circumstances, the baby had lost, or abandoned, part of her human inheritance during that struggle to be born. Her brain had been starved of oxygen. The medical profession call it MBD—Minimal Brain Dysfunction—but it was hard for a lay person to see what was minimal about it. The child was very late to walk, and then hardly ever talking, and too dull for school; but the one thing she could do was to follow her father about everywhere. In a way that was apparently typical of the characteristics of her condition, she attached herself to one focal point in her environment, and this was her father and everything to do with him, and him only. Other people she scarcely noticed, and often would be unable to hear if they spoke to her. But everything her father said and did, and everything to do with his care of the birds absorbed her. She was devoted to him, and she loved the birds.

You would see her father go down the path, and as soon as she was old enough to walk by herself there she'd be just behind him. He was a fine looking man, but he never married anyone else. He just let his sister keep house for him. His name was Dan Pugh.

Chapter Two

WHEN BETHAN WAS NEARLY FIFTEEN this routine was still much the same as it had been when she was five. When her father came back from the pit and had had his tea, she would follow him down the garden path to the loft, and when they reached it, Dan would go in first and Bethan after.

"Close the door, there's a good girl," he'd say. And she'd close it. She always waited until she heard those words. She would stand there, her mouth hanging very slightly open with concentration, her eyes as big as saucers and her hand on the latch. As soon as her father told her to close the door, she would turn her body right round, putting both hands to the work of very carefully pressing down the latchet and then releasing the fastening exactly into place. Behind her the birds rustled in the boxes. They responded to a visit like grass to the wind. They turned their heads from side to side. A pair blew down onto the floor of the loft snapping wide their wings, one two. They made their small soft noises. Powdered minerals, grain husks and straw scented the air.

"Now then." From a crouched position, pouring out feed and not looking up, Dan spoke to his girl. "Have you got the ring ready, Bethan?"

Pugh could stay sitting on his heels for a long time without feeling any strain because although he was unusually tall for a

Welsh miner they all learned from a young age to adopt that position when working at the coal face underground. Perhaps his ancestry was not from Iberia but—as the school master was always saying, getting out his copy of Geoffrey of Monmouth's *Chronicles of the Kings of Britain* and pointing to the page—from vanquished Troy. That would account for the tall frame, the black hair, the pale skin of Welshmen like Dan Pugh.

"Bethan?" he said again. He was getting to the last of the feed tubs. One of them had PUSSY written on it. He looked up sideways before straightening his back. She was standing with her hand already out, the red registration ring already in her palm.

"Good girl," he said. He put down the grain and stood up. "Wait there."

She remained exactly where she was. Dan reached into a nest, and from the side of the unprotesting mother bird he lifted a four day old chick. He took the claw in his hand, bunching it together and folding back the thumb.

"Now, Bethan." The girl made a little sound in the back of her throat. She moved the ring intently through the air with something of the concentrated deliberation of a conjuror, lined it up carefully with the end of the little bird's claw and slipped it along onto the leg.

"Good girl!" her father said again. "You know exactly how to do that now, Bethan. There are grown men in the valley who couldn't do it half as well."

Her face shone with joy at his words. Dan was busy putting the bird back into the nest and didn't look at her. He was reciting a familiar litany to Bethan as he worked, saying how that ring would be on the pigeon's leg now until it died; that it would be there when the bird soared up in the clouds, and flew over the mountains and perhaps the sea. Bethan listened with the spell-bound charm of a child listening to nursery rhymes. When her father turned back he took a deep breath, smiling and rubbing the palms of his hands together.

"Water next."

The girl turned and walked softly towards the door.

"Open it," he said.

He could see that she knew the next move before he spoke, and sometimes he longed for her to make that leap, and perform the next action with spontaneous independence like other people. But she probably never would. And of course, if someone else spoke to her she didn't seem even to hear what they said. With him at least, she never missed a word. She only waited until it was spoken and then she would do exactly what he asked of her. If he was in the house and he said, "Fetch me my shoes, Bethan, there's a good girl," she'd be off straight. She'd come back and put them on the floor in front of him very carefully, side by side. Then she would wait again. He'd run out of things to tell her to do. A little crease of humour would show at the corner of his eye.

It happened yesterday evening his sister's voice called from the kitchen. "Bethan. You can come here and peel these potatoes." The girl didn't move. You would swear she hadn't heard a thing. Dan looked at her. He raised his eyebrows. "Did you hear Aunty Betty?" Bethan turned her head a little, her eyes wide and enquiring still fixed on her father.

She didn't look like her mother at all. Her hair wasn't even dark, but a dull blond that hung straight and heavy to just above her shoulders, with a frizzy thickness to it. Her skin was opaque; a sort of corn colour. She had the same hazel eyes as her mother, and they were huge, but clouded where the stream of intelligence had been muddied up.

"Bethan!" Betty appeared in the door. "Did you hear me now?"

"Aunty Betty wants you to peel the potatoes," Dan said in a quiet voice, with a little raising of his brows again, and a slight nod towards the kitchen. Bethan turned at once then, quite content, and lumbered off after her aunt.

Chapter Three

WHEN BETHAN WAS FIFTEEN, DAN bought a twelve month old bird from John Strachan for her birthday. At that time, in order to conform to the law she still attended school for half the day, but would spend most of the time in the playground by herself. The teachers were very good, and if it started to rain they remembered to come out with an umbrella, and entice her with sweets to come indoors. On the few occasions when her father had been able to stay with her it was possible to integrate her into the school activities to some extent. She would be given books to hand out, and would sit, apparently attentive, in a chair. But as soon as Dan was gone she seemed to lose her ability to see or hear anyone.

Not that she was unhappy. She merely drifted apart. At the end of the day Betty had to fetch her, and she would then follow her aunt home. They had achieved that much.

Bethan's birthday was in October. When the sun came out it cascaded down, the colour of rusty water out of an old tap. The bracken had turned brown on the mountains, both in front of and behind the house. The one in front was a bare mountain without trees. Its entire charm lay in the washes of colour or cloud shadow that poured over it. It had streaks of purple heather, patches of russet gold or green from the bracken, and rock sticking out like rounded bones. But the mountain behind had paths and shale; it had rowan trees with scarlet berries, and sheep who cropped the turf and clacked with their hooves against the stones. It had thorn trees and the ruins of some cottages, and a delicious little stream that tumbled over stones and moss. Most people liked the back mountain best.

On Bethan's birthday her aunt was kind to her. She remembered Beth and the suffering that poor woman had. She had got on very well with her sister-in-law, and Betty didn't get on well with everyone. "Oh, it was terrible," she'd say to her friends when they talked about what had happened, taking off her glasses and wiping them as if there were tears on the lens. "Terrible. And all for what?"

So when she fetched the culprit from school on that particular day of her birthday she talked to her more kindly and told her that she had baked a cake, with icing and candles. The child would always respond to the mention of any form of sweets. If her father was absent, it was the only way to communicate with her.

On this day Dan was on the morning shift, and so already back from work and waiting in the kitchen when they got back. After the cake and the candles, he said, "Now I've got a present for you, Bethan, but it's down the garden." He went out of the back door and she followed him. There was a bench just by the loft that Dan had made to sit on when waiting for the birds to fly in after their exercise. The birds were exercised nearly every day. That's why you'd see them if you went up either mountain and looked down on the village during about half an hour after the day shift was over. Various teams of pigeons would be flying together, wheeling over the rooftops in their loose packs, changing colour as the blade of the formation tipped on the turn and every bird caught the light for an instant under its wing. The men could recognise each others' birds from a phenomenal distance.

While their birds were out in this way, Dan and Bethan would clean the loft and the boxes and do anything else that had to be done; and then they would sit together on the bench and watch them in the sky. When they were almost ready to come back to the loft, the male birds banged and clapped their wings in flight—a noise caused by the wing tips meeting over the shoulder.

This afternoon of Bethan's birthday, when Dan and Bethan got to the end of the garden there was a box waiting on the bench. It was quite a plain cardboard box, with holes in it, but it had a bright red ribbon tied around and knotted with a bow.

"It's your birthday today, isn't it Bethan," Dan repeated. "This is your birthday present. Open it, Bethan," Dan said. "No. Wait a minute. We must take it into the loft first." He let her carry it, and they went into the shed. There was plenty of light from the wire mesh flap opening of the side wall through which the birds flew out when it was hooked up. "I'll hold it for you," he said, taking the box "Look now." He showed her how to pull the end of the ribbon, and when it fell away he held the box firmly while saying to her, "Lift the lid now. That's right. Lift it up."

She bent forwards. Sitting in the box on a layer of straw, was a beautiful pale grey hen bird, with a scattering of white across the top of the head and down the back, and check white flights against a blue bar. Quite unafraid at finding the box open and the large pale face of the child hanging over her, the bird cocked her head, and looked about her first with one eye and then the other. Her eyes were caramel coloured, and as bright as jewels.

"Pick her up," Dan said gently. "You know how to do it, Bethan. Take her out of the box. She is your bird." The child, breathing almost as heavily as a cow in a field of parsley, put her spread hands on either side of the bird in the box. The hard and soft structure, the mixture of silken feathers and the baskety resistant quills, held firm against the grip of her fingers. Although her hands were small she could lift the unprotesting bird out, and held her correctly so that the little legs poked out between her fingers, and the creature was secure.

Dan's own breath was quite taken away. Look at her! A sort of effulgence had spread over the child's face, and she simply stood holding the bird as it moved its little head this way and that and made gestures of settlings, and stirrings of contentment.

"What will you call her?" Dan said. The girl didn't answer, and he coughed to clear his throat, waiting. "She'll have to have a name."

There was a long silence. He could count the number of times Bethan had ever spoken. She might not speak now, in which case he would use the bird's registered name of Abercwm Flyer. But eventually Bethan lifted her glowing face and said, "Birthday."

"Birthday?" he repeated, with some surprise. "You mean you want her to be called Birthday?" Bethan gazed at him as if she was hearing celestial music. There was no doubt about it at all.

"Well," the man said. He lifted his eye brows in that way he had when he was amused, while a suppressed laugh pinched the outside corner of his eye. "Birthday it is then. Welcome to the loft, Birthday."

The young bird was put in a perch that Dan had prepared. He had already decided on a mate for her. They had a cock bird called Black Rill, with dark checkered feathers and a very strong eye. He put this bird together with Birthday in the vacant compartment among all the others. At that point all but four of the boxes built against the wall were full.

"Shall we enter Birthday for her first race in the new season, Bethan? In April?"

He talked continually when he was with Bethan, like someone carrying on both sides of a conversation. Like the Minister in chapel with God. You never could be sure, after all, how much Bethan might be able to understand. The girl couldn't ask questions like other children. One could not tell what she might be wanting to know. So he kept up a running commentary of information, stories, and general remarks. Betty might criticise him. "You're like an old woman who talks non-stop to her cats," she said more than once. "And that one doesn't understand a thing." All right then; he didn't mind. Let his sister say what she liked, but he carried on as before.

"Birthday is twelve months old now," he continued on this occasion to Bethan. "Still got a little bit of down on her head, but did you look under her wing? No. Well, look now." He picked the bird up again and spread the pinions wide. "Look under there. Beautifully full feathered. She'll be ready to race by the beginning of the season if we can time her chicks just right. Now she'll have to go in a cage on the roof for two or three days so that she can see around her and get her bearings before we let her out to fly. And then, what with the new mate and being more familiar with where she is, she will lose her inclination to fly back to her old loft."

He was fetching a small wire cage as he spoke, and then holding it for Bethan to put the bird in. "Once she's out there in the cage, you'll see her turn her head this way and that. She will notice where the sun rises and sets. She'll look over towards the end of the valley, where your friend Mrs Isaacs teaches at the infant school, and the stream where you used to sit with your feet in the water when you were a little girl. And she will look on the other side. She'll see the Price's farm and the back mountain. She'll get to know where she is."

He fetched the short ladder and put the cage on the roof, latched down on the edges with a sliding catch, before letting the other birds out for exercise. Then out they came, flying straight up into a loose pack, circling the loft a few times before widening the trajectory of their flight. Dan stared into the sky until his eyes watered. "I think they're going to fly down to Weeks's farm," he said. "Yes, there they go." And away the birds went.

Dan and Bethan cleaned the loft. The shadows lengthened. They sat down on the bench Dan had made, waiting for the other birds to return, listening to voices calling just below in the street, the bus going by, Jenkin's dog barking.

"What is Birthday doing, Bethan?" She got up to look. Birthday was perched inside the wire, peering out this way and that with her little bright eyes.

"She's doing the same as we are," Dan said. "Noticing what's going on." He was silent for a moment, and then he said, "We must watch out for cats. Miss Thomas kept three of the last batch of kittens, and the ginger tom from the other side of the chapel is back."

Eventually a scattering of bird shadows flowed over the two of them once more where they sat. The pack wheeled nearer home and swung away again; wheeled and swung. A cooler wind—the forerunner of darkness—sent a chilly shadow across the rough grass. The spinach in Betty's little garden patch had almost had it. It was time for Dan to go to the pub. He felt ready for soft light and the smell of beer and the company of other men. And as the thought came into his head, almost on cue the first pigeon folded its wings back like a falcon, and disappeared in a steep dive through the open flap of the loft. One by one, in a race, the others followed, cascading down. Dan got to his feet. He gave Bethan the grain tin and she shuffled it softly. Four birds had landed on the grass and shifted tantalisingly about; even spread their wings and did another little curvette over the loft roof. Dan shook his head. "Remember what I said, Bethan? There are only two places for a pigeon to be: in the sky or in the loft."

He took a whistle out of his pocket and blew on it softly; a sound that was comforting, somewhat wild and triste; a sound calculated to appeal to birds. The procrastinators allowed themselves to be driven like chickens into the loft, followed by the man pocketing his whistle and the child with the grain tin. They closed the doors.

"One more job to do," Dan said. "We must fetch Birthday down and put her into her box with her new mate for the night."

He took down the wire cage, and he and Bethan carried it inside the loft and transferred Birthday into her perch. There was a shallow bowl ready for nesting. From among the birds now slackening their attention to the feed on the loft floor, Dan picked up the cock bird he had selected for Birthday's mate, and put him in the adjoining box. Almost immediately the cock started crooning deep in his throat.

By the time that Dan and Bethan had closed the loft door and were walking away towards their house the cock bird started to brush with his tail and drop his wings in front of the hen. And outside, the night, just as predictably, first wooed, and then settled onto, the earth.

Chapter Four

THE FOLLOWING MORNING WAS, FOR some people, a day like any other. Betty, for example. She kept everything very clean and tidy, and had quite enough to do. "We've got the Welfare calling today," she announced, "and if Bethan behaves like she did last time, I'm not answerable for the consequences."

Dan looked at his sister from the chair in which he was reading the paper. She was collecting the dishes off the table. She had perfect skin, which Time had as yet only rendered slightly leathery. On important occasions she painted her lips with a colour called Mayfair, which was always in stock in the chemist's. Her brother noticed that she had got it on this morning.

"But I'm on night shift from today," he said.

"It's nothing to do with me," she rather snapped back. "I don't ask them to come, do I? For all the use they are they could stay away and not waste my time. As I've said before, I can't see why it's any business of theirs if Bethan is – like she is." Betty would have said 'twp' if she hadn't been talking to Dan, being the local word for stupid, but she knew better than to use it to him. "We look after her, not them. They don't do anything to help. Nothing at all. She's never ill anyway, but when I wanted to go with the choir to Llanebry would they send a woman to look after Bethan for two days? No fear! It was Margaret had to come in. And Margaret wanted paying because of Billy's music lessons. Move your feet Dan. So I think it's an absolute cheek that they think they can just announce that they are coming today and I have got to make arrangements to suit them."

"I'm sorry if it's awkward, Betty."

"Well it isn't. But it might have been. And look what happened last time!"

"It wasn't Bethan who caused the trouble Betty. It was that Welfare Officer from Cardiff. When are they coming anyway?"

"At three."

"But I've got to clock in at five to two for my shift." Dan protested, looking worried. "I'd better go and speak to Bethan. I sent her down to the loft with the grain."

He got up and went into the garden. He could see Bethan as soon as he was out of the back door. She was looking in at the birds through the wire mesh. He ran his hand through his hair in a gesture both weary and amused. He started up the path.

When Bethan saw her father, she came running towards him. There was a lack of coordination in the way that her ankles and feet moved. Her body got thrown forwards and now that she was almost grown up a smaller man might have felt quite intimidated by her. She stopped short, and Dan could definitely see something new shining behind the habitual slackness of her solemn face. He hadn't thought that it would make quite such a difference, when he decided to give the bird to her, but now he realised that he was looking at a girl who Owned Her Own Pigeon. He gave a short laugh and put his arm around her shoulder.

"How's Birthday today, Bethan?"

She smiled. He couldn't see it because she kept her face

down, her neck hanging.

"You know I'm on night shift for the next four days, so Fred will have to come and exercise the birds. But we'll put Birthday on the roof in her cage again now, and you and Fred will have to bring her in after the exercise."

They had reached the loft and went in.

"Look. Birthday's mate has already put some straw in the nest." Clean wisps were laid neatly across the bowl, and Birthday was sitting on them. Bethan reached up and put one of her little hands on the bird's shoulder. The cock was on his feet, but Birthday didn't move.

"Work to do. Here's the scraper," Dan said. She responded at once, as always, to her father.

"You do the floor, Bethan."

Down she went.

He swept the droppings into the pan, replenished the water tubs and the feeders. Outside, they went together over to Betty's garden patch and scattered the contents of the bucket over the soil. He gave Bethan the rake for her to scratch it in, and started on the subject of the Welfare Visitor.

"Betty tells me that the Welfare Visitor is coming again today."

Pause. He did not expect any response, but he knew that she was listening. She continued, in that clumsy, but always, in the end, quite exact way to rake the soil.

"On one occasion you didn't like the Welfare Visitor, Bethan. Do you remember when that was?"

The rake suddenly stopped.

"I'd have preferred to be here to help you this time, but I'm on night shift. Like I told you, I've got to clock in at two today. So now, will you be a specially good girl. I know the Welfare Visitor who will call today. He is a friend of mine, you see. A friend of Dad's. Not like the other one. So you don't have to be afraid of him. I'll be home later and nothing can happen to you."

He waited a minute, and decided to repeat it one more time.

"Be a good girl for the Welfare Visitor and he'll go away nice and tidy. Now rake that little patch there, and that will do."

The memory of that previous visit played itself through in Dan's mind when he set out in his work clothes at two o'clock, his great boots firm on the slag encrusted path that led from the other side of the road to the pit head. He only had Betty's word for the opening scene; her at the door, and this young fellow with a briefcase. In those days they sent them by bus, and he had just walked down from the Shepherd's Arms. Dan had returned when the Welfare Officer had finished what he called his examination and was just pronouncing on what he intended to recommend by way of a future for Bethan. After Dan had hit him, his lips swelled up and he could no longer pronounce words like "mandatory" and "care."

The Doctor had had to be called. He and Dan between them laid the man on the kitchen table rather than let his blood get on the chairs.

"What a dreadful lot of trouble you've caused, Mr Perks!" Dr Thomas said, dressing the Welfare Visitor's mouth. "Don't try to move your lips now. If you try to say it wasn't your fault I'll have to do the stitches over again. Keep the dressing still. And you should know better than to disturb a patient with Minimal Brain Dysfunction. Didn't you read her notes before coming here? She is very docile; a typical passive example of MBD. I presume you have read your text book: defects in orientation and memory; day dreaming; insufficient motivation in pursuing goals such as household tasks and school work, and a tendency to become very attached to just one person. In Bethan's case that person is her father. And if it's therapy which in your wisdom you were thinking of bestowing on her by separating her from him, you must be mad. And if you threaten a devoted father with taking his child away you deserve all you get. So now, don't go back and complain to your superiors about being hit, or I'll see to it personally that you get the sack. It won't be difficult. You've made such a mess of things here that I'll only have to tell the truth. Don't move now."

Then Dr Thomas had turned to Dan and said, "Let me see your hand."

Dan held it out, and the Doctor took it in his own very delicate fingers, and felt along the metatarsals, and the rough hewn skin that had all day been wielding tools under ground. He cleaned the grazes on the knuckle bones, and dabbed on some antiseptic.

Meanwhile the Welfare Officer groaned because on top of everything else he had tripped backwards and chipped his coccyx on the fender.

"You fell down the outside steps because you put your foot on a cracked stone," the Doctor told him severely. "Now I'll drive you back to your office in my own car. You'll be able to stand once we get you upright."

And that was the end of the matter.

The Welfare had continued to send people regularly since then, but no more ambitious young men with theories about Care. The ones arriving today—to whom Betty now opened the door—were straight forward pleasant individuals. The man was in his twenties, and accompanied by a young girl who belonged to the office in the same way as the chairs did, and the tea-making machine. She was useful and had her place. They sat in Betty's kitchen for twenty minutes until Bethan, who was keeping a look out for Fred, dived suddenly out into the garden by the back door.

She went without even saying thank you to the young

woman for giving her a present. For, surprisingly enough, this Welfare worker had a sister of her own with the same disability as Bethan. That very day she happened to have bought a hair slide with a bunch of red lacquered cherries stuck on the bar, intending to give it to her sister. But seeing Bethan, she decided to give it to her, and buy another tomorrow. Aunty Betty had put it in the child's hair, although to her mind the cherries were rather ridiculously big. It was there now as Bethan stumped down the path towards the loft and Fred, seeing her, turned in his tracks and said, "Hello, girl. How are you today then? That's a pretty hair slide you've got."

They went together into the loft. He held the door open for her to go in, and closed it after her.

"Right now, We've to put – Birthday, is it? I've heard all about Birthday. Is she already in the wire cage on the roof? I forgot to look." He opened the door and peered up. "Ah! Right you are. I see her."

He went out, climbed up the ladder and replenished Birthday's feed and water in the little cage. Then he came down again and propped open the wire mesh side of the loft to let the other birds out for exercise. They flew away. Then Fred and Bethan together worked away in the empty loft until all the jobs were done.

"I'm off down to the shop a minute," Fred called over his shoulder to Bethan once they'd finished. "I'll be back before the birds return."

Bethan sat down on the bench, her eyes fixed on the little wire cage on the roof. Birthday was shifting about, looking here and looking there. Over the dry stone wall that backed onto the next garden the ginger tomcat sprung down clear of the brambles and lay crouched in the grass, also watching the bird. The children were out of school. The buses came and went.

Bethan got up and wandered back towards where Betty had her washing line. A group of boys aged about eleven were playing on the open piece of ground by the side of the shop. She watched them, while behind her the catch of Birthday's cage, which Fred had only partly put back in place, worked its way loose, and the bird fed from the grain tin attached to the wires. When at last the door swung open Birthday, with a soft alertness, jerked her little head to one side and looked out. For a moment she settled again. But when a gust of wind blew by, she advanced to the edge of the cage.

The tomcat, who had been watching the caged bird from the very beginning, slid round to the front of the shed and crouched beside the soil bucket. He had his eyes glued to Birthday as if there was an invisible pathway between himself and the delicious bird, extruded from his very soul.

The pigeon stepped onto the roof of the loft. She gripped the roofing felt with her neat claws. The cat could see the red brown tag of her registration ring around one leg, and every other minutest morsel of detail. The bones under his fur slithered into a new alignment that provided more torque from which to spring.

It was a beautiful afternoon as far as the weather went. Fred was remarking on it as he placed a small bet in the shop down the hill. "I must be getting back," he said. "Dan's birds to see to."

"How's the girl?"

"Oh, she's the same as ever."

Birthday flew down onto the bench. Bethan heard the loud snap of her wings. She turned around at the very moment when the cat, having coiled his inner spring to such a pitch, launched himself from the ground. In slow motion Bethan saw him rise in a murderous curve. But before the sound that had started up in her throat had had time to break through, something hit the cat in mid air. It was something small that struck him hard near the eye. He collapsed. The weight of his own body brought him crashing down within inches of the pigeon, who clattered her wings, but moved not very far away.

A terrified wailing sound came out of Bethan's mouth. The pigeon nervously stirred. And then a small boy, looking very pleased with himself, strutted into the garden swinging a catapult in the direction of the unconscious cat lying sprawled in the grass.

"Never mind, Bethan. Don't cry. I got him in the nick of time. He didn't do any harm. I got him with my catapult, see?" He swung it again by the thick elastic thong.

"It's a pity that you don't often talk, Bethan, because I would very much like you to be able to tell John Daniels and the others what I just did there.They might not believe me."

He swaggered right up to the cat. It was not dead; but having said that, it was going to be a long time before it felt well again.

"That's what a catapult's for, you see," he said, showing it to Bethan. "CAT a pult. For shooting cats."

At that moment, Birthday flew up into the air. Rigid from head to foot, Bethan watched to see if she would fly away. The whole wide world was around Birthday. Between that vast expanse and herself not one single bar or mesh of wire existed. Above, the massive dome of the sky was clear with only a few clouds put there as if on purpose to make more clear the alluring perspective of space. A light breeze ruffled the grass. The bird moved her head, and blinked one eye. A child called in play from way up towards the end of the valley. A distant motor went past the far end of Fforchaman road. One clawed foot stepped forward and then stopped. Birthday opened her wings, and then suddenly she was up, giving the small boy Emrys the impression of air and feathers all mixed as if they burst out from an exploding pack of cards. He expected her to be off. He could already hear himself; "She'll only have gone to her old loft won't she, Mr Pugh; you heard that, Bethan, don't cry, we'll go and fetch her home, won't we Mr Pugh. Look, the cat could have eaten her and then there would have been something to cry about. I've seen them do that, they get the blood and feathers everywhere, when I'm grown up I'm not going to have a cat near my house, if my wife likes cats she'll have to go back to her mother I mean it Mr Pugh..." But before he needed to even open his mouth, Birthday had dropped down to where those brightly lacquered cherries shone in the sun, and landed on Bethan's head.

That was how Fred found them when he returned; the boy bragging and swinging his catapult, the Tom cat still unconscious in the grass, and the pigeon sitting on the girl's head.

Chapter Five

"WE WERE LUCKY THAT TIME, Bethan," Dan said when he heard about this incident. "Lucky that Em was nearby, and lucky that Birthday didn't fly away. That shows that she has a good, stable temperament. And that she likes her new mate, and the loft. And your new hair slide."

He said this last in the characteristically solemn tone with which he was accustomed to overlay a private joke when speaking to Bethan; a tone that had crept more and more into his conversations with her as the longing for her mother receded from him.

"But we mustn't take any more risks. We must wait until Birthday has laid her first pair of eggs before we let her out with the pack for exercise. She'll come back then for sure."

In the meantime the racing season being over and Winter approaching, Dan spent more hours in the pub. It was not that he neglected Bethan, but he liked the company of other men. Fred Potts was his particular friend, but he had many others, including Owen, the father of the boy with the catapult. Dan bought him a pint by way of thanks.

"Emrys is too young to drink it," Owen said, holding the glass tankard up to the light. "So I'll drink it for him!" But he gave Em sixpence when he got home.

"And there's no point taking offence on behalf of the cat. Men who are fond of birds can't stand them, and that's the end of it. Did I ever tell you about my uncle's linnet? Ah well, that's lucky, because everyone up in Porth Nant has heard it a dozen times but I'd forgotten until my sister reminded me yesterday."

He turned to the counter and put some money on it.

"Another round, Gwyn." And turning back again, "It was like this, you see. My uncle met a man when he was away from home who kept a linnet in a little cage. This man would go into his local pub and put the cage down on the table, whereupon the bird would begin to sing. And it would sing and sing, to the wonder and delight of everybody. If it was here between us now it would be doing it." And he pointed at the grooved sinews of the table top like a man amazed. "My uncle became so enchanted with the bird he wanted to buy it, but the man wouldn't sell. All the same, he couldn't stand the amount of pestering he got from my uncle, and in the end he gave in. So from then onward my uncle had it.

"He took it everywhere with him then. He was never without it. No sooner would he come back from work than he'd up with the linnet, and take it down to the pub. Like the other man he put the cage on the table and off it would go. Singing, singing, singing.

"Then the war came. The war to end all wars. Let this fellow Hitler just remember that! My uncle had to go off and fight and he couldn't take the linnet with him. 'Look after it for me, Dad,' he said. 'Be sure to look after my linnet and see that it always has food and water.'

"Half way through the war he came back on leave, and the first thing he did when he walked into the house was to say to his mother, "Where's the linnet?" She looked very awkward, and said, "Oh, your father's down in he pub." So off went my uncle and found his father sitting with his mates, but no linnet.

"Where's my linnet?" he said. And then he heard the terrible story. His father had left the cage on the kitchen table and the cat had managed to open the latch, and killed it.

"My uncle went home without another word. He stoked up the kitchen fire until the oven beside it was blazing hot. Then he opened the cast iron door, threw in the cat, and walked straight out of the house back to his regiment. And he was killed in 1917, so he never returned."

There was a chorus of protest at the end of the story, and Owen drank his beer like an actor indulgent to the shouts of an audience who would be throwing a few rotten tomatoes next and he didn't care. But it happened that on this particular evening the schoolmaster was making one of his rare visits to the Shepherd's Arms to play chess with Jack Servini in the corner, and as he passed by he picked up the tag end of the story. So he stopped and asked, "Would you say, from the cat's point of view, that, apart from the way he died, it was right for him to die at all?"

Owen was a bit flummoxed. Willing to answer the question but guessing there was a catch in it, he said, "Well, the cat's got to die sometime."

"Ah!"

Olave Richards was a popular man. As school master of the valley school, he was far too clever for his job, but curiously content nevertheless to spend his daylight hours teaching horrid little boys like Emrys Morgan, and his evenings with literature and philosophy; not to overlook that lovely woman, Iris, his wife. He sat down now on a chair that he hooked under him from the next table. The large wooden room got its light partly from the blazing coal fire in the grate. But just at that late moment, after a dark and rainy day, a burst of rich evening sunlight cast in at the window a few bars of gold.

"About the cat," he said. "Bearing in mind what we happen

to know about Owen's uncle – that he was angry and punishing the cat – what we have here is just an animal whose life on earth is terminated by a higher power. Now what does that remind you of?"

"I don't know, Mr Richards."

"God." He held up an admonitory finger as he said it. "Doesn't it remind you of God and Us?"

"Are you coming to play over here or not, Olave?" interrupted Servini shouting from the corner.

"In a minute. I'll be with you now." And, to the bar man, "Gwyn, give my friend a drink."

The smell of cider as well as beer hung in the air. A sudden gust of wind outside produced some shouts from the street and the clatter of bottles falling over.

"Carry on, Mr Richards," Owen said.

"Well then. I think that our human fate is similar to the cat's. We let superficial details delude us into thinking otherwise, but like the cat, we are born without having the faintest idea why or where from. Then we live for a while believing all the time that somewhere or other is a Being stronger than ourselves, who will come and shut us up in the oven whenever he feels like it!"

The men didn't know whether to laugh or carry on listening respectfully.

"All right," Olave said, making a concession. "Not an oven. We make a more respectable business of it with our graves and funerals. But where's the real difference between a cat who is suddenly killed for doing what is in his nature to do, and we, who whether we err or not will have our lives taken from us in the end, and in a manner that is just as arbitrary. We don't need a war to do it. They say Hitler's going to make us fight again. But whether he does or not it all comes to the same thing in the end."

Fred went discreetly off round the back to relieve himself. "I think he's been drinking," he muttered to the bar man as he passed by. He meant, of course, the other sort of drinking, that he went in for himself at times, but not today. There was a sort of drinking that left him legless, whereas perhaps in Mr Richard's case, an overindulgence in alcohol would attack a different part of the anatomy. When you thought of it, drink could be seen to have the tendency to take away from a person whatever was his most precious quality; the strong man his strength, the intellectual his reason, the beauty her serene and unlined face. Another time, in appropriate company, he would point this out, but for now Fred merely made his way to the lavatory, from whence he could hear the brass band practising in the basement.

In his absence the school master delivered the crux of the argument. "What do we call a living creature that does not have the right to decide for itself its own comings and goings? Answer? Either a pet, or a slave." The statement went down on the table between them with the same snap of precision as a glass of beer. Olave looked from face to face. "We like to think we are God's pets, rather than His slaves, but if I had any choice I'd refuse to be either. I object; very strongly. It's not right. Civilised countries have come to realise that slavery is wrong, and among ourselves we don't allow it. And what's more, if I took a man as far as Swansea on the same terms as we are parcelled off here and there by death, or what we call divine will – not telling that man, as a dying man is not told, where he was going, nor allowing him to communicate with his loved ones when he got there any more than our dear departed are allowed by God to contact us – I'd be prosecuted. We apply a stricter morality to what we do to each other than we do to the actions of Providence. By a long chalk. So never mind the cat. Just you remember that God will take you all, in your time, and sometimes the process is as nasty as an oven and the destination is certainly a damn sight further than Swansea."

After a moment's silence, Dan said, "Well, there it is, isn't it. What can we do about it?"

"Ah!" Olave had been about to leave well alone, but now he spoke again, so that they all looked back apprehensively at the swarthy folds of skin around his mouth, and the glitter of his eye. "What does a man do when he finds himself enslaved, or imprisoned? He fights! He doesn't say, 'Oh, this is where I'm meant to be.' He says, 'I must be free!'"

"But it's different when it's God's will."

"No, it isn't!" the school master insisted. "Someone's told you that, to stop you fighting for your freedom. Fight, I say. Not with the fists, but with the mind." He suddenly noticed his watch. If he didn't get on with it he wouldn't have time for a game with Servini.

"I must leave you," he said. He smiled that very charming smile of his. He got up in a way that a drunk could never possibly have managed. He crossed over the room and sat down opposite Servini.

Chapter Six

ALSO AT THIS TIME, AND because of the incident of Birthday and the cat, Bethan found that she had acquired her first childhood friend. She had never had a friend before, but now Emrys, intoxicated with his own marksmanship and the way in which he had saved Birthday, began to hang around the loft in every spare minute, but especially during the time when the birds were out being exercised. He would strut down the path swinging his catapult, having jumped over the wall, or come round the house bent double so that Betty shouldn't see him through the windows.

He invariably had a very tattered appearance. It wasn't that his mother didn't care for him, but he was the sort of boy who was bound to catch his trousers on a nail or a piece of barbed wire if there was any about. He had dark hair like his mother, but it grew in amazing directions. He had one sister who was old enough to work in Servini's. She complained that her brother had made her life a misery asking for free ice creams after school ever since she got her job. But Em's new mission, as cat patrol for the Pugh's pigeon loft, now took up all his spare time, and his sister was getting some peace.

"Hello Bethan," he'd call, as soon as he got round from the dairy where his mother was too busy with the churns and Owen and the cows to make sure that he did his homework before going out again. And as soon as he caught sight of Bethan, "I've come to make sure everything's all right." Or if Bethan was absent, he would employ his time practising with the catapult, shooting stones at targets that he rigged up on the lid of the bucket. When, as invariably happened, Bethan reappeared, he'd turn round and grin at her, swinging the leather thong.

He thought she was pretty. A precocious eleven year old can admire a girl of fifteen, and what he noticed was her pale thick hair and huge eyes. He was the first male person who ever observed in that way, how the light would catch on the heavy fringe of her eye lashes, or marvel at the clean pale glimmer of her neck.

He didn't care at all that she didn't answer him. He was used to it.

"Yer! Did you see that?" He'd swing round to catch her reaction to some feat of marksmanship accompanied by a resounding clatter from the metal bin. "Do you notice, Bethan, how the cats don't come here any more? That's because they daren't come near me! They walk a mile out of their way rather than cross by here now. The village is full of cats limping with exhaustion."

The first time Dan was back on the day shift after the cat incident, the boy was already in the garden when Bethan came down the garden path behind her father. Em stood his ground.

"Hello, Mr Pugh."

"Emrys. How are you?"

"Just been keeping an eye on things," he replied. He tried a swagger but it came off a bit lame, like the performance of a clown whose shoe laces have been tied together by accident instead of on purpose. But Pugh responded with dignity.

"Very good of you, Em," he said. "Bethan and I appreciate it."

The boy cheered up at once, and at that very moment one of the Tabbys from the Jenkins's garden appearing for an instant on the wall, he let off a stone and got it smack in the ribs. From then onwards Em continued to go over to the Pugh's loft almost every day after school. It became the accepted routine. He was very talkative, and this seemed to be quite a pleasant change for the father of a child who never spoke at all. Emrys asked endless question and Dan, in his patient way, would answer as he worked at cleaning the boxes, or when all three of them sat on the bench.

Em helped with all the chores, and as he worked he rattled on about everything, from the tortures of arithmetic to his sister's boy friends. Sometimes Dan stood outside the loft looking at the sky, dragging his fingers over the skin of his jaw. If he didn't like the look of the weather, but thought it would hold long enough, he let the birds out for exercise with an eye to the wind, and the cloud formations. He also looked for hawks. A man up the top of the valley had lost a prize bird not so long ago.

As the year wore on it would begin to rain more often while they were waiting for the birds to fly home. Big slate grey spots of water dropping onto the stones and the last green leaves of Betty's harvest in the vegetable patch. At any minute it could turn to a deluge. And when the wind came and whistled that mean sound in the north, he worried about how it might blow the birds off course.

"Bethan!" Betty's voice could be heard thin and sharp from the back door. "Send that girl in, Dan. It's raining." And perhaps at that moment the pack would wheel over from the further end of the valley, slicing through the rain with staunch wings. Their bright eyes would be protected with the seven eyelids of the pigeon, each one a thin film that can be dropped down to protect the eye, and maintain visibility in bad weather.

What infinite satisfaction the man felt when, with his odd little companions, he watched the returning pigeons cascade in through the open side of the loft. He would let down the prop at one side of the opening as Bethan let down the other, and the mesh panel was latched shut. Then, with the birds safe inside eating their fresh feed and preening their wings, he would walk back down the garden path to his own house.

Chapter Seven

THE BEST TIME FOR TRAINING pigeons is not the late Autumn and Winter. But that year Dan, who was keen to begin training Birthday for the Spring races in the following year, decided as soon as she had her eggs in the nest to look out for a fair day on which to take her ten miles or so from home. This way they would test out how well she could find her way back to the loft. He talked continually to Bethan about this and other matters as they tended the birds. Nowadays, when Em was with them, the previously one-sided nature of the conversation when Dan was alone with Bethan would take a more conventional turn.

One day, as he was carrying the bucket across to the vegetable patch with Bethan, Emrys glanced down the path and said, “Oh, watch out. Here comes Mr Evans.”

A small man, smiling nicely, raised a hand as he approached. “Hello,” he called from a distance of about ten paces. “I got your message. What do you want me to do, then?”

Dan carried on with the scraper, pausing just long enough to say, “I’ll be with you now.”

“Hello Bethan,” Mr Evans said when he had come up to the end of the garden. “I hear your new bird is settled in very well." His eye wandered as he talked and came to rest briefly on Em. He winked.

The girl kept her face turned away from Mr Evans. Within seconds of seeing him she had put down her side of the bucket and Em had carried it the rest of the way. He came back without stopping to spread it, and stood by Bethan. When Dan put down the scraper, Mr Evans stepped over towards him and started to speak. As soon as he moved Bethan suddenly turned her face up towards the sky and made a moaning sound. It was quite a soft noise. Em looked at her.

"What is it Bethan?" he said. She wouldn't look at him, and he had to step round her to get a look at her face. His thin legs and socks poked out from under the short trousers. "Don't cry, Bethan," he said.

Mr Evans cast around him with an indomitable look that also had an edge of sadness. "I don't know," he said to Dan. "When I was a boy we weren't so namby pamby. They used to crowd around in those days when there was a chicken to be killed. I learned to wring a bird's neck when I was six, mun."

Pugh gave him a pitying glance. "Never mind the girl," he said. And then, in a louder voice so that she could hear him, "Bethan, Mr Evans has only come to take Gypsy and Scram to his loft to fly them. He'll do them no harm. He's got extra room. I told you, Bethan, that we should need more boxes for Birthday's nestlings in the Spring."

But it was to no avail. She still gave out small moans, and her cheeks were wet with tears. Combined with the absolute stillness with which she held her body facing towards the back mountain, slack but upright and as immovable as a statue, it was an unnerving sound. A flash of anger showed in Mr Evans's eye. It came and went like the wink.

"My birds are exercising now, girl," he remonstrated, throwing his arm out and pointing at the sky. "I look after them. There they are, over by the school. Look at them. Turn round and look at them."

But she wouldn't.

There was a silence. Then, "I'm sorry," Dan said. "You'd better come inside with me and have a cup of tea."

As Mr Evans walked by he moved his hand in his pocket, against his thin shanks, where he had once told Em that he kept the penknife used for pushing down the chicken's throat to kill it. Did he expect something like that to be forgotten? And then he would talk reasonably about the need to keep numbers down in the loft here, or put a chicken in the pot there, and you couldn't really gainsay him.

Dan looked miserably at Bethan as he passed her. He hesitated in his stride. Em was holding Bethan's hand.

"All right," Dan said, as if in response to a spoken argument. "All right." He turned back to Mr Evans. "I'm sorry, John."

"You mean you won't give them to me?"

"I can't can I?"

"What do you mean, you can't? A girl like that! She doesn't understand, mun. She's... I know you're her father, but be realistic now."

He could see by the hard look that had come over Dan's face that he'd better hold his tongue. And there that idiot child stood; enough to make your flesh creep. What did he do with her anyway? Followed around everywhere by that thing. All these thoughts went through his mind, and would find expression when he was back with his particular friends. But at this moment standing on the uneven stones, only a certain look floated over his face like a sour light. He said nothing more.

"Take this," Dan said pulling a coin from his pocket and pushing it at the other man. "No. Go on. I've wasted your time. I'm sorry, you see. Take it."

He took it. Said nothing. He gave a small valedictory jerk with his chin by means of a goodbye, with his lips turned down, and went off down the path.

"Well, Bethan," Dan said when he was gone. "Now what are we going to do? I can't give those birds to anyone else. Not after refusing them to Mr Evans. And you want Birthday to hatch some chicks, don't you? That's the way to make her race home, when she is hatching her chicks. And it's not fair to just let her get the eggs all the time and not hatch any."

One more small moan and he put his arm around her shoulder. Then he rested his cheek against the top of her head, and stroked her face with his other hand. She fell silent. Her limbs returned to their natural position. He took a handkerchief out of his pocket that was fresh from Betty's laundry, and dried her face.

"I've got an idea, Mr Pugh," struck up Em.

"Oh, you're still here are you," the man said with a certain grim humour.

"I could help you out, see," said Em. "My Dad's got a rabbit hutch that's empty. If he'll give it to me, I could keep two birds. That's how my uncle started. He's told me often; he began with two birds and raced them out of just a hutch in the back yard. I'll do the same."

"Well..." Dan considered. "What would you think of that, Bethan? Would you be willing for Em to have them?"

He knew she would. "Very well then, Em. They're yours if your father will let you have that hutch. They cost a bit to feed, mind. What will you do about that?"

This was a serious question, and one to which Emrys gave much thought. A week after the encounter just described, the word went out that Emrys Morgan was going to charge for singing the solo in the annual competitions against the three counties choirs. Everyone remonstrated with him, but he was adamant. They even considered using another boy. But in the end the desire to win overcame all other objections and since neither Em's father nor the school teachers could change his mind, the men clubbed together and paid him a fee. They did this in secret, of course. They were more than a bit ashamed of it.

"You wait 'til his voice breaks," one of them said. "I'm going to give him the biggest hiding he's ever had."

"Grown men like that being held to ransom by a scruffy little kid!" the women said, because inevitably they got to know about it. They said the boy's father should teach him a lesson, but Owen was not the sort of man to beat his son. He did plead with him though. He even attempted to blackmail him over the rabbit hutch. But Em said that would only mean he'd have to increase his fee in order to get the money to buy a new hutch, and so he gave in.

To return to that afternoon; when Mr Evans had gone, Dan said, "About Saturday. Provided the weather holds I'm taking Birthday on a training run. If you want to come as well Emrys, we're catching the ten o'clock bus over to Fforest Fach. We'll have just Birthday and her mate in the basket."

"Oh, that'll be great, Mr Pugh," Em exclaimed. "Won't it, Bethan. I haven't been up to the beacons for months. There'll be skylarks. Will there be skylarks, Mr Pugh?" And for the rest of that afternoon he talked of nothing else.

Chapter Eight

ON SATURDAY MORNING THE WEATHER was as bright as Spring. Sometimes you could almost mistake the air of late Autumn for that of early Summer; the sharp and slightly breezy tang of the old year as against the razor sharp sweetness of the new, like catching sight of an aging beauty at a distance and mistaking her for a young girl. Dan and Bethan stood at the bus stop with the basket waiting for Emrys. "I hope he doesn't miss the bus," Dan said more than once.

The bus came, and still he hadn't appeared. It went up the valley another hundred yards, turned round just past the Shepherd's Arms, and started to come back again. Fred Potts would be coming down to the Pugh's loft soon after eleven, ready to let the birds out and take care of things while Dan was away.

"I think Emrys is going to miss the bus," Dan said, but at that very moment the boy came tearing up from the side-turning near the river carrying a paper bag by the scruff of its neck and shouting out, "Wait for me! Tell the driver to wait, Mr Pugh."

He jumped onto the platform in the nick of time and away went the bus. They sat in the front seats, Em behind Dan and Bethan. "Are you wondering what I've got in this bag?" he started up the minute he'd got his breath. "I've got some sandwiches, and three of Mam's fairy cakes." He thrust the bag at them, between the two head rests. "I made the sandwiches myself. They're fish paste. Do you like fish paste, Bethan? Does Bethan like fish paste, Mr Pugh?"

When the bus got into town there was another wait, and then a new driver got into the cab and set it off again in the direction of Fforest Fach. The country in those parts consists of bare sweeps of hill covered with rough grass and rocks, and punctuated with miniature valleys full of streams and hazel trees. Dan got to his feet while the bus was climbing up the steepest road so far. The wicker basket creaked as birds and bus and man all lurched to keep their balance. Bethan followed, with Em behind her.

"Shall I ring the bell, Mr Pugh?"

"Go on then, Em."

There was a single woman waiting at the stop to get on. It defied the imagination to work out where she'd come from. All around, the heath-like uplands were bare with not a sign of a single house. Em took a good look at her as he jumped down. She had blue eyes and a wart near her mouth.

"Now then," Dan said. "We'll walk just a hundred yards or so up there. Come on Bethan."

The girl's eyes were shining. She walked over the rough grass with her big sandals planted firmly at each step, Em running after them breathless from having watched the bus until it disappeared.

"When we've eaten our sandwiches," he shouted, "I'm going to fill the bag with whinberries. Do you like picking whinberries, Bethan? Does Bethan like picking whinberries, Mr Pugh?"

"Yes, I think so," Dan said.

"There's a good patch of whinberries, Bethan," the boy

said, pointing off to the right. "We can come back to it. Let's remember where it is." He stopped just for a minute, apparently fixing the point with various landmarks.

"What time do you think it is, Em?" Dan asked.

Neither of them had a watch.

"Just after three minutes past eleven," said Em.

Dan stopped in his tracks and turned round. "You'll cut yourself one of these days, Emrys Morgan."

"No, honest, Mr Pugh. You saw that lady getting on the bus. She was wearing a watch and I had a good look. Three minutes past eleven."

Dan nodded. "Oh, well then..."

Em ran after him again. "Where do you think she came from, Mr Pugh? Don't you think it a bit suspicious, her standing there all alone in the middle of nowhere. I couldn't see any houses. Perhaps she was a ghost."

"In what way suspicious, boy?"

"I don't know." But he was giving his mind to it.

All this while Dan had been striding forward across the tussocks of grass until they reached a pile of rocks bundled together; not gathered there, but bursting out of a mound. There he stopped and put down the wicker crate.

"Is this where we are going to fly the birds from, Mr Pugh?"

Dan gave no answer for a moment. He was looking at the sky. Then, "Yes," he said, still looking up. He put his hands in his pockets. The larks were singing everywhere. The wind, sun laden, rustled over the flowering heads of grass. A sense of space and freedom beyond expression held the land and the sky and the horizons apart from each other. Em noticed it. He looked at Bethan with admiration. From his point of view, being much shorter than she, Bethan was wearing the heavens like a hat. The blue sky seemed to sit on her pale hair, or rather wafted around it, depending on your fancy. She was as tall for her age as he was small for his. She was wearing her slide with the cherries.

"Well, let's get on then," Dan said, like a man waking up. "Who's going to open the basket and let the birds out? Will you, Bethan?"

She turned her face silently towards him and he seemed to be able to read the answer as if it was written there, because he said, "All right. I will." He smiled. "Ready now?"

He undid the latch of the basket, and set back the lid. For a moment the two birds merely stirred, but stayed inside. Then Birthday put her foot on the edge, spread her wings and dropped onto the ground. Her mate followed her. Breathless, the three humans stood and watched. Birthday walked experimentally across the rock. All the while, her bright eyes were fixed first this way and then that. Black Rill followed her. Then with a loud snap of wings they both flew up into the sky and circled.

Will she go straight, Dan thought to himself, or will she...? Oh! And he laughed a quiet whistling laugh as Birthday, spotting the red cherries, came down on Bethan's head just as she had done on the famous day of the ginger cat, and many times since. Dan had always said one should look out for a bird's special peculiarities; like Gypsy, who would eat peanuts out of your hand, or Pie who would go every time for the privet in the hedge. And here was Birthday who had taken a fancy to the red lacquered cherries, so that Bethan would never now let Aunt Betty do her hair without that slide.

"Oh, Bethan!" Dan laughed, "Right on your head, girl."

But it was only for an instant. The cock bird was circling his mate, anxious to be off, and she rose and joined him. Within seconds they seemed to have located some unerring path in the sky, and away they flew, home to their loft.

"Well," Dan said, after a moment's silence during which all three of them stared after the departing wings. "So what time is it now, Em?"

"About a half past eleven, Mr Pugh?"

"Yes. That's a fair guess. They'll be home in about ten minutes; maybe nine. But we are just lumbering human beings who have to take a bus and go round and round, and one way and another since we can't be fast let us be slow, and enjoy our picnic. Let's have a look at your sandwiches Emrys, if you'll be so kind, and Betty made us some cake."

He pulled up the legs of his trousers and sat down on the rock.

"Do you want to sit down, Bethan?" She sat.

Em handed round his paper bag. The food tasted extraordinarily good. "Did you really make these yourself, Emrys?"

"Of course, Mr Pugh. I said so," said Emrys with his mouth full.

He was a remarkable boy. Olave Richards didn't really count him among the brightest ones in his school. He was always mentioning the Morris twins, and a girl who lived over at Aber. One was good at mathematics, and the other two did Greek and Latin. But Emrys, if he didn't have a particularly distinguished grasp of school work, seemed to have an extraordinary grip on life. He was telling Bethan now all about how he was going to sell the nestlings he'd get from Gypsy and Scram, and he'd been training two other boys who were quite good shots with the catapult, and offering their services, for a fee, to lofts in particularly cat ridden locations during the exercising time of the day.

Dan heard him say now, "I asked Mr Richards if we could come out of school ten minutes earlier to give Wil time to get up to Farson's end by four o'clock but he wouldn't." Bethan nodded. Perhaps she understood. "Do you see that clump of heather over there?" He stood up. "Watch now, Bethan. I'm going to hit right in the middle of it where that snail is hanging onto that stalk there."

"Emrys!" said Dan.

"Honestly, Mr Pugh, I can see..."

"You can not."

"All right, then. There COULD be a snail there. And if there was a snail there it would help mark the spot for Bethan."

"Mark the spot with something else, then."

"My bus ticket!" He ran over to the clump he had in mind, and jammed it between the dry twigs. Then he came back to the rock.

"You think you can hit that?" said Pugh.

Em was somewhat taken aback. The clump was twenty yards away and the target was almost invisible. He looked sideways at Bethan who was staring up at him from the ground with her mouth slightly open and a shine in her eyes.

"Definitely I can," he said. He unhooked his catapult from his belt. There were a few small stones at his feet and he carefully selected one. He stood at the ready and glared at the heather clump. Then he slung the shot and it went smack into the middle and cut the bus ticket in half.

Chapter Nine

WHEN THE WINTER MONTHS REALLY set in, imprisoning the world in a regime of short days and long nights and air the colour of wet slate, Dan had to put aside further training of the birds until the Spring. Just the daily exercise and the routines of cleaning the loft and grooming and feeding the birds took up a reasonable amount of time every day, but he went off early to the Shepherds Arms, and Emrys was sometimes allowed to do his homework in Betty's kitchen to keep Bethan company.

"As long as you don't ask me any silly question!" Betty said. "None of your arithmetic or geography. It's cheating to get grown-ups to do it for you anyway."

"I wasn't asking, Miss Pugh" said Emrys. "I wouldn't dream of it, would I Bethan. And I am extremely good at arithmetic, Miss Pugh. Do you know what two thousand three hundred and sixty five divided by five comes to?"

"There you are, Emrys Morgan! I tell you not to ask me, and you do it straight away."

"But I'm not asking you Miss Pugh. I know the answer myself. It was just a riddle. To amuse you."

"I don't need amusement thank you. I am busy enough doing all this washing and ironing. No! Don't you dare tell me now. I don't want to know. If you won't let me alone you'll have to go back to your Mam and do your homework there."

In the Shepherd's Arms Dan was drinking a pint with Morgan. "Emrys is up there now," he said. "Betty is letting him do his homework on the kitchen table."

Morgan laughed. "He'll be driving her crazy, mun."

"Well. Betty can take care of herself."

"In some ways, yes. I'm not so sure how useful a sharp tongue is when it comes to Jack Isaacs, mind."

"Go on! Has he got his eye on her now?"

"I don't know. I saw him looking at her; just my own idea, and I didn't say anything to anyone else. Best not. But we all know Jack. And the funny thing is that there's not a woman in the valley capable of standing up to him. They go weak at the knees and that's it. I wouldn't be Mrs Isaacs for all the tea in China."

"Was he looking at her legs then?"

"Yes, that's it. Betty has got nice legs, you must admit."

But then they started to talk about rugby with the others.

And then there was Christmas to look forward to. Olave Richards said that God's genius in arranging for the birthday of Jesus to fall in the middle of Winter when people needed cheering up proved that human beings could have full confidence in divine authority. But in his mocking way Olave himself was the main inspiration of the school Christmas activities; the plays, the art works, the decorations and the singing.

"There have been complaints about you, Emrys Morgan," he said after school a day or so before the choir competition. "I have been told that you are trying to charge a fee to sing at the four counties."

"Yes, Mr Richards."

"What do you mean, yes Mr Richards? You are charging a fee?"

"Yes Mr Richards."

"Why?"

"I need the money, Sir."

Olave Richards pushed out his bottom lip with his tongue. He frowned. His very long and thick black eye lashes came closer together. He scratched his right cheek bone with one finger and nodded.

"I see. What for?"

"Feeding my pigeons, Mr Richards."

"Right." The school master nodded again. Then he turned round and walked off without another word. After all, that sort of straight forward answer and independent thinking was exactly what, as a school master, he was trying to teach the boys. He couldn't punish Emrys for it. If there was anybody Mr Richards felt like correcting forcibly at that time, it was his new assistant, Mark Roberts, who held that Blake was a better poet than Shakespeare. He'd warned Roberts that if he taught one class on those grounds he'd get the sack; he didn't care about employment contracts or compensation. Out he'd go. Given the chance to administer a stinging wallop in the pants to Mark Roberts or Emrys, Olave Richards knew which one he'd choose.

Fortunately he could always get over this or any other vexation from the school days routine in the company of his friends, first of whom were his extremely beautiful wife Iris, and second, Marco Servini, the owner of the Italian ice cream shop in town. For many years now Olave had been meeting Servini on Wednesday evenings to play chess, and this custom was particularly precious to both of them in Winter. Servini lived almost next door to Morgan the milk and, of course, by definition, Emrys and Olwn. He and his fellow countrymen who had all settled in Wales—where identical attitudes to women and music made them feel at home—were responsible for the high standards of ice cream making in the whole principality. The newsagent and sweet shop at the other end of the village was a Larimo, and Servini had a rival tea shop and ice cream parlour owner in town in the person of Raffa Ferrari. But from Olave's point of view it was the discussions of music and politics he cared for. It was as much the conversation as the game which the two men looked forward to. They exchanged books. They argued literary theory. Just now they kept up minutely with news of the tensions in Europe and Germany. And they talked about their work, which in both cases was incongruous when compared to the abilities of the man doing it; but in which both of them took great pleasure nevertheless. Richards loved being a school master, and Servini was very content to sell good ice cream. However, sometimes there were tedious interruptions to the flow of ideas and Richards' obsession with the iniquities of modern educational theory was one of them.

"Don't let's get onto that again," Servini said when Olave's thoughts veered once more in this direction. He tapped out his pipe against the side of the chimney. The ash scattered in the grate where Iris would clean it up the next day. "When all is said and done it must be a matter of opinion."

"Later on, yes. When they have learned enough to make the comparison, yes. But to set the bias of his own very political point of view on unformed minds before they have learned, and hamper the impartial absorption of the original work; that I don't agree with."

"How is Iris?" said Servini. "I haven't seen her tonight."

"And do you know he has told the boys to call him by his Christian name in class? Have you any idea where that will lead? Have you?"

"Check mate," said Servini.

"It will lead to this kind of thing; let me give you an

example. Here's the teacher. He says, 'now, I want you to call me by my first name. My name is Mark. Your name is Henry?'" Then Richards lifted his voice to imitate the higher register of the boy; "'Yes, Sir.' 'Not yes Sir. Call me Mark.' Very well. 'Yes, Mark.' By and by Henry misbehaves. 'Who's that talking?' says Roberts. 'Henry, what did I just say about Blake?' 'I don't know, Mark,' Henry pipes up, sprawling on his desk. 'I was talking, wasn't I!' Next thing I've got Roberts in my study complaining that the boys don't respect him, and he needs a higher salary to enhance his dignity and enable him to cope with the strain. It's your own fault, I tell him. You wanted them to treat you like an equal, but you forgot to mention that they have to come up to your level and not you go down to theirs."

"Check mate," said Servini again.

Richards looked down on the board like a man suddenly waking up. He studied it for a moment, and then moved his rook and cut off the black castle's line of fire.

"Oh," said Servini.

Iris came in to stoke the fire. "I'm going to bed, Olave," she said. Olave scarcely looked up, but Servini let his eyes rest on her when she had her back to them both as she checked the latch on the window. She was wearing a woollen dress through which the lovely shape of her haunches was revealed at she leaned forward. The catch was stiff. The glitter of the night-lit panes of the window held fragments of the life around them like fish in a glass bowl. If you gave yourself time you could pick out shards of gold from the street lamp down the hill, reflections from wet tarmac, sparks from the fire, the brass scuttle, the underwater glimmer of Iris's face.

She turned round and caught Servini's eye before he could snatch it away. With a slightly haughty look and at the same time a little peremptory smile, she lifted his gaze off her in just the same way as she might have removed his hand if he had allowed it to stray onto her knee in a darkened cinema; a venture that he had several times been on the brink of. Others thought the same. When she was fourteen she went to the cinema with her friend Mary, and an apparently absent minded man sitting beside her seemed to mistake her thighs for his own when he put his hands down. She had been too polite to correct him, but she told her father about it when she got home and he said, "Remember, Iris. A man always knows where his hands are!"

"Good night then," she said.

They both replied.

"Come on," Richards said to Servini. "It's your move."

The door was closed behind her. He looked down at the board.

"My grandfather used to read Dante for hours at a time when he became an old man," Servini said, apparently at random. "But I've forgotten how to really understand Italian, and poetry in translation is always more or less like washing up water to a good soup in my opinion; not completely useless in its way, but entirely unsuitable as a replacement."

"I agree with you," said Olave, and they talked after that about poetry without any more reference to school matters until the game was finished at half past midnight.

Servini didn't have far to walk to get home, and for once it wasn't actually raining. He pulled the street door of the Richards' house shut quietly behind him, and looked up once. The bedroom light was on, and shone through a pattern of large marigolds on the curtains. He longed suddenly for his own house, and made a search in his coat pockets for his key. Just as he did that the street lamps went out. Over his left shoulder, on the other side of the road, the land dipped sharply down towards the narrow valley floor. One more line of houses, and then just where the river beautifully cut through hazel trees and rocks and fern, his own house and the street where Em lived was arrived at cheek by jowl with the colliery wheel, and the narrow rail track laid along the far bank. The earth which was black under Servini's feet in the dark was just as black in the day time. The coal seemed to be turned up to the surface on the backs of worms, or carried on colliery boots and dropped from buckets.

The leather soles of Servini's Italian shoes skidded on the steep decline. When his grandfather came from Italy with a group of his bankrupted compatriots they settled here, as I said, because they shared the typical Welsh man's attitude to women and singing. It was enough to make them feel at home. After a short time Servini's generation no longer missed the vineyards and the sunshine. Some of them had become miners, but most of them kept shops. He himself was something of a scholar. He wrote for the local, and sometimes national, newspaper as well as selling ice cream. He swore now in Welsh as he almost fell near the bottom of the lane. His voice, or the tread of his feet, woke up the Morgan's dog, and as it barked Em's two birds, fast asleep in their rabbit hutch, shuffled and crooned.

Every time Emrys let them out they flew back to Dan and Bethan, and this was driving Em mad. "Why do they do it, Mr Pugh?" the boy complained. "I've given them good food. They've got everything down there."

"Well, just be patient," Dan said. "If you like, Em, you can keep them down there and feed them, and then when they win a race they can fly back here and I'll collect the money."

"Very funny, Mr Pugh, if you don't mind me saying so," remarked Emrys bitterly. "But tell me now, what can I do?"

And then this very night, when at one remove he heard Servini on his way home because of the dog barking, which woke him up, he at last thought of something. He'd let Gypsy and Scram hatch two nestlings. Then, when the young birds were ready to be weaned, he would sell Gypsy and Scram to the cousin of a boy he knew, who lived the other side of Fforest Fach. That would be far enough away for Gypsy and Scram to be resettled just as Birthday had been. The boy was quite well off, and his father had enough room to do it. All it would need would be a bit of persuasion. This all came to Emrys in the batting of an eye; between the time that Servini grabbed the top of the fence to stop himself from falling and the moment when the dog barked. Then it was silence and darkness once more.

Chapter Ten

In Betty's kitchen Fred Potts was almost as familiar a sight as Dan himself. They had been close friends, those two, since their school days. Once upon a time, long ago when he had been in his early twenties, Fred had cast an eye over Betty, drawn by the idea of having Dan's good-looking sister for a wife. But the moment passed. It passed for him in a series of half-meant evasions; an instinctive side-stepping; he hardly knew quite why. She was such a smart woman. He admired her. He looked up at her now. She was coming over to where Dan and he had spread out the maps and racing schedules on the kitchen table after tea, in order to discuss the next season's races, and which of them they would enter, and with which birds. Betty was bringing over a piece of cake specially for Fred, because Mary, his wife, had gone to visit her mother for two days and Betty was convinced—or so she said—that he needed feeding up. He said, in his pleasant open way, "Well, thank you very much, Betty." He tried to sweep away a bunch of papers to make room for her to put down the plate, and a sheet fell on the floor. Bethan, who stood as always silently between himself and Dan, trod on it.

"Get out of the way, Bethan," Betty said, snatching at the floor after putting down the plate. She had to push the side of

Bethan's leg before the girl responded. Having Bethan around was like having an awkward piece of furniture that always got in the way—an over-stuffed armchair, or one small table too many. It was as if the girl wasn't aware of the fact that she was inside her own body and needed to move it out of the way.

Other people, of course, thought that it was very easy to deal with a retarded child who was docile, like Bethan. Or like Bethan usually was. In fact, there were the occasional fits of temper. Now, that was something to be reckoned with. Who stopped to consider what a time Betty had when one of those fits was on her? Not so long ago there had been a scene over the ridiculous slide that the social worker had given Bethan. You would expect a social worker to know better; to have a bit of insight into just what problems might be caused by a gift like that. But no. She had no idea of the trouble she had made. Never mind that the slide looked absurd, with those huge red cherries on it in all weather; it was impossible nowadays to persuade Bethan to go out of the house without it in her hair. And after all, there are times when it would be nice if the girl could look as near normal as possible. There were enough problems in that direction, without her insisting on always wearing a great clutch of bright red baubles in that mop of hair of hers.

All these thoughts lay behind the gesture with which Betty now pushed Bethan's leg aside. It was almost a slap that she gave the girl. Fred saw it of course; and Betty's covert quick glance at her brother's unconscious profile as he remained bent over the map, saying "Here it is, Fred. We couldn't find it because of this mark. But can you see it now? That's an A. You see?"

Fred looked briefly where Dan pointed, but his mind was still aimed in the direction of Betty, and he looked again at her as she walked out of the room. He rarely raked over old coals, but as he watched her now he noticed her ankles; how fine they were. She had on good stockings. Her hair was smart. She hadn't put on weight. She was eerily like the girl he had once almost courted. It was enough to make him break out into a cold sweat to think of it, but just imagine—when he woke during the night, it could have been her beside him instead of Mary.

"What's the matter?" Dan was saying. "Don't you think it's a good idea?"

"What's a good idea?"

"To try Birthday in the long distance race from Scotland in April. Bethan wants to, don't you Bethan?"

"Not to put in Pied Jack then?"

"I don't know. It will cost a bit. Jack doesn't look much better to me than he did nine months gone, and then he was only sixth. And Birthday's dam flew second from Loch Kree. What about your checkered hen?"

"Too far. I'd prefer this one for her. Let me see now..." Fred moved his finger down the list of races on the printed schedule.

"That's two hundred miles. Hadn't you better try Birthday on a shorter race first?"

"Maybe." Dan looked doubtful. "Yes. Maybe. Then when is the next one from further north?"

They plotted and planned, eventually refolding the map in its original creases and stacking the race schedules in a dark blue folder. Betty had come to collect Bethan for bed. "Bed time, Bethan!" from the open door in her no nonsense voice; not the same voice as the one that offered cake.

The child gave not the slightest sign of having heard her aunt. Fred and Dan at that moment were deep in discussion about the French races. Neither of them had ever entered a bird yet for a flight from the continent. It gave them a thrill to roll the names over between their teeth: Nantes and Pau,

Brittany and Zanzibar. It might as well have been Zanzibar.

"Bethan!"

Both men looked up quickly. That stinging tone belonged to the days when they were boys who could receive a cut across the hand with a ruler.

"Go on Bethan," Dan said gently. Just now, in his thoughts, he had been on some sun soaked railway platform in France where a stranger with a smiling face might have been unloading a crate of his birds tied with a tag for the French marking station.

"It's bed time now. Be a good girl for Aunty Betty."

Bethan looked uncertain.

"For me then. Be a good girl for me, and go nice to bed now. Give Dad a kiss." She bent down. She put her mouth against his cheek but she had never learned to give a kiss. What is a kiss? Both lips pressed together and then a little sound like a bird makes when it is in or near its nest. She couldn't make the sound, any more than she could play tennis, or add up. But he loved that silent pressure of her lips against his cheek. He smiled at her, his own eyes dancing. He had seen the humour of the occasion again. Familiar as it was, he was still tickled by Betty's comic stare as she stood in the doorway waiting. Now Bethan would walk across the room with her silent heavy tread and pass through the doorway as if in the entire world there was neither father nor aunt, no up nor down, day nor night, but only 'Bethan goes to bed. Lights out.'

And Betty could be very amusing. Even Fred gave a chuckle as he saw her now. She had always had a talent for mockery, more often cruel than kind although not, of course, on this occasion. She knew better than that. This time it was just something in the way that she turned after Bethan and then cast a last glance into the room with her hand on the door knob and one foot kicked up behind, that made both the men laugh.

"I don't know what I'd do without Betty," Dan said. "She's very good to the girl, you know. Dealing with someone like Bethan day in day out isn't easy."

"No."

They talked on for a while, and then, just as Servini had done, Fred bid his friend good night and walked home.

Chapter Eleven

IN JANUARY, WHEN THE LEES of the old year are still being poured off and a rancid mixture of sleet and cold dust clouds the eye in that part of the world, there are still some people who see the knotted buds of new life trapped in the bark, and smell the Spring. Betty wasn't exactly one of them. But the urge to move faster, a sporadic elastic sharpness of anticipation in the way she looked out on life made her responsibility for Bethan more irksome. During the long hours when Dan was at work, Bethan was always in the corner of Betty's eye; the vacant point of no departure to which all her own comings and goings had to yield. Just in the natural order of things she was bound to get snappish.

One morning she returned from a visit to the shops to find a strange woman on her door step. Leading to the door a steep little path climbed from the street, the valley being so narrow and the buried roots of the back mountain already pushing up the ground at this point. To the left the garden path, running parallel to the street, was where Beth had walked pregnant with Bethan. And later Dan, when his shifts were over and he had had his bath and tea, with Bethan close behind him first as a little stumbling infant and now such a big girl, would go down the same path to the pigeon loft.

"Hello," Betty said, looking up towards the front door at the woman standing there. "Are you wanting me?"

"Miss Pugh?" the woman asked.

"I'm Miss Pugh," she said, coming up the path.

"From the Welfare Office. Miss Clark."

Betty had caught up with her. "Go on in. The door's open," she said. The path was too narrow to change places. Inside, Bethan was alone in the kitchen.

"She's quite safe," Betty said. "She doesn't do anything," and she shepherded Miss Clark ahead of her.

But she had been caught off her guard. Or if that was too strong a way of putting it, just a bit off balance. The Welfare Office always notified her in advance of a visit. They didn't appear unexpectedly when Betty, fresh from an interesting excursion to the shops, had other things on her mind. The established routine was that once every six months Miss Pugh opened the door to one or other of the social workers from town, when she had had her hair set at the hairdresser's the day before. She would invite the visitor in, holding the door with both hands. "Mind you don't slip. I've just done the floor."

The lino would be glassy. The visitor would give his or her shoes a fierce brushing on the mat and step in, past Betty, who would say, "Go straight through, if you don't mind the kitchen."

Getting herself back on track this time, she said to Miss Clark "Go straight through if you don't mind the kitchen."

Miss Clark didn't mind. She stood by the table waiting for Miss Pugh to catch up with her, and there standing near the back window was Bethan.

"Hello," she said. "Are you Bethan, my dear? I am Miss Clark."

"Bethan!" Betty said with sharpness. "Aren't you going to

say hello to Miss Clark?"

She knew very well that she was asking the impossible. She simply wanted to demonstrate to Miss Clark not only the fact that Bethan wouldn't answer, but what a nuisance it was to her, Betty Pugh, to have such a lump to deal with. So she cast in—not with the deliberate intention of sowing a falsehood—a scattering of words capable of giving Miss Clark the impression that Bethan could answer if she chose. Miss Clark knew better. She had opened her briefcase and taken out some notes which she now glanced at. 'Minimal Brain Dysfunction. (MBD) Family interviews can help in understanding the structure and relationship of the family. Items to observe. 1) Does the parent (or relative) get any pleasure from the child. 2) Are they critical of him/her? 3) Are they over-involved and suffering even more than the child? 4) Do they present in over emotional and dramatic display? WHAT TO EXPECT: MBD without hyperactivity: apathy: day dreaming: insufficient motivation in pursuing goals such as household tasks, school work etc. Also defects in orientation and memory; inappropriate affection.'

"Bethan is very attached to her father I believe."

"Very," said Miss Pugh, still wrestling with the disconcerting feeling of not having caught up with events. Over this business of Miss Clark's visit, she was in the wrong frame of mind. Any outing—and this morning's trip to the shops was no exception—always involved Betty in gossip, and her sharp wits would delight in the sort of talk that sent her home in a frame of mind rather like the heightened spirits of a highwayman after a successful encounter. Many were the times that she had lightened the pockets of reputation for this person or that. And now, following just such a morning, she had difficulty adjusting to the sober mood needed for dealing with Miss Clark. In response to the comment, "But she's no trouble,

I take it?" before she had time to stop herself Betty had said, "Oh! You can call it that. People say readily enough, when they don't know at first hand what it is like to have such a..."—she lowered her voice suddenly and much too late— "girl to look after, that it's easy. Well, it's not, you see."

Her voice carried recklessly on. "She won't do a thing for me unless her father tells her to. I've got to ask him to ask her before he goes to work if I want her to do the smallest thing for me in the house. She can do jobs like cleaning the floor, you see. Or peeling potatoes. I said to her yesterday, 'Help me to polish the Silvo off the teapot, Bethan, there's a good girl.' But she wouldn't. 'Dad would like you to help Aunty Betty. You know he would. He just forgot to mention it.' But I couldn't persuade the girl to so much as take hold of the duster. I can pick up her hand like this, you see, and try to close the fingers round the cloth but it will get me nowhere." Nowhere except to put herself so on edge that she could no longer bear the sight of her niece. Then she would go off out with her shopping bag, bursting for a talk with one of her cronies while Bethan would still sit, or occasionally stand in the window, or walk down the garden to the pigeon loft by herself.

"I see," said Miss Clark. She paused, and glanced over at the child She looked really very pleasant and harmless. She looked as if she might help Miss Pugh. Miss Clark took off her spectacles with their pink plastic frames, folded them gently, and laid them on the table and then said, with a little smile, "The question is, how will Bethan spend the rest of her days? She was fifteen in the Autumn so she will graduate, as it were, out of one category in our office and into another. If she has an adequate home, well and good. But if there are any serious problems, there might be other options we should consider."

Betty perceived a signal, both of danger and opportunity, in what was being said. She needed to work it out, and she could have done if she had had any warning. Miss Clark continued, "Have there been any violent incidents?"

Betty told her about the quarrel over the cherry slide, partly to let Miss Clark know that social workers could also make mistakes. There it was in the girl's hair now. Betty would never attempt to make her give it up again. Oh no! She had herself to consider. At her age, if she fell it was exactly the sort of thing that caused trouble later on, like Mrs Williams up in Graig Row, crippled with arthritis after her husband was such a bully all those years. "Why?" asked Miss Clark. "Did Bethan push you?" "Oh, yes. Nearly had the kitchen table over. It bruised the side of my ankle as it was." Betty held out her leg. She had very good pair of ankles on her. Everyone had always said so.

Miss Clark wrote this down. As it happened she also made a note of the fact that Miss Pugh did not like looking after her niece and that there were family problems, with too strong an attachment to the father. Betty watched her writing, wondering with some slight unease what it was all about considering that it took as much as five minutes to put down. She started to try to correct the impression she might have.

"She's a lovely girl, mind. Don't imagine I don't love her. I do. I really do. We get along very well, don't we Bethan love?" Bethan gave no response. Miss Clark had just come to the end of her sentence, and as she gently closed her note book she looked up and seemed to absorb the thread of complete uncommunication between the two of them. She moistened her lip with her tongue and stood up.

"Well, thank you for your time, Miss Pugh, and thank you Bethan. I will be writing to the girl's father, Miss Pugh, with the results of our deliberations in a week or two." And then she was gone.

After Miss Clark left, Betty found herself feeling curiously low; almost ill at ease. She kept going to the window, twitching back the curtains. Scuds of fine rain began blowing down the valley. When Dan came in at two fifteen he was wet. He went to change his clothes. She had his dinner ready for him.

"Bethan been a good girl?" he said with that humorous tilt to his voice, and his eye on his daughter. She had her gaze fixed on him as always. Not smiling, but now that he was home the aura surrounding her had shifted from blank vacancy to something else. You could say she was happy.

"We'll have to take the umbrella when we go down the garden to the loft," he said.

Bethan loved carrying the umbrella.

"We don't want to get wet again, do we? We could let the birds out just for half an hour, I think. They won't want to be long today. Come and sit down, Bethan."

She sat. Betty put a plate of food in front of her. "What's this?" said Dan. "Shepherd's pie and chips. Delicious."

Bethan looked at him. He put his fingers out flat on either side of his own plate and shifted it; an habitual gesture to do with just registering his intention to begin eating. Bethan did exactly the same. Then she watched him picking up his fork and when he did it, she also lifted hers. Betty came back to the table with the teapot and sat down.

When the meal was over Bethan put her coat on. Dan slung an old waterproof cape over his shoulders and they went off down the garden with Bethan holding the umbrella. Looking up to the right as he went, Dan could just imagine how the stream would be tumbling down the back mountain where it crossed the path under a slab of slate; how the sheep, their greasy coats soaked on the outside, would be huddled under the thorn trees, or foraging still across the rain sounding slopes, the occasional clack of their hooves against a stone muted by the hiss of water.

"Lovely weather, isn't it," he said, tossing the remark over his shoulder to Bethan not entirely in jest.

At the door of the loft he helped her to fold the umbrella, and in they went. The delicious grey shadow, full of folded wings, and the gentle sounds that come from birds who shuffle on their perches and croon and stir themselves enveloped Dan and his daughter. He went briefly out again and fetched two scrapers. He began to clean the floor but decided against doing it until the birds had been let out.

"They may not want to go," he said to Bethan as they lifted the wire mesh panel and hooked it back. But the birds, except for two hens sitting on eggs, stirred themselves. They stretched their wings, hopped a little way, and then leapt into the air. They circled closely once or twice.

"They'll be back very soon," Dan said. "Let's get cracking while we have the chance, Bethan. You do the boxes and I'll do the floor."

They worked away for a few minutes. The job didn't take long. Dan changed the water, fetched the feed, refilled the hoppers. It warmed them both up to be so busy.

"Won't be long now, Bethan," he said, "before we can let Birthday hatch a fertile egg. Only another month and a half. Then we'll let her keep two eggs, and when the time comes you can see them hatch, and you'll be able to hold the baby birds like you did before. But you've forgotten that. Don't you remember Gypsy's chicks? No? All the better. It will be like a new experience for you. When the fledgling is ready to chip out, you can hear the little creature inside the shell tapping, tapping away. And then, when it emerges – well, you shall see, Bethan. And that's just when we'll race Birthday on her first long distance. We'll test how she does then."

The rain stopped. The moon already showed in a pale shape that could have been caused by peeling off a small flake of the sky. Over the end of the valley the birds wheeled for home. A tiny song bird in a bramble set up a most untimely singing. The notes, so sharp and sweet, trilled in two long phrases, and then stopped. Dan heard it. He felt a surge of energy. The pigeons wheeled briefly again and flew down and into the loft.

"Yes, Bethan," he said, "Spring is on its way. It won't be long now."

Chapter Twelve

DAN PUGH VERY RARELY RECEIVED a letter. When he did, it was to do with Bethan, and would come from what they called the Parish in those days; the Local Authority, or the Mental Welfare Officer. Such an envelope came at the end of February and Betty took it in. She laid it down on the kitchen table. Dan had left for work several hours ago. The day shift started at six a.m. in the dark.

She let go of the letter slowly. Her hands were bleached from doing the washing. Her strong fingernails never broke and she kept them well trimmed. She pressed them lingeringly down on the edge of the paper. The letter was franked as usual by the local Welfare Office and therefore, in theory, no different than usual. But a feeling of unease, like indigestion but located in the spirit, oppressed her. She remembered Miss Clark's visit. She repeatedly walked back to the envelope during the morning, turning it over.

When Dan came home and sat down to dinner, he found the letter by his plate. He opened it. Coming in with a dish in her hand at that moment, Betty's glance flicked over him as fast as a lizard's tongue. But there seemed to be no sign of Miss Clark's visit. She spotted nothing to alarm her. The letter appeared to be a routine communication from the department.

"Look at this, Betty," Dan said. "They want me to go into the Local Authority Office with Bethan next Wednesday." He would be on night shift starting Tuesday.

"You'll have to go," he said to his sister. "You take Bethan into town, and explain that I'm on night shift, Betty."

"They don't say what it's to do with though."

"Well, she's fifteen now. I suppose we have to expect them to make some changes. They may alter the payment in my book, or offer something. Who knows?"

"Do you think that's it?"

When Wednesday came Betty set off with Bethan. But she returned without her.

Dan was asleep when his sister came home. He had trouble waking when he was on night shift and had to sleep during the day. "Where's Bethan?" he said after a while, but Betty gave him no answer. She made out that she was busy. But her hands shook. She gave an angry toss of her head.

The second time Dan asked, she came across the room ready for battle.

"Now, look here, Dan."

He opened his eyes wide with surprise, and fixed them on her. The impact cut her off. In the brief interval of silence, instinct warned him that something was amiss.

"Where's Bethan?" he said, in a much more urgent tone of voice.

"They said she'd got to stay in Fforest Fach," Betty replied. "They said she needs to go to the Junior Training Centre and they want her to be resident during the week."

"What!"

"Well don't look at me like that! It's not my fault," the woman said. "I told them you'd not agree but they wouldn't listen. They can decide apparently if someone like Bethan has needs that are not being met in her home environment. That is what they said."

"They said what?" Dan's eyes blazed but his voice was still quiet. "You took Bethan in, and they demanded to keep her there. And you let them. Just like that."

He threw his glance around the room, breasting the impact of Bethan's absence now that he was fully aware that she was gone.

"I had to," said Betty. "I told you, I had to."

"What about her clothes? What about her things?" His voice rose each time. "What about me?"

There was a pause between each of these questions, like intervals in some terrible music. In each gap Betty felt the blood drain from her body. It showed in her face, that took on a raddled streaked look in a matter of seconds. Nevertheless she answered gamely. "They said all that was taken care of. They said there's no need to worry. She can come home at week ends. Usually."

Dan leapt to his feet. He towered over his sister. The front door opened without anyone knocking and Fred Potts came in. He was accustomed to walking in.

"Hello!" he called out, and then, at the door of the kitchen, stopped. "What's going on?"

"Tell him, Betty," Dan shouted.

Her voice trembling and shrill, Betty said, "The Welfare have kept Bethan. They say she's got to go to the Training Centre to learn to work."

"They said more than that Betty. Tell us what else they said. WHAT HAVE YOU BEEN UP TO?"

Betty was ready to fight back. "What do you mean, what have I been up to? What am I ever up to but watching after Bethan and you day in day out. I wash, I cook, I shop, I clean. It's all very well for you, Dan Pugh. But it's not easy for me on times, and Miss Clark – that woman who called here – she saw it. It wasn't anything that I said."

"What did you say then?"

"I only answered her questions honestly."

There was a pause but Dan said nothing, and she was obliged to go on. "Miss Clark asked if Bethan was ever violent and I HAD to tell her about the scene we had before Christmas, over the slide."

"What do you mean, you had to tell her? You had to tell her about the way you goaded Bethan, picking on this small business as if it was so important, until she got confused and you fell over your own feet?"

"No! Bethan tried to hit me. You know she did."

"She did NOT. You know very well that you tried to snatch the slide out of her hair, and she hung on to it. That was all, Betty. She moved her arm suddenly to stop you, and only knocked you by accident."

His sister was crying now, but Dan ignored her tears. She pulled a handkerchief out of her apron pocket but he had his eyes fixed on her as if he could only see the thoughts in her head, and nothing else.

"What, besides that, have you told them, Betty?"

His voice was full of menace. He was another man.

"Fetch the doctor, quick," Fred Potts was saying to the next door neighbour. He had gone back to the front door and out across the path between the two houses.

"I'm going to bring her home," Dan was saying, putting on his coat in the kitchen. Fred got back in time to hear him say this.

"You can't," he interrupted. "Listen now, Dan. If they've issued an Order, you'll be breaking the law, mun. Think first."

"I'm fetching her home."

"The doctor's on his way. Speak to him before you do anything."

"Yes Dan," said the next door neighbour, who had come in. "I've sent Margaret. Wait until he comes."

Dan paused. He tried to calm himself. Like a drowning man who hears, slicing through the water, the blades of oars plied to rescue him, he tried to keep his head above the fear of losing Bethan; of harm coming to her.

"Doctor Thomas will know what to do," Fred reiterated. "Listen to him, Dan."

Margaret had already rung the Doctor's front door bell, which was answered by the maid who listened standing on one leg with her right foot tucked behind her left knee and her hand on the latch like she always did. Leaving the door ajar she went to the room where doctor Thomas, who hardly ever had a full night's sleep without calls, was resting in an armchair after his lunch.

"The doctor's wanted at number 6 Jubilee Place," she said to his wife. The Doctor stirred, saying "What is it?"

"Bethan Pugh has been kept by the Welfare. They won't let her come home and her father is threatening to go a bring her back by force."

The doctor got up straight away.

When he arrived a matter of minutes later at the Pugh's house, nothing had changed. Betty was still crying in a corner and issuing shrill self-justifying remarks that no one heeded. Dan was still standing.

The Doctor came in through the door bending his tall head, although if he had stood up the lintel would have been just high enough. He had taken his hat off, and looked around him with a peculiar expression. As soon as he had appeared, the attention of everyone was focused on him. Even the neighbour's dog, which had been attracted by the sound of voices and the open door, ran up to him.

He put his hat on the table and sat down on a chair. "A

letter came a week ago?" he said, in response to Betty. "Can I see it."

It was put in front of him.

"It's not my fault, Doctor," cried Betty. "I haven't done anything."

The Doctor read the letter, and looked into Dan's ashen face. He stood up.

"Sit here," he said. "I want to have a look at you."

The assembled people continued to contribute details of the story, as he took a small torch out of his pocket, shone it in Dan's eye, and felt his pulse. He said to the nearest person, "Fetch a glass of water, please."

"And then I was asked to sign a form," Betty said. "And I told them her father wouldn't agree but they said there were procedures or something. How was I supposed to know what to do?"

The doctor didn't answer her but handed Dan two tablets to take with the water.

"Have you ever been short of breath before?" he said to Dan. "No? Well, I'll have to look at you another time. Come up to the surgery next week. Now put your coat on. We'll go and fetch Bethan. You too, Betty."

A child came running after him with his hat. "Oh, thank you," he said, as he took it from her. His face took on a faint quizzical expression in the brief instant that he and the child were face to face. He put the hat on. He looked surprisingly dashing in it; more like a film star than a village doctor.

On the drive into town he stopped twice to make calls. At one house they had a telephone, and he used it to call a colleague, a Doctor Stanley, to whom he explained this situation *vis á vis* Bethan. He stood very upright, his shoes well polished, one hand in his pocket. "I know this man," he said. "He's a patient of mine." He listened for a moment or two to what was being said in reply. Then he remarked, "Pugh's sister is a bit of a trouble maker. She's perfectly all right in the normal way, but there was a new visitor from the Local Authority who I suspect enticed her into some nonsense, Do you know a Miss Clark? I see. Well, I can guarantee that that child, Bethan Pugh, is well looked after at home. No. There's no problem with her father. On the contrary. Good. I'll see you there."

He went back to the car and within a minute or two they were drawing up outside the Welfare Centre.

The lights were on inside the building. They had an exceptionally yellowish glare, like street lamps. This was not the building where Dan and Betty normally brought Bethan for her occasional examinations or remedial therapies. They knew it only by repute, as a desperate place where hopeless cases would be taken in. The supervisor, a Mrs Craddock, was a stranger. To Dan's eye, straining across an unfamiliar place and situation, her comfortable outlines and blond coiffure brought no solace whatsoever.

"Bethan Pugh is in ward three, doctor," she said. "It is the Mental Welfare. There's a new manager since December who came in to replace Mr Powell."

"Wait a minute," the doctor said, not to her but to Dan who had started towards the far door as if he intended to go straight in and fetch his child. He laid just the tips of his fingers on the man's arm as he said it, and Dan responded as if that light touch had the power to root him to the spot. At the same moment, Dr Stanley arrived. Mrs Craddock watched with satisfaction as this new man shouldered his way familiarly through the swing door, with his notes in his hand, his red hair, his white coat. As the chief medical authority at the Centre, he was, in a sense, her doctor. Her property. She watched the friendly greetings between the two doctors with a smile on her lips. If it had been up to her to decide what to do with that tragic lump of a girl in the ward, who had refused to eat or sit since she arrived and had even defecated in the middle of the floor, she couldn't have done it. This environment made a nonsense of real life. Sometimes it was a benign conversion, replacing cruelty with kindness. But it certainly excluded the process whereby Mrs Craddock, the fallible female human creature, took personal responsibility for any of life's eternal problems.

"This is Mr Pugh," Doctor Thomas said. "The girl's father. She suffered damage at birth, and I have been caring for her throughout her childhood. She is classified as having Minimal Brain Dysfunction, but without hyperactivity, so that she is not difficult to control, is she Miss Pugh? That was a mistaken impression that a new Welfare Visitor who had no experience of the family gained as a result of a misunderstanding."

"Oh yes, it was," said Betty, looking absolutely stricken.

"Shall I have a look at the records?" Dr Stanley said. He took them and concentrated on them for a moment or two, for the sake of appearances. He knew Joe Thomas. If the Welfare Officer had said Bethan Pugh was a homicidal lunatic, he would still have crossed it out on Dr Thomas's say so, and released her.

"And you would recommend that she is taken home now, and the decision reviewed?" he queried, for the sake of Mrs Craddock who was listening.

"Definitely." Dr Thomas said. "It could do a lot of harm, in a case of this sort, to disrupt and alarm her." Stanley nodded. "Let's go into the ward then. You as well, Mr Pugh." He led the way.

The room they finally emerged into was airy and spacious. Half a dozen beds were grouped down one end of it, and in the middle of the floor where there was an empty space, stood

Bethan. There were about six children and young adults in the ward, but they were sitting around a table eating, with two nurses attending to them. Only Bethan was stranded on her legs, motionless and apparently almost unconscious, some distance away from them.

"We can't do anything with her, doctor," one of the nurses said, standing up as she spoke. "She's the worst case we've ever had, isn't she Jane."

Nurse Jane nodded. "Oh yes." She was preoccupied with a spillage at the table but wanted to tell the doctor about the incident in the afternoon. "Yes. You don't need to go over that," Dr Stanley said. "I spoke to Mrs Craddock."

"But Doctor, there something really peculiar about her arm. Will you look."

Dr Stanley went over to Bethan and said something to her, but without eliciting any response. "Look at this," he said to Doctor Thomas in a tone of professional curiosity. He had put his hand on Bethan's arm but it was rigid. While appearing to be quite slack, the arm could not be moved. Gently, but using considerable strength, he tried to lift it as a preliminary to leading Bethan across the floor, but he couldn't make any impression. He tried once more, bracing his feet.

"What does that remind you of?"

"Post hypnotic suggestion," said Dr Thomas.

"Exactly. You know, I'd very much like to get Anderson down from Cardiff to see this." But his companion touched him on the arm, and he paused and said, "Well... Of course the girl's interests must come before scientific curiosity; but how do they cope with her at home? I should have to prescribe muscle relaxants here, and two nursing staff would be needed merely to get her into bed."

Doctor Thomas turned to where Dan Pugh was waiting where he had been asked to stand in the doorway. "Look at this," he replied to Stanley, and he beckoned to the girl's father, and stood back a little himself, drawing Stanley with him.

Dan stepped forward. He came to where Bethan was standing. He stopped just in front of her, a little to one side, and put his hand on her shoulder, then her cheek.

"Bethan," he said.

When the Hindus talk of Prajna, meaning breath, the presence of life in its ultimate sense, perhaps this is exactly the process they visualise; the godless human form whose state of suspended animation becomes suddenly enlightened by divine awareness. At the sound of her father's voice and at the touch of his hand a breath rose visibly through Bethan's body. One could trace the alteration as it seemed to flow under the skin. She slightly shifted one leg and a smell arose because the nurses had not been able to completely clean her clothes or reach the part of the floor she was standing on.

"We're going home now, love," Dan said. "Doctor will take us in his car. Give me your hand."

He took it, and led her unresisting towards the door.

Chapter Thirteen

THE NEXT DAY WHEN DR Thomas called at the Pugh's house, Bethan was out in the loft as usual, helping her father to see to the birds. Betty went to the kitchen door to call them, but the doctor said, "No. There's no need for that, Betty. I'll go down myself."

She looked after him as he walked along the narrow concrete path. He hadn't said anything about her part in yesterday's drama, but he called her Betty. Not Miss Pugh. His voice, turning her name over like that—Betty—had in an instant breathed balm onto the sore place in her spirit.

Self-justification had not been able to do it. She had tried that last night. With red eyes and a red nose, telling Dan angrily that she had nothing to be sorry for, she had snivelled off to bed. She had planned the next day to call on the consolation of her own particular friends who understood how hard it was to be rammed by Fate into the place vacated by her sister-in-law, and condemned, day in day out, to care for a backward child.

But now she felt that what she really needed was the doctor's sympathy; the understanding that he had expressed before, at other times, combined with the expectation nevertheless of certain standards on her part. As she watched him walk so elegantly away from her towards the loft, the elasticity in his step quite amazing when you realised he had been up half the night with Ann Matthew's baby, feelings of contrition took the place of defiance in her breast. Rather irrationally, she was overcome now by remorse for having let HIM down. She would put the kettle on. She'd get out the cake tin. He wouldn't stop, but he might put two of her fairy cakes in his pocket, like he did once before.

In the meantime Dr Thomas had reached the loft. Dan and Bethan were so busy in there they didn't hear him coming. He could hear Dan's voice and then, rather incredibly, a squeal of childish laughter. He wondered what was going on. He glanced around him before going up to the wire mesh and looking through. It was a soggy sort of day. A veil of moisture hung in the air, scented with the smell of wet grass and tinged with the smoke from coal fires. It blurred the edges of the mountain, and gave a watery double note to the sound of bus wheels and voices from down below.

And then to turn from all that and look through the wire mesh side of the loft and after a moment of adjustment to make out in the shady interior the tall figure of Dan holding a little egg up to Bethan's ear. They both saw the doctor at once.

"Who's the proud mother this time?" the doctor asked. "You're not going to tell me that's Birthday's egg are you?"

Bethan took in a radiant breath as if the doctor must be a magician.

"It is?"

She was still silent but she would burst with holding in the word she wanted to utter unless her father spoke it for her. "Yes," Dan said. "And the little chick inside is already tapping on the shell isn't he, Bethan. I held the egg up to your ear and you heard it. It made you laugh out loud it did."

He was putting the egg back under the bird as he spoke. The doctor looked kindly into the child's great moon face as she continued to stand, her mouth slightly open, her eyes shining, her fingers laced together. Not much wrong there then, give or take a disaster like Minimal Brain Dysfunction. She seemed none the worse for her bad experience of the day before.

"So no problems?" he said to Dan when he came out of the shed, and Bethan was sent off to tip the rakings from the nest boxes into Betty's vegetable patch. "She doesn't seem badly affected."

"Not at all," Dan said. "If anything... do you know, just now I was holding that egg up to her ear for her to listen to the chick inside tapping away like they do. The egg feels quite hot; especially against the ear. She laughed, and what's more..." He paused, stupendously. "And what's more, a look came over her face, doctor, I swear it, of real intelligence; even unusual intelligence. Something amazing. Her look went all clear, if you know what I mean. It gave me a shock. My heart banged in my ribs. I thought that perhaps some miraculous switch had gone on in her mind and made her whole. I waited for her to speak, you see. She was going to. And then, before my very eyes, whatever it was left her. Just like that. The light of intelligence in her face was shaded over again by something else. Gone." He sighed; pressed his lips together in a way very characteristic of him, nodding slightly. Acceptance. "She was still smiling, mind," he added. "There you are! You saw her."

Time was getting on and there were other calls for the doctor to make.

"Well, I thought I'd look in and make sure she had settled down after the trouble yesterday," he said.

"Thank you very much, doctor. She seems to have forgotten all about it."

He let a little incredulous smile settle on his face as he said this, and just for a moment the two men looked at each other in silent companionship in the face of life's mysteries. But then they had both to go their separate ways.

But Dan had not forgotten all about yesterday. In the afternoon when he was back down the pit, he thought about it. Not particularly about Betty. He more or less forgave his sister. He knew her too well, and he was quite fond enough of her. No. What he was concerned with was the same old problem—the fascinating problem—of trying to understand how Bethan's mind really worked. Because there was something special there. Perhaps that special, or peculiar, consciousness locked in Bethan's unique mind the very thing all mankind needed to know. Because there certainly are things we need to know and can't get at. He couldn't fathom it. Could it be that her mind was whole in one sense? Was she perhaps trapped in a different element altogether; like dolphins, whose functioning brains are much larger than a man's, but being to so great an extent cut off from human understanding by the fact that all their skills take place in the element of water, are deemed to be inferior. And what might Bethan's element consist of? What magical restructuring of the atmosphere might suddenly unravel the spells that held her mind in thrall?

But when, at the end of his shift, Dan got home again, he forgot these ideas. To come back to life above ground was to have the banalities of human existence barge into you again at every turn, like shoppers hurrying down a crowded street. Here was his bath. Here was Betty with a timid smile and a pie as well as bacon.

He might as well accept it all for what it was. The child was asleep now. They never had any trouble with her at night. She lay down her head on her pillow and closed her eyes until the morning. Be thankful for small mercies.

* * *

As the beginning of the racing season in April approached there was more talk of birds, both between the men working down the pit and in the Shepherd's Arms. More than rugby or football, or Mr Hitler, or the possibility of war in Europe. The men all discussed the various pigeon races scheduled for the coming season. They discussed the Fed, their own and their friends' chances in various competitions, the relative merits of known birds in the valleys. The pigeon fanciers in Cwm knew the geography of Great Britain and France from that unique point of view. They knew the prevailing winds and the train time tables of every town from Rouen, from Nantes, from Thurso, from Torquay, and the location and boundaries of all the Pigeon Fanciers' Federations. If you had given Owen Morgan a map of the battle of Waterloo and its surrounding areas, he would immediately pinpoint the spot from which Rothschilde's homing pigeons were released to fly back to London with the news of Napoleon's defeat. The fancier's reading matter was made up of innumerable books closely printed from start to finish with numbers in columns denoting distances, yards per minute (y.p.m.) dates, and times. On any evening there might be as many as twenty men in the pub in various groups planning, arguing, boasting, and laying bets.

The best local performer at the time was a man from the end of the valley near the school, called Jack Isaacs—the same as had been observed by Owen Morgan eyeing Betty's legs. Jack Isaacs kept enough sheep to count as a small sheep farmer. Not far from the last house in the terrace, yards away from which the road surface crumbled into mountain soil, stones, and the dry long grasses, stood his little cottage. He kept his pigeons in a yard where the sheep loved to thrust their noses. When he went out to check his birds last thing at night, he couldn't hear a single bus or car, or the men tramping home from the Shepherd's Arms after closing time, the drunk ones singing. All he could hear was the water in the rocky stream that ran down past the school and on to the pit head; and the spacious billowing of the wind when it has the broad shoulders and flanks of mountains to run on, and only hazel trees and thorn in its way.

It was Jack Isaacs who had put forward the name of the fancier who sold Birthday to Dan Pugh. Five years previously he himself had had a bird that came fifth in the long distance from Nantes. No one else at that point had ever entered a bird in a race from France, and all the pigeon fanciers who worked down the pit had asked Dr Thomas for sick notices on the day that Jack's bird, Cwm Streak, was due in. What's more, they kept all their own birds out of the skies to avoid impeding Cwm Streak's vital last minutes before landing back in her own loft. At three in the afternoon there wasn't a wing to be seen. Thrushes and sparrows and blackbirds, certainly, darted among the gardens and low hedges, but in the higher air there was an unfamiliar vacancy. No teams of large birds cutting, like a flight of knives, from one thermal to another. No packs from one end of the village flying towards a pack from the other, mixing and deftly separating again to whirl off intact. The skies looked very odd without them. And on the ground, here and there, groups of men stood waiting, talking, and keeping an eye open all the time for the return of Cwm Streak.

Evans had thought she'd not get in before dark. There were eight men standing in Dan's garden—and Bethan of course, although she was only ten at the time—looking out from that vantage point towards the front mountain, from which direction the bird would surely come. A difficult route through the mountains at the home end, according to Gareth Swyer. "It's that one," he said repeatedly when they had the maps out, pointing with the stump of his amputated index finger at the highest range between Cwm and the Severn Estuary. "I reckon we've got the most difficult route in from France."

But towards four o'clock Owen Morgan, with his binoculars, had seen a black spot of wings over Trebont. The spot grew and grew until everyone could see how the bird had to work to keep going forward after five hundred and thirty miles of flying. There was a wind, too, blowing in the wrong direction from the Weeks's end and you could actually detect the moment when the bird felt the pressure of it on the pinions, but sliced sideways and then flew on. Reaching the end of the valley and her own loft, she came down into Jack's hand, or you might almost say fell down, without any delay. Seventeen hours, five minutes and three seconds on the wing. He had her racing ring off in the instant and slotted into the clock. He had a ten bird Toulet that he shared with Tom Price. And then it was all the business of feeding the exhausted bird, putting her in a special place, keeping her warm.

"I don't suppose we'll ever see another one like that," Evans said to Jack Isaacs almost every time they met.

"Maybe. Maybe not," Jack would invariably reply, not liking that remark. What did the man expect him to do now? Die? Wring the necks of his other birds? He was as keen now as anyone who had not yet had a winner.

He came over to the table where Dan and Fred Potts were sitting with Owen arguing over the relative merits of a fifty or a seventy five mile tryout for Birthday. He pulled a chair over and sat down with his pint.

"I reckon she could do more than that," he said.

"You do?"

"Her dam was the Federation and Open Combine winner, remember. And her grand dam was the long distance Marvel Check Hen. It was only because that breeder let his stud go to wrack and ruin that she could be bought like she was. I think she could do the distance from Scotland in May. Feed her up, mind. And are you using linseed?"

"That's a big risk to take," Fred argued. "You don't want to lose her."

"I'm not suggesting straight away. Work up to it of course. How about the fifty mile North Wales Fed., then one hundred two weeks later here, you see." He pointed at the lists. "The Carlisle is still in the first half of April."

He was a handsome man, Jack Isaacs, in his forties and married; and has already been said, very apt to spend long hours on the mountain with one bird in a wicker basket and another one in the bracken. He hadn't been found out yet, or at least not by his wife.

Gareth, when he could get a word in, said, "What do you think of my chances with Gloriette, Jack?"

"I haven't seen her since February that time. Has she got rid of those pipey feathers under the wing? If she's well feathered now..."

Dan left while they were all still at it. He had promised Bethan to get home before her bed time, and Fred came with him. They carried on the same conversation as they walked down the hill. They passed Servini on his way up with his betting book in his pocket, and stopped to talk to him and discuss the different ratings given to the birds.

"Odds like this on Lightning!" Fred exploded, in response to one item of information. "Go on, mun, he's been telling you stories. Gareth hasn't had..."

"You can't be sure," Dan interrupted him.

"Yes I can. And he's got this new idea. Called the jealousy system. You've heard about it."

"It sounds cruel," Servini commented with a mean Renaissance smile. "But he's expecting results."

"Let him expect then. You stick to Jack Isaacs. That's my advice." And off they went.

Back in Betty's kitchen they were able to lay all the paperwork out on the table again. They sat down there, the two of them with Bethan in her flannel nightdress and dressing gown between them, licking their pencils and getting down to work like a couple of tax inspectors. The forms had all to be filled in for the races which they had decided upon, with the names of the birds and all the other details, and the postal orders included in the envelopes. Betty brought them biscuits and a pot of tea. Dan had applied for one form for Emrys Morgan. He was too young yet to belong to the Fed. "It's just as well," Dan joked. "Scram will fly back to our loft, won't she, Bethan?"

The child panted with her lips turned up at the corners, which was how she laughed when she was joining in with a joke.

"Not if she's got an egg in the rabbit hutch!" Fred pointed out.

"Oh, I hadn't thought of that!" Dan said "He's sure to time it right, as well. He's a sharp one, that boy." And he laughed again, and put down Em's own house and street number.

They reached the end of it just before ten o'clock. Bethan was still up. Betty had gone next door. They finished by checking over all the dates, including Birthday's entries for April 20th and the 27th. Birthday's mate, Black Rill, was included, and seven other birds from Dan's loft, and ten from Fred's. Birthday's entries were the last to be completed. April 20th and the 27th for the two short races, May 5th for Scotland. Bethan's name went on the forms as owner. Dan held her slack fingers on the pen inside his own firm fist, and they got all the letters into the box.

"Time for bed now then," Dan said. "Here's Aunty Betty, back just in time."

Fred left for his own house. It was dark of course, but a

different kind of darkness from the hard tinselly glitter of mid Winter. Any pigeon fancier loves the beginning of the racing season. He could smell the moist yellow curl inside the husk of the old bracken round about, and to him that meant not Spring as such, but the first race. He smelled it now. He walked up the village—the same route as he and Dan had taken together when they were as young as six and seven years old on their way to school. If their footprints could still have been visible he would have seen that he several times trod in them again before turning off to the house where he now lived. He opened the door, and shut it after him quietly, but didn't lock it. He went upstairs to find Mary.

Chapter Fourteen

WHEN THE MOMENT CAME FOR Birthday to be sent up North for the fifty miles North Wales Fed—her first race—and at the beginning of the season, Dan was very much on his mettle. As he saw her put into the racing basket ready to be sent off to the marking station, he said, "Put her down nice and gently now, Bethan. She'll be quite happy."

He hoped that she would be happy. He thought that such a sound intelligent bird would go on her first race with ease. But you never knew. Bethan handled the bird very well. Her small fingers were wrapped very firmly around the mottled grey body, which vibrated with little crooning noises as she was settled into the basket. Dan lowered the lid.

"She'll come home," he said, as if Bethan and not his own conscience, had sounded an uneasy question. "Birthday knows her way round here now. And she'll want to get back to her nest, and her mate. She'll be in such a hurry, Bethan, we'll see her coming over the front mountain in no time."

When all the pigeons from the valley were loaded into the baskets, and all the baskets were loaded onto his van, Owen Morgan drove off to the railway station in time for the afternoon train. Those men who were on the morning shift had friends to load their birds for them. But Dan was on nights just now, and so the following morning he came home from work and after hardly any sleep he took up his place by the loft with Bethan and Emrys. The birds had been released from the North Wales station at nine. All they had to do now was wait.

On these occasions everyone's eyes were glued to the point in the sky overhanging the left shoulder of the front mountain where homing birds came in from all destinations except Ireland. How many times, when Bethan was very small had Dan stood on that spot with her fingers locked in his big hand and his eyes so fixed and narrow that he almost forgot that she was beside him. But now, when Bethan was flying her own bird for the first time, she claimed his attention almost as much as the sky, there was something so remarkable about her. The child breathed through her open mouth and gazed towards the horizon as if not just one pigeon but the whole phalanx of God's angels was about to appear over it. He had difficulty keeping his eyes away.

"Don't be disappointed now, girl," he couldn't help saying, "if Birthday is slow this time. Don't forget, it's her first race."

But the caution wasn't needed. Five minutes later he saw a black speck appear just to the left of the expected quarter. Himself, he guessed that it would be Jack Isaacs' bird, although it was far too distant yet to identify; or so he thought. But Bethan made one of those extraordinary sounds, between a grunt and a laugh and a murmur, and she clapped her hands, and knowing her as he did Dan realised that she could recognise the bird. He looked with astonishment from her face to the tiny dot still so far away. It was yet so small that the effort of staring overlaid the image and for a moment he could see nothing at all. But Bethan could. It was ten seconds more before Dan could get anything like an identification from the wing flap and the flight pattern. Twenty, more like.

Bethan had her hands clasped in front of her, and her face glowing as she watched the magical descent of Birthday from the primrose soft sky to the stones and shale, the rough grass beside the loft. The bird came to her hand and Bethan stood there, incandescent with joy.

"Take the ring off now," Dan said. "Let's be quick Bethan."

He held himself back, to let his daughter remove the racing rubber from the bird's leg.

"Bethan's won, hasn't she, Mr Pugh," Emrys was shouting, hopping about with his catapult dangling out of his pocket. From his point of view, just over four foot off the ground, he could see the shell-coloured flush of excitement under the nape of Bethan's neck, and the shining pale blue of her lowered eye.

"Run to the Post Office now, Em," Dan said. "Come on. Don't lose a second. Your legs are younger than mine."

And off Em went scrambling down the bank, a short cut over the stone wall, his boots pounding across the tarmac at the bottom until within only a yard or so he could see the post office clock. He shouted out the time. His voice could be heard easily. It was distinctive. Half way through the word "o'clock" it shot suddenly from soprano to bass.

"Three o'clock exactly."

"Very good, very good" said Evans, who was time-keeping outside the Post Office. He was already writing it down in his book.

"What have you written down, Mr Evans?" asked Em.

"What do you think, boy?" the man said.

"I can't see."

"You've no need to see." He licked his pencil. Em grabbed the edge of the page.

"I'll disqualify you mind!"

"Sorry, Mr Evans," said Em, still trying to look.

"The trouble with you," Evans said, capitulating and letting him have one quick squint at the page, "is that you're a bit small, aren't you."

"I'M FOUR FOOT."

"Yes. And you're also twelve and a half years old."

"Where's the problem, Mr Evans? I'll be six foot by the time I'm twenty. All I have to do is grow three point two inches a year. It's nothing. It's only that much, look." He whipped a card out of his pocket that was marked with the exact length, and which he always kept on him. "Anyone could grow that much in a whole year."

"I don't," Mr Evans said.

"That's just being awkward, if you don't mind my saying so, Mr Evans. But I can't stop here arguing." He had kept half an eye out for birds all the time and now three or four pairs of wings began to appear and he was off. Even at this distance he thought he could detect Gypsy among them. He rushed up back to the Pugh's garden.

"I've got to go, Mr Pugh. I won't be far. Gypsy is coming in and I've got to head her off," he shouted. He ran back down to where the road forked, the one turning towards his own house, and the other carrying on toward the Pugh's and from there up the valleys. The front bird flew past on his way up to the Price's loft. You could hear the men calling, and Tom Price's daughters, ready to run for the Post Office as soon as Lightning was in. But Emrys stood full square, and when indeed Gypsy was in the sky just ahead of him he was jumping up and down on the cinders bordering the lane as if he could levitate and get himself right in front of her there.

"Go on, Gypsy," he shouted. "That way," pointing to the right and down the lane that led to his own place. But just as she reached the crucial spot you could see the bird shift in the air just that fraction to the left, and as sure as can be it was to the Pugh's loft she was homing. Desperate, Em ripped off his jersey, rushed to the other side of the road and flailed in the air with it, and shouted. His exact words were, "Not that way Gypsy, you bloody bird! That's not your home any more." Half the village heard him swearing.

"You shouldn't have said that," Dan remarked later on when Em was back at the loft with him and Bethan, and they were trying to pass the time until the official results came through to the Post Office from all the other contenders.

"I don't care," Emrys said.

"Well, your mother wouldn't have beaten you if she hadn't been just coming off the bus at the time."

"I don't care," Emrys said again. But Mrs Owen had a strong wrist.

"Put a newspaper down your pants next time."

"She won't let me."

"Well, you don't want to let her see, mun!"

"She's too quick," Em said. "Just my luck."

There was a pause.

Dan took out his watch yet again.

"You wouldn't think the telephone had been invented, would you Mr Pugh," Em said with just as much bitterness in his voice as if his mother controlled that as well. "We should have heard by now."

"It takes time to get all the birds in and compute the figures," said Dan. "Two more minutes and we'll go down to the Post Office to wait." He looked at where Bethan was standing over Birthday in the nest just as she had done from the moment the bird re-settled. Birthday crooned from time to time, and the quick eye that had charted streams and rocks and treetops from such a height darted from time to time up at the child. Dan was loath to interrupt such absolute communion.

"You stay there, Bethan," he said. "Em and I will go and wait at the Post Office." They set off, the two of them. They found a small group gathered there again. Fifty yards or so further up the road the Shepherd's Arms wasn't due to open until six o'clock. Those waiting included some runners from lofts further off—children and cousins and a few men.

Evans, making the most of it, stood holding the book until eventually the bell rang and the postmaster came out with the telegram. He passed it over and Evans tucked the book under his elbow to have both hands free. But when he saw what was printed in front of his eyes he forgot himself.

"Good God!" he said, staring up from the paper.

He needed to shave right down to his Adam's apple, that man, and it worked away bristling in his throat when the other men said, "Come on!What is it?" Or made a grab for the paper.

"No you don't!" he shouted. "All right, all right. It's Birthday. She's won."

"You mean in the whole Fed?"

"It says here. And 1505.8 yards per minute."

"1505.8? Go on!"

Someone else grabbed the paper off him.

"It's true, Dan," Fred Potts said.

"Let me see. It can't be printed right."

"Get off, Megan. And you, Tom Phillips. Your Dad will be waiting for you. Who was second now? Just a minute. That's it. Barley's Loft from Monmouth and—I can't make that one out. We don't know him. Off you go." The young ones went dashing off. You could hear their voices a few minutes later shouting ahead of their feet, thin and distant; "Birthday. Birthday."

"I wouldn't set so much store by it," Dan said that evening to Fred, "because it was only fifty miles. But 1505.8 y.p.m.! Well!"

"You've got a rare bird there, Dan."

"Bethan. Bethan's bird don't forget," Dan said. Fred looked at her where she was standing in her usual place just beside and behind her father's elbow.

"Oh yes," he said kindly, smiling down, catching his tongue for a second in the gap between his front teeth. "Bethan's bird indeed. She's a proud girl."

Chapter Fifteen

ONLY THREE WEEKS AFTER THAT event, Birthday came first again, this time in the two hundred mile race from Scotland. First, mind. Not second, or fifth, or tenth. First. Any of these places would have been quite remarkable, but she won out of a total entry of all the feds who competed. She was the only bird racing from Cwm that day. It was like the historic occasion when Jack Isaacs' bird flew in the much bigger race from Nantes in France; other pigeon fanciers kept the sky clear for her. No other birds flew. They also had all the figures worked out in advance this time since with a longer race it was easier to get it right. They knew Birthday's overall speed from the minute she landed. "I'm telling you," Jack said, "that bird is quite remarkable."

There were five or six of them gathered on the narrow spine of land beside Dan's loft when the race was over and the results had come through. Birthday was in a small enclosure of her own, to feed her up after the long journey. But she seemed so bright eyed, so plush under the shining quills. She fed from Bethan's hand. As soon as Dan let her out she jumped again onto Bethan's shoulder, or her hair, pecking playfully at that famous cherry slide. To see the great girl laugh like that delighted Olave Richards who came by to add his congratulations to all the rest. He had brought his camera and took a photograph of her. "What will you buy with the prize money, Dan?" Owen Morgan said.

"He's going to buy me a Kenwood Food Mixer," Betty sang out as she appeared that very minute on the path with a white tray of mugs full of tea. "Fetch the sugar, will you Bethan? I left it on the table."

"It will be Bethan's prize money," Dan said, putting his hands round Birthday to return her to the nest. "But I'm sure Bethan will get you what you want, Betty." And then, in an aside, he added to Bethan, "Fetch the sugar for Aunty Betty will you, love. She's left it on the kitchen table."

Not long after this it began to be whispered that Dan might put the bird in for the race from Nantes, in France, in the late Summer. "Well, he can afford to do it," Owen Morgan pointed out. "The prize money for one race pays for the next. That's the way it goes."

Dan also had a visit from men up from one of the notable breeding lofts near Cardiff two weeks after the Carlyle Fed, who were ready to buy the next chick that Birthday would hatch, at a good price. A day or so later Dan went off in the van with Owen Morgan and Bethan and came back with a new Paloma clock that kept every man in the Shepherd's Arms transfixed for a week. It had the usual thimble—a glass tube about two inches long and half an inch wide, into which the race rubber is put when it is taken off the bird's leg, just like a ten bird Toulet. But when the thimble was posted into its slot in the mechanism, the clock started to record the time of the pigeon's flight, with a little illuminated picture of a bird that moved with flapping wings across a disk. In addition to that, it produced a written record like a bus ticket.

"You'll wear it out before July at this rate," Dan said, joking. But he made no effort to stop them. During the day time he even had the twins down from Jack Isaacs' to see the clock. He felt sorry for those girls. Their mother was just beginning to realise that Jack did more than look after sheep and pigeons when he went out on the mountains, and it was souring her temper. The twins caught feral pigeons before school, by laying out food for them alongside a strong thread tied in a loop. Edith was the one best at snaring them. As soon as the bird put its foot in the loop, she would twitch the thread tight and catch it. One morning she and Megan got ten pigeons and shut them up in the outside lavatory before going off to school. But those birds, in the time they had there before Mrs Isaacs found them, made an incredible mess. Edith and Megan got home from school to a thorough beating, and were made to scrub out the lavatory, not to mention the fact that they lost all their birds.

But Jack promised them a chick each. That was the worst of it. It was his fault that their mother was developing a foul temper—his philandering that made her so miserable that she scolded Edith and Megan for every little thing. And yet he would come into the kitchen in his boots, smelling of oil from the sheep, dried moss and wool in his pockets, not closing the door to keep the dog from the kitchen, and charm the whole lot of them out of their tears and scolding in seconds. As a matter of fact that month he had his eye on Iris Richards, and Mrs Isaacs knew it. She became extremely watchful. But Olave sent Edith home from school one day with a note, saying that Mrs Richards thanked Mr Isaacs very much for offering to show her how he trained pigeons on the mountain, but she had decided against taking an interest in the fancy. Mrs Isaacs read the note when Edith gave it to her, and then left it on the kitchen table. Later, after Jack had come home, when she was standing in the pantry with the door open, she watched his reflection in the mirror. He sat down at the table. Noticing the paper for the first time, he took it up and read it. Then thinking that with luck the girls had left the note and his wife had not yet read what was written there, he stuffed it quickly in his pocket. How do you cope with a man like that, whose nature is loving but greedy? If beauty and the physical play of life and the ecstasy of desire were coinage, he would take his wages, but then afterwards be just unable to keep his hands out of the till.

When the twins Edith and Megan came down to Jubilee Place after school and asked to see the new clock Dan was very gentle with them, as he was to everybody. But in his dry way he also pitied them a little. He took special care as he showed Edith and Megan how the clock worked, and then went with them and Bethan back down to the loft to see the birds.

"I'm going to be a pigeon fancier when I grow up, Mr Pugh," said Megan.

"So am I."

"I never had any doubt about you, Edith. And when your Dad gives you the chick where will you keep it?"

"In the loft of course."

"Well, you mind your Dad knows which one is yours. You might rear a chick like Birthday after all. That would be a fine thing."

"Is Birthday really Bethan's bird?"

Megan was walking putting her right foot on the grass and her left foot on the path which involved crossing her legs over with a hop at each step.

"Ask her."

"Is Birthday really your bird, Bethan?"

Bethan nodded her head up and down, smiling and making a little sound that could have been yes. Or no for that matter. It was the body language you had to watch with Bethan.

"That means yes," Dan said. "And her name and her

signature is on all the paperwork."

"Go on, is it really?" said Megan. She was very impressed, and looked admiringly at Bethan for the first time, and Bethan, on her father's instruction, carefully lifted the latch of the loft, and opened the door. They all crowded into the little space. An indiscriminate murmur and rustling of wings greeted them. Most of the birds were in their nest boxes. Black Rill jumped down onto the floor of the loft, and landed with a gentle clip of his claws against the wood. He foraged for grain, expecting something extra.

"I see Birthday," said Edith. She was very sharp. "I seen her before. She's this one isn't she?" She laid her little hand softly where the scattering of white marks across the top of Birthday's head made such a pretty contrast to the pale grey of her overall colouring. "You don't mind me smoothing her do you Bethan?"

The big girl was excited. You could see a build-up of unexpressed ideas almost inflate her skin as if she was a balloon. Her lips parted and smiling, her eyes aglimmer, she made a sudden soft noise and put her hand on Edith's hair. It was a joke! Her father, the one and only simultaneous translator of her language, chuckled out loud and said, "There you are, Edith. Bethan is stroking you and you are stroking Birthday. If you could just fly off now to Scotland and back in – well, what shall we say? Twelve hours? You'd be a prize pigeon as well."

At that moment the siren blew from the pit head. It was a long mellow sound—not shrill—that could be heard right up at the other end of the valley, giving ten minutes warning before it would blow again for the next shift. Men in their wives' kitchens heard it. Men out the back digging a bit of soil or doing some planting, heard it and prepared to put down their tools. The landlord of the Shepherd's Arms, that opened its doors at the same time as the pithead swallowed up the evening shift of men, let a heavy barrel slam down so hard on the bar that a board on the floor beneath it sprung half an inch, pulled a nail, and a little scattering of dust fell down into the empty practice room below where later on the silver band would be rehearsing for the Eisteddfod. And even in the pigeon loft Dan heard it. "There you are!" he said. "Dad's got to go to work now." And out they all went again into the garden.

Chapter Sixteen

FROM ABOUT THIS TIME ONWARDS Jack Isaacs was preparing Cwm Streak for Nantes at the same time that Dan was preparing Birthday, and he offered to help in every way he could. This was how it came about that he visited the Pugh's house regularly throughout May. He would sit at the kitchen table with Dan, and probably Fred, with Bethan standing in her usual place between. They would study the maps of France, discuss the relative merits of feed supplements that could get the birds in fighting trim—linseed, garlic, honey, ginseng, B group vitamins, marmite—and regularly from the kitchen, sometimes just bringing a hot drink or a snack or, on occasion, a round of beer, would come Betty: Betty with her ankles and shapely legs, taking a chair sometimes with a bit of darning or a woman's magazine, where Jack Isaacs could see her.

He had just said, "Don't put Birthday on one of these new transporters, Dan. Send her by train. That's how I'm sending Cwm Streak."

"All right then."

His eye flicked over to Betty and back again.

"The money's here, look." And he points with his finger at the small print in one of the many booklets open on the table.

Or on another occasion when Betty came in with a cake,

"Hello Betty," Fred says. "Is that for us? Oh, we're being treated today!" They were, too. Betty stood beside Jack to slide the dish onto the table. As she leaned across him, to reach the middle of the board, her soft upper arm very nearly touched his face. He smelled lavender on it. "Now don't you eat all that, Bethan," she said, in a dulcet tone that marked her words as belonging to her guest and not the great big clumsy girl. "Leave some for our visitors."

Alternatively, the discussions went on in the pub. Curiously enough, the war, whether it was imminent and what effect it would have, was rarely mentioned. They weren't that interested. You'd have thought they could go on racing pigeons even if the entire Continent was covered with fighting men. Every now and then someone would pipe up—"But what if war is declared? We won't be able to race from France will we? They said on the news last night..." And then as likely as not he would be told to be quiet, or those gathered around Dan would go up to his loft to argue some point with the bird herself under inspection. Then Birthday would sit content in Bethan's hand, the wattles on her beak as white as two small pieces of coral. With her quick eye darting to and fro, and her heart beating steadily in the silken basket of her breast so that Bethan could feel it, she would be examined in such detail, I doubt if any racehorse in the land ever had more attention.

When they went up to Jack's place, Owen Morgan might go with them to see Jack's wife who was his sister. And in the pub, they could consult Olave Richards about the French side of things; that is, the distances, the language and pronunciations, and any other details they could think of. Olave and Iris spent their honeymoon in Lille, so they were reckoned to be experts on all things French, leave alone the fact that in school Mr Richards taught the language, and even read Madame Bovary in the original. At around the twentieth of May there was a spell of unseasonably bad weather. Those maps that showed the average speed and trajectory of prevailing winds were borrowed from the geography room in school and studied from a pigeon's point of view. Emrys was almost always with them once school was over. "Don't forget to keep an eye on the cats," Dan would say to him. "We men are going down the Shepherd's for a pint." "That's all right, Mr Pugh. Bring us back two packets of crisps and Bethan and I will clean out the nesting boxes as well."

Em talked non stop to Bethan just like her father did, and she listened, but not in quite the same way. "Come for a walk with me up the back mountain, Bethan," Emrys said yet again one evening when the loft was closed and the birds all in. But she would not follow him. "Look how lovely it is," he protested. "My mam won't expect me back for another hour. And you don't have to worry about my homework. I've done it. I know everything now about rock formations in northern Spain, and I'm onto calculus. Do you know what that is? Mathematics. Miss Price says I'm the best in our class. She gave me a boiled sweet yesterday. But I hate boiled sweets. I gave it to Edith Isaacs and she shared it with her sister. Their mother won't let them have sweets. Can you imagine that? What a way to behave, not letting your children have sweets. I get them every day from my auntie, and Mr Servini gives us ice cream. Edith sucked the boiled sweet for five minutes and then she gave it to Megan. I said, Gosh, you girls. Surely you get some pocket money now and then, and you can buy some sweets and eat them on the sly. But no. Their mother's cousin keeps the sweet shop, see. She'd tell on them. Some people have miserable lives." He paused, thinking about it. "Don't you think some people have miserable lives, Bethan?"

But she wouldn't go up the mountain with him. He'd get over the wall and half way up the path and he'd look round and she'd be still standing by the shed. "Come on," he wheedled. "There's a new lamb up there. You'd like it. It's so small you could hold it in your arms almost like Birthday. Lambs are very nice as well, you know. You've no idea how soft and pretty their fleece is until you've touched it. And we might find some cress in the stream. Wouldn't your Dad like some cress for his tea? I'll pick you a bunch of those little yellow flowers that grow up there as well."

Useless. She wouldn't budge. But he didn't give up. He felt sure that one day Bethan would go with him. He thought that nothing would be nicer than to sit with her on the cropped coarse grass overlooking the valley, and lob pebbles at the sheep, and hear the whine of the colliery wheel combined with the gentle rustle of the wind and the far-away voices of people up the valley going about their lives.

While everyone was waiting for the big race, there were other smaller races every Saturday, and Emrys himself at last had a chance to enter Gypsy in the local Fed. He worked for his father to earn the entry money, washing down the cow's udders before milking. He had spent all he earned with the choir on feed, and now that his voice had broken he could not expect any more earnings from that direction.

"Emrys," Owen said, looking down at his son, "I'm going to give you an extra sixpence."

"Thank you Dad. Oh, make it a shilling will you?"

"That's enough of your cheek. You haven't asked me what you're going to have to do for the sixpence."

"You said it was extra."

"That's right. Extra for doing extra; the dairy accounts on Tuesday."

"All of them?"

"It won't take a minute with your arithmetic. And I want to take your Mam to the cinema."

"Two shillings!" said Emrys.

"Two shillings!" Owen was genuinely shocked. "I'll get your sister to do it. She's been learning how to keep the books at Servini's."

"She makes mistakes. Mr Servini said. I heard him. He said to my mam that Olwen's head was full of romance."

"Oh?"

"And Olwen goes out with her young man after work. You're more likely to see her in the back row of the cinema than here doing your sums for you, Dad."

Owen looked down affectionately at the boy; the well covered milk-fed dairy man, and his bright-eyed little sparrow of a son.

"Well then," he said. "The labourer is worthy of his hire, I suppose, and Miss Price says you're very good with your sums. No mistakes mind! One and sixpence."

"Two shillings."

"Oh, all right then." And off he went.

* * *

One evening when Dan and Fred and various others were in the Shepherd's Arms, there was a knock at Betty's door.

"Come in!" her voice called out. "The door's open."

She had just turned on the oven, and through the open kitchen door she heard some footsteps and then Jack Isaacs' voice saying, as in surprise,

"Hello Betty. I thought we were meeting here tonight."

"Oh!" she said. She straightened up. She wasn't a woman who could be caught not looking her best. She wore a fresh apron and if one strand of her hair had fallen loose all the rest was very smart. No doubt the pink in her cheeks came from dealing with the oven, but wherever pink cheeks come from, they do make the eyes sparkle.

"They're down the Shepherd's," she said. But she came towards the kitchen door. "Have a cup of tea before you go. You look as if you could do with it."

He did look a bit parched. He was short of something at all events. His eyes had a smokey look to them. When they rested on her, the effect on Betty was as if she had stepped into a lift which had suddenly plunged downwards. She literally put one hand out to stop herself from falling; from giving way at the knees.

"Are you all right?" he said. He took a step towards her, holding his pale bottom lip in his teeth as if perplexed. But he wasn't. He knew exactly.

"Oh yes." She gave a little breathless laugh, with her hand on the edge of the table. From the top of her hair, to her smooth immaculate skin, to her red lips, fresh clothes, slim legs and ankles, she looked quite delicious. Jack Isaacs wanted to have her like a fox wants a chicken.

"Are you sure?" he said, putting his hand on her bare arm.

As soon as he had done that she went very still. He felt as if a magnet held his skin on hers. The only thought in his mind was this woman. He could have lived his entire life until this minute longing only for her. He stood still and close, giving up all semblance of casual politeness, and struck right down into her soul with those eyes. He tightened the muscle of his arm a little, and she tipped helplessly towards him. He put the other arm around her.

"Betty," he said in a strangled whisper, and heard and felt the whole bundle of fresh starch, flesh, scented hair and all that he had in his arms very nearly oxidise so that he could breathe the whole thing up.

The house was empty. He took her upstairs.

"You knew they were in the Shepherd's Arms."

"Yes, I knew," he said.

Chapter Seventeen

TO FILL IN THE TIME while everyone in the valley waited on tenterhooks for the race from Nantes, there were a number of other smaller events, and of course, there were stories and dramas to do with the pigeon racing world at large, and whatever there was of note going on in it. Of all the stories of the season there wasn't one more telling than that of Owen Morgan's uncle who lived in Berry. He went into the Shepherd's Arms on the Wednesday on purpose to tell it, but Jack Isaacs had already heard, and, as he was on the same shift, so had Evans.

"Well, I won't bother then," said Owen. "I'm not very happy about it anyway. I'm fond of the old man. He was my mother's favourite brother."

"What do you mean – 'was'?" said Fred. "Has he died then?"

"Well, you don't know then?"

"Come on, say what it's about. Wait a minute. Dan? Come back. Listen to this before we go."

"What is it?" Dan said stopping by the door that was propped open to let the air in.

"My uncle, down in Berry," Owen said. "Do you remember the bird he has. I told you he had this wonderful flyer, fast and tough as could be."

"Oh yes, I remember that," said Dan, walking back in. "Isn't he the one who won't come to the hand or go back into the loft when he returns? That's a fatal defect in a bird. It might as well be dead."

"Well he is now," said Owen.

"Your uncle?"

"No. The bird." He paused a moment, looking at them. He had got his audience now. He said,

"My uncle has been trying to train him, but you already know how when that bird got back to his own loft he would not go in for love or money. I've seen him do it myself. He circles around in the sky, waiting. That's no use to a racing man is it. Until the bird is in his hand and he can take the racing rubber off and put it into the clock or hand it in at the Post Office that racing pigeon is not home in any useful sense of the word. It was breaking my uncle's heart, to have such a brilliant racer – because that bird was really fast – and then to be so frustrated in the end."

"What's he done then? Has he wrung it's neck?"

"Don't spoil my story, mun. Let me tell it. My uncle John really set his heart on that last Fed from Scotland. Absolutely set his heart on it. He laid a big bet as well. My mother's furious with him, I can tell you. But he was quite right to be certain that if he could only get the bird to come down when he got to the loft, he would win. He entered Berry Boy, paid his fee and he's been training him ever since for this one thing; to go back into the loft. He felt that it was now or never. He said when he discussed it with his friends that Berry Boy would be so tired when he got home that for once he would come to the hand like a rational bird. He scraped and saved and got together all the money for the Fed that was organising the race, and the entry fee which was high because of the distance, and so on. And the bet.

"When was it now – last Tuesday. I think Gareth's Bridal Lee was the only pigeon entered from near here. Anyway, Uncle John was waiting by the loft with some friends, and they spotted the his bird flying in in record time – absolutely record time – coming over the bit of plough near the railway bridge. And the timing was really brilliant. There wasn't another bird that could touch him. "I can see his wings are heavy on him," the old man said, wishful thinking. "He'll come down this time."

"He got out his whistle, and when the bird was just above, he blew it softly and rattled grain in the can. Apparently Berry Boy didn't even bother to look down. As if the roof of his own loft was a spindle and he was flying off it, he swung off on a great loop over towards the next village. But then he thought better of it and came back. "Down you come. Good boy!" the old man was shouting. Not a bit of it. Berry Boy flew right past again, and circled. There was food for him in the loft, and his mate and his rest, but he stayed up there.

"And then at last the old man went into the kitchen and came out with his gun and shot the bird clean through the eye. It fell to the ground. There wasn't a head left on it. And he took the racing rubber off that damn bird's leg, and sent his boy running to the Post Office."

There was an outcry in the Shepherd's Arms, even from those few who had heard the story already. Some of them laughed. "Wait a minute" Evans was shouting out. "That's illegal!" "Oh, get on with you!" Fred Potts said back at him. "Wait, wait" shouted Owen. "Look. It was fair enough in my opinion. The bird had flown the race, and this was the race rubber belonging to him. There's no rule about a headless pigeon." There was going to be another outcry, but he shouted them down. "All right. Don't you worry. They made one up on the spot. They disqualified him."

Dan was shaking his head, half laughing, half sorry, all the way home. He and Fred Potts were speculating on how the old man was going to pay his debt. He'd have to find some soft hearted friend, because that syndicate run by Fairweather had no pity at all.

"I wonder how much he's lost by it," said Fred. "Owen had better look around for friends of his who are in a good mood these days to lend a bit for six months or so."

"In that case we'd better tell Betty," said Dan. "I don't know what's come over her, but she's making cake three times a week, taking Bethan to the cinema, gave me beef on Sunday... Maybe she'd give him the money!"

"Oh?" said Fred. "I hadn't noticed."

"Well that's probably because she's hardly ever in. Have you seen her this week? She's out all the time as well, but when she is at home she's as happy as a lark. Let's go straight into the kitchen now because I want to look at our calculations for the final regime of food supplements for Birthday before the big race."

When they got in Betty was not at home, but within five minutes the door opened again and there she was, pink cheeks from hurrying, and saying that she'd been up to the grocers which, as it happened, was on the way to the Isaacs' farm and that part of the mountain where Jack grazed his sheep. Dan seemed hardly to notice, but Fred, in view of the conversation they had just had, took a good look at her. He thought she didn't look happy at all. In fact, she could have been crying. She dashed about, and seemed to have a lot to do, but he had a definite impression that she was upset. It made him purse his lips, and raise his eyebrows, turning it over for a few moments, until his attention was demanded at the table, and he sat down.

Between Pugh and his daughter the conversation went like this: "What do you think, Bethan? Linseed or Ginseng to go with the Patent Flying Force?"

He'd look up from his chair, enquiring, into the face that hung over him, and the eyes that shone so much in response. At such moments her skin seemed to swell under the pressure of what she wanted to say but could not express. But there was no frustration in it. It was more like the essence of a moment just before a person, knowing that they had something delightful or particularly useful to contribute, might revel in a dramatic pause on the brink of their reply. Only, with Bethan, the punch line was withheld somewhere in space.

Her father could always hear it though.

"You're right, love," he'd say the next instant, as if in response to an audible reply. "We should give her the Linseed and Ginseng, and forget the Flying Force until Wednesday. Do you agree to that, Fred? Now where does Betty keep the bicarbonate of soda? Betty?"

He had to go and look for her, and found her in front of the mirror in the pantry putting lipstick on, and her best scarf draped around her neck.

"Oh, are you going out again, Betty?"

"It's such a nice evening," she said, "I'm going over to Pugh's farm to see the new baby."

She would not get as far as the Pugh's. Near the old hut by the stone quarry she might find Jack Isaacs waiting for her now, after all. On the other hand, she just might not. For the sake of the first option, she was all bloom, an effervescent current of anticipation quivering just under her skin and giving her eyes a sparkle. But for the sake of the second option there was a deadly venom ready to break out now as she remarked tartly to her brother, "I've been listening to you and Bethan going on and on, and if I don't get out I'll go mad. What am I saying? Not you AND Bethan. Just you. You talk to that girl as if she can understand and talk back, and it's daft. Don't argue with me now. I'll just be glad when this race is over."

If Jack failed to turn up altogether, like he did last time and said it would never happen again—but what had she been doing this afternoon if not waiting and expecting him and he hadn't come yet—then what should she do? Lurk around among the stones and small rowan trees until a group of school children come upon her and she has to make out she's looking for a special leaf for the bloody birds? Should she absorb again those long drawn minutes when everything—the sky, the wind, the turf, the rocks—became pregnant with despair? Pregnant? That wasn't the problem. That couldn't happen to her. But this other thing, that stung like the serpents that got under the skin of the Jews when they were wandering in the desert, did happen.

"Where do you keep the bicarb, Betty?" Dan asked.

"In the cupboard where it's always been," she said, and she went out the front door.

"Well," said Fred. "I don't think she's a particularly happy woman today after all."

"No" said Dan. "It seems it didn't last. Pity. Never mind."

Three quarters of an hour later Betty was lying in the bracken with Jack. Tall and thick and green, it hid them from sight and she could gaze up at the sky and see out of the corner of her bliss-filled eye at the same time, the coarse white of his shirt; feel the arm that she was lying on under her neck. He wore an old waistcoat that had belonged to his father, of black hopsack that had developed a greenish tinge, and was sewn with wine dark satin across the back. It had four pockets, and Betty felt as if a piece of her heart had dropped into every one. When she had met the twins in the Co-op one day last week, she gave them, secretly, a bar of chocolate that she had just bought. Megan looked up at her with astonishment. As they walked away Edith said, "What's come over old Betty vinegar then?" Megan had stopped just outside the door and was dividing up the chocolate. They took the long way home, to eat it where they might not be seen.

Jack began to whistle through his teeth. He had his eyes on one tiny white cloud, and sniffed the very first wicked little wind of evening that scythed over the grass; that just bent and scented the wild seed heads on the dry coarse stems. In a moment he'd look at his watch, but for now he felt like whistling *Dafydd y Gareg Wen*. He started softly, but he was dying to let rip. "Hush," giggled Betty. But when he got to the last exquisitely melodic climb of notes, that he could do perfectly with each interval so exact it pierced the heart, than he let the full sound out. He lay there in the long green bracken, and whistled loud like a mad blackbird, holding Betty struggling and laughing in his arms.

Emrys heard him. He was half a mile away, but he heard him. He'd brought Gypsy up here to train her, where her old loft was safely out of sight. He had his older brother Gareth with him. "That's Jack Isaacs." Emrys said. He began to walk over in the direction of the sound. "Come on, Gareth. We can ask him about that mark on Gypsy's claws." But Gareth was ten years older than Emrys, and he knew better than to go looking for Jack in the bracken. He didn't say anything, but he made out that he had a rough place on his boot that had blistered his foot, and he wanted to go home to his wife, and let Em make his own way to the dairy.

Chapter Eighteen

THE NEXT TIME BETTY SAW Jack was when he came with Olave Richards, Servini and Owen and the four of them went straight down to the loft. Betty knew that Jack was in the garden. It was her that he had come to see, not Bethan and Em who were tending the birds until Dan got back from the pit in about half an hour, or Birthday. She would come out soon with a basket, to pick beans. She tidied herself in the pantry mirror, put a dab of scent behind her ear, and went off. The four men were discussing the directional instincts of birds when she drew near, and whether or not, when the stars were no longer visible, their magnetic pull might still be felt. When referring to a mechanism as sensitive as that, would you call it psychic or physical? Olave Richards insisted that the definition of the difference between the two was often in the ignorance of the observer and not the thing itself.

"We'll have a chance to find out when Birthday flies," Betty said tartly over her shoulder. "It's only eight months Dan's had that bird, and he seems to think she could find her way home from China."

They laughed, but Jack cast a slightly anxious look at Bethan.

"I don't think we need worry about Birthday getting lost,"

he said. Betty, who had her eye on him even though her back was turned, wanted to needle him. "Oh no? Birds get lost all the time. Look at the pigeon that your girls caught last week. It came from Finland. If a bird from Finland wandering about in Cwm eating the rubbish that Megan and Edith use in their traps isn't a lost bird I'd like to know what is!"

"A bird?" Fred asked. He had wandered up in the last ten minutes and was standing between Betty and the loft. "Did they find a bird? A racing pigeon you mean?"

"Yes. Didn't I tell you?" Jack said. He hadn't told anyone except Betty, and that was no accident because he didn't want anyone in the village to know about it. It looked a wonderful bird and he was hoping to breed from it before having to return it. The bird's registration ring could not be taken off its leg or forged and so he couldn't keep it exactly, but he was taking his time about notifying the Fed.

"We had that bad weather at the beginning of the month," Owen said. "It'll have been blown off course."

"Oh indeed!" Betty took him up. She was bending over. Her thighs ghosted through her dress as Jack looked at her. But he also heard her voice. "You men won't even consider that a pigeon occasionally hasn't got the faintest idea which way to fly. It couldn't possibly be that perhaps that bird was bred in a village up there, and along comes a man like my brother who thinks that homing is some magical power invested in this wonderful bird, and he sends it off like Birthday is going to be, five hundred miles or more the second or third time it's been out of the loft."

"You sound really worried, Betty. Won't Dan listen to you?" This was said with a very slight ironic overtone, but she didn't catch it, or she didn't choose to.

"Oh, I don't care," she said. "You know me. I'm not really one for the birds. But if that one gets lost I'm off to stay with

Morwen in London. There wouldn't be room for a sane woman in this house for a while."

Somehow the conversation had turned a bit nasty. It wasn't what Betty had intended. The little group were silent when she finished speaking, and the backwash of her own words caught her unaware with a miscalculated rebound that caused her to cock her head rather like those birds she had been talking about; a little movement at the same time lively and defensive.

"Come on, Bethan," she said in a nice loving voice. "Come into the kitchen with Aunty Betty. I bought some of your favourite sweets when I went up for the bread."

Occasionally if she enticed her like this, Bethan might follow her. So it was this time, and the two of them in single file retreated towards the house.

A quarter of an hour later Jack looked into the kitchen door on his own.

"I'm off," he said. "The others have already left."

"Wait a minute."

He waited. She came over and stood by him, smiling.

"Watch out," he said quietly. "Where's Bethan?"

"She's in the other room. But what do you think she's going to do anyway? Go round the village gossiping?"

"She has feelings all the same," he said. "You don't know what they are."

"Oh, I know what feelings are like!" she said, the skin under her eyes seeming to reflect the light of a nearby fire as she pushed gently against him with her arm.

"I don't mean that kind of feelings," he said, getting drawn in a little. He stroked down the side of her face with the tips of two fingers. "But it's not kind to talk in any way that can worry her."

"Oh, you're like my brother!" she brought out on a breath that was exasperated as well as indulgent. "Can't either of you see that she is what she is. She can't hear reason, and take part in a conversation. Dan goes on and on as if she can. It drives me mad on times." Jack didn't respond. Or at least not in a way that Betty was capable of noticing. He ran his fingers reflectively several more times down that smooth lavender scented cheek before moistening his bottom lip with his tongue in the way that almost floored her with desire, and saying, "I must be off then."

Oh, those words!

"See you tomorrow, Jack?"

"Yes."

"By the hut?"

"All right then." He had no hesitation about promising. It was the easiest way of dealing with the present moment, and besides, he probably would. And off he went, whistling between his teeth. His sheep dog, waiting for him at the gate, pricked her ears and with an anticipatory whimper and excited stirrings, attached herself to his heels for the walk home.

Chapter Nineteen

When the time came to send Birthday to France, however, Bethan gave no sign of anxiety, and presumably she never did hear what Betty said about birds getting lost. She lowered Birthday into the travelling basket just as she had done several times now, and she watched with a smile as, hand in hand with her father she stood on the pavement and Owen Morgan drove away in his van, taking Birthday on the first leg of her journey. At the railway station she would be loaded on the next train for Cardiff and after that another. The porters were used to handling the birds. They lifted the crates gently enough to break no bones and brusquely enough to avoid holding up the train, and Birthday on her bed of straw would hear the baskets creak and the croon of other birds, and the shunt of the engines.

But there was still no respite for Betty. Even Jack, when she saw him, wanted to talk about pigeons. Two days before the race Emrys was in her kitchen complaining to Dan about what Servini had said to him when he confided his ambition to race Gypsy from France.

"I wasn't saying I intended to race her tomorrow," he complained. "But he said she didn't know the difference between east and west, and would as soon fly to Poland as back here. Did you ever hear anything so stupid? I'm sorry to talk about one of your fellow grown-ups like that, Mr Pugh, but you agree with me, don't you? Gypsy was a bit muddled between our garden and yours but that's different from getting Poland and Great Britain confused. I told him, I've been training Gypsy on the mountain, where she has to get her bearings without being tempted by seeing her old loft and she does very well. You saw her, didn't you, Miss Pugh? That time when you and Mr Isaacs were collecting herbs."

"Let Dan have his tea now," Betty said sharply. "He's been up and working hard since five in the morning. And take that whatever-it-is off the table."

"Sorry," said Em, picking up his beetle box and a paper bag full of stamps. "Will Birthday be across the sea yet, Mr Pugh? Imagine her being in a train in France now. It seems wonderful, doesn't it!"

"You heard me, Emrys," said Betty. "Go on. Take Bethan with you."

Em looked at Bethan. She stood quietly just as usual, with her thick hair canted forward because of the way she hung her head, her soft mouth slightly open, eyes fixed on her father. "Shall we go out then, Bethan?" the boy said. "We can go and see the other birds. Cheer them up a bit."

Dan looked up and just gave Bethan a nod. "You could let the other birds out for exercise if you would please, Emrys. You and Bethan. It's just about time. Then they'll be ready to come back in and not keep me hanging about. I'll be out after tea, just to tend to the birds before I have my sleep."

"Think of that, Bethan," Em said as they went down the path. "Birthday's probably on the train in France at this very minute. They have different trains over there. They eat garlic. We only give it to the pigeons but the human beings eat it over there. My Dad says French men are small. Napoleon used up all the tall ones in his army. Do you know who Napoleon was, Bethan? He was a great General. My grandmother says she remembers her grandmother telling her that if she didn't go to sleep at night and stop talking to her sister, Napoleon would come and beat her. As if even a girl would be stupid enough to think an army general would have the time to travel all that way for such a thing! When I'm grown up I'm not going to be stupid like that." He paused for a brief think, and swung his catapult around his fist reflectively as he walked. "When I grow up, Bethan, I might marry you," he said. "I like you better than all the other girls. You are really pretty, you know. It embarrasses me to say so, but I thought I should. Do you like me, Bethan?"

Surprisingly enough she turned a big smiling face over her shoulder and actually said,

"Yes."

Em was so amazed to hear her voice he nearly jumped out of his skin.

"Good heavens, I've done it now!" he said to himself under his breath. "I'm engaged."

He was unusually quiet for a while, and when Dan came out he was practising with his catapult while Bethan picked flowers in the ditch. She would gather a handful of ragwort and daisies and then forget about them.

"Come on then," Dan said. "I thought you two would have cleaned the boxes by now."

He went into the loft, followed by Bethan, and soon they were all busy with the scrapers and the brushes, and the water and grain. Two birds were left inside; Black Rill on the nest incubating the egg which Birthday would race home to, and another hen bird also.

Emrys was unusually quiet. Dan reflected on that remark about Betty collecting herbs with Jack Isaacs. He pressed his lips together as he worked, a small grim smile, saying nothing. Surely Betty... Yes. Betty. What could you do? Just keep quiet he supposed. Maybe when Jack had worked his way through the whole village he'd move to Brecon or Swansea, and start on the women there. Sell one farm and buy another.

"So what's keeping you so quiet, Emrys?" he eventually said. The boy straightened his back and stood there with the small brush in his hand.

"Mr Pugh," he said. Somehow around the middle of Em's body there was always an accumulation of extra shirt, the bulging contents of his pockets, often a package looped onto his belt, that gave him a generous girth; north and south of these arrangements he was as thin as a stick. "Mr Pugh," he said. "Bethan and I are going to be married."

There was quite a long pause before Dan said, with an expression of serious attention to Em's words, and his eyebrows raised a little, "Now?"

Emrys gave his future father-in-law a very sharp stare right into the eyes, but encountered only the solemn respect and attention that one man ought to give another at a moment like that.

"No. Not now," Em said. "But are you willing, Mr Pugh?"

"Very pleased, Emrys," he said. "But I hope you agree that we can see how things go for the next ten or fifteen years, and then who knows? Very likely it will all work out exactly as you say. Until then we can keep it as a bit of a secret between us. Right?"

Emrys didn't quite know what to make of that, but somehow he began to feel better. "Right," he said. "I'll take the bucket out on the vegetable patch shall I Mr Pugh?"

"Yes please. It's time the birds were coming in." And with that the three of them went out to where the pack was already flying in a tight circle over the garden. Then they dropped in a cascade of wings through the open side of the loft, while Dan and Bethan counted them in; Dandy, Checkmate, Barbarey, Coral... He released the stay catch and let down the wire mesh over the shaded, murmurous interior, feeling the need for sleep catch on his eyes, like husks of corn floating in the air.

Chapter Twenty

IN THE MORNING IT WAS another bright day. Summer in these parts could mean scuds of rain soaking the dark hidden crotch of the valley, with its matted bush and wet stream, for days on end. But this year you looked at the land and thought not of the human body, but of heaven, and wings, and sky. On the top of the mountain there were larks in their hundreds, measuring the turf far beneath them with their piping threads of song. Those wild ethereal eyes would see, long before anyone else, the heroic wings of the wanderer returning from France, and witness the steady dip and pull, dip and pull of wings like oars navigating a celestial ocean. From the point of view of mere human beings, it was necessary to wait until returning racing pigeons breasted the front mountain before you could see them. That is unless you climbed the back mountain and stood as high as you could up there and got a slightly longer view. Emrys had decided to do this, and when the great day arrived, at about two o'clock he climbed up the path behind the Pugh's house in company with his father and Servini.

As on that other famous occasion when Jack Isaacs had entered a bird in a race from France, all the other local fanciers had kept their birds in the lofts to leave the whole sky free for the returning combatants. Not a wing was to be seen from Cwm to Merthyr Tydfil, unless you lowered your gaze to the hedgerows and bushes and took in sparrows and blackbirds. Over the front mountain even the clouds had been folded up and set aside, and the pathways of heaven were as clear of traffic as terrestrial ones when a member of the royal family was expected.

Jack Isaacs was the other fancier who had a bird in this race. He didn't rate its chances very highly, but having once entered that time before, he couldn't let it go. The romance was irresistible to him, like that other one.

Today he was glad to be occupied on his own bit of turf, with his little girls going wild with excitement, and his own wife around whose waist he put a remembering arm, and found it more pleasant than Betty's. Maybe this was what philandering was about; to remind a man of what he liked best.

Elsewhere in the village, groups of people were gathering everywhere to watch the outcome of the race. Like all crowds, they gathered too early. There was the usual knot of people around the Post Office, then in Dan's garden perhaps ten, including Dan himself, and Bethan, and similarly in all the gardens along. And now, after all that optimism and determination Dan had his doubts. The sky even here, looked so vast. Eight months he had had Birthday. He had bought her from among the possessions of a man who had had to leave the area suddenly and who had sold the entire contents of his loft after a period of complete inaction as a fancier. Consequently Birthday had had less training than just about any other bird of her age that he knew, and precious little of that on this home ground. If the bird had not belonged to Bethan he would have been more philosophical about the chance he was taking. But seeing as the girl loved this bird so much, should he have run the risk of such a long distance race? Standing there, listening to the casual gossip around him as he waited, he seemed to hear again all the endless conversations of a life time to do with the homing instincts of birds, and the eternal mystery of it all. All the stories of lost birds.

"We've got a long wait yet," Fred was saying, looking at his watch. "The very earliest Olave Richards and Emrys calculated was three thirty. Around then."

"Are you tired Bethan?" Dan said. "Sit on the bench? Only if you want to." She made a sound that could have been "wait." She radiated that mysterious pent up, and yet satisfied state of excitement which was uniquely hers. She wore her famous slide. From where he was up the mountain Emrys could look down on the Pugh's garden, and he could see Bethan, and the cherries in her hair. A second later he nearly choked, because he was eating a biscuit at the moment when his eye caught something.

"Careful, Em," Owen said, giving him a great thump on the back.

Servini turned round on the path, looking at him.

"What's that, Dad?" Em managed to shout between coughs. "Look!" His father, who was about to give him another clump between the shoulder blades, looked up and saw, indeed, a mark in the sky that could have been a pigeon. He looked at his watch. "Not yet," he said. "Come on. Be realistic."

"Dad!" Em shouted, as if he was a hundred yards away. Owen put his thumbnail against his mouth, and stared hard. "I see something," shouted Servini. He had the black eyebrows and bony features of a costal Italian cut-throat, and you were suddenly aware of it if you saw him standing in the open air with his eyes lit up with excitement.

"Bethan!" Emrys yelled down. "Mr Pugh. We can see something."

His shrill voice caused the little figures below to turn from the front mountain and look up instead behind them, as if staring at the source of that distant yell would make it clearer.

"There's a bird coming," screamed Em.

"It can't be one of ours yet," Olave Richards said to Dan. "That boy's not so good at mathematics as I thought."

"I'll go to the kitchen and get our sandwiches," Betty said. "All this excitement makes everybody hungry. Come and help me with the plates, Bethan." And as of course there was no response, she said again sharply, "Bethan!"

"Oh," Dan said, in a quandary. "Better leave her here, Betty, just in case."

"In case what?" Betty said. "In case that bird can transmigrate itself like Houdini?" And before there was time for anyone to laugh at her witticism, they all saw it; they saw a bird in that dip on the left shoulder of the mountain, and it was definitely a pigeon.

"It's Birthday!" Dan said. And he swore quietly in the back of his throat, like a man seeing a ghost. "It's Birthday!"

For several seconds something resembling the collective fear or bewilderment of mere humans in the presence of the supernatural certainly gripped them all, whether they had heard Dan's astonished words or not. Down by the Post Office, all along the edges of the valley, not a voice was to be heard, and then shouts and yells went up. The screeches of Edith and Megan, Emrys' boots pounding and kicking stones as he raced downhill, the call of Servini's great tenor from his thin neck, and a chorus of bellows from the colliery yard.

"Well, my girl, it's Birthday!" Dan said in an awed voice to Bethan. "It's Birthday." Bethan had her fingers twisted together, her eyes blazing with joy. She was breathing heavily and looked as if she would jump up and down, but her feet never left the ground, although her knees bent and straightened.

As Birthday flew closer, dropping down over the pit head track, planing across the open end of Fforchaman Rd, and circling her own loft, excitement reached a fever pitch beyond what anyone there could even describe. Long before there was time to work it out, they knew that Birthday had not only won that race, but set a new national record. Every man held his breath as she landed; as Dan took the racing ring off her leg and slipped it in the clock.

There was a near riot after that. In the Post Office, Mr Bryant was juggling wires and headphones, with his fingers trembling. Normally calm and deliberate enough to send any reasonable man mad, he was beside himself, and in danger of fusing the entire county.

"Birthday, the racing pigeon, property of Miss Bethan Pugh," he finally announced, shouting into a crowd already intoxicated with the news which he had not announced yet, "is declared the winner of the international competition race from Nantes with a record breaking time..." and then his voice was drowned out by the cheers and yells, and he gave up.

Chapter Twenty-One

"I HOPE YOU'VE GOT THAT bird insured," Dr Thomas said to Dan when he called later that week. "They're worth a lot of money, I understand, prize racing-pigeons!"

"Luckily there's no danger of her being stolen or anything like that," Dan said "There's not much point in stealing birds, doctor. You can't get the original registration off the bird without mutilating it. And also you might think they look all the same, but to us fanciers each mark is different. Birthday is registered as belonging to Bethan and that's the end of it."

Bethan was not in the house. Her father had asked her to take some grain down to the loft, and there she was when, standing in a quiet fashion gazing just around her, she noticed all at once the doctor's car. There weren't many cars in the village in those days, but even if there had been Bethan would not have mistaken that car for any other. The highly idiosyncratic recognition system that was hers seemed to be released by very sensitive triggers which always took others by surprise. Something in the whole demeanour of a person—their spirit most likely—would either clear a channel for communication between her and them, or block it. In the latter case she seemed genuinely unable to hear their voice, and once or twice, for example, she had walked into Betty as if she had been unable even to see her.

But where Dr Thomas was concerned, she recognised not only him but his car, his hat, his bag. She ran now down the garden path and into the kitchen through the back door, arriving just as he was doing up the clasp of his bag, so that her breathless scamper broke through his train of thought. The crepe soles of her sandals squeaked as she pulled herself to attention, and she gave out a little pent up noise that was part breathlessness from running, part laughter and expectation.

"Oh, so you're here Bethan," the Doctor said kindly, straightening up and taking a full view of her. "Well, I must say, you look a fine girl and every inch the owner of a prize racing-pigeon!"

The child stood basking and wriggling under his gaze, her eyes and skin glowing. Her hair stood out in a bush around her face, and every now and then between her parted lips, a little exclamatory sound bubbled out.

"That's it is it," the doctor said, smiling and seeming to understand her. He didn't. He only understood her feelings, and he pretended, out of politeness, to understand more. "Well, I'm sure this village has never known a bird like Birthday. Do you want to show her to me before I go, Bethan? I think I've got time."

He followed the ecstatic child down the path again. Dan and Betty stayed in the kitchen. "I don't know how he finds the time to be so kind to her," Betty said. She was much kinder herself for the rest of that day.

Meanwhile Bethan was holding Birthday in her hands. The doctor was tall, and had to bend over inside the loft. He caressed the bright intelligent little head of the bird with one finger. On the scale of human intelligence, this little creature rated rather low, just like her mistress. But there were secrets locked up in both cases.

He noticed once more the asymmetrical scattering of white marks across the pale blue grey; the intricate bars and checks of the folded wings, and said to Bethan, "Oh, this is a lovely bird! What a wonder that she has been to France and back, Bethan, while you and I were just sitting here. She flew high up in the clouds and the sunlight and over the sea and all. How did she find her way? What a clever bird!" Bethan listened to every syllable. She remembered what he said. "She could find her way anywhere I shouldn't wonder," he added, and his comment sank, unaware, into some profound space from which he had no idea that it would ever return to puzzle and torment him to his dying day. He gave one last stroke to the feathers. "Will you be putting her back on the nest now? Is it safe for me to open the door?"

Bethan promptly set down the bird in the nest again, the familiar conformity of her fat fingers around the bird's unafraid body as she did so striking the doctor as something like a poem. He opened the door and stepped out. The fishmonger's cart went past on the road below, and knowing from long habit roughly what time it must therefore be, he looked at his watch and swore softly.

"I must be off, Bethan. Oh dear, oh dear."

He hurried nimbly down the path, and straight through the kitchen. "'Bye Dan. Goodbye Betty. I'm late." And he was gone.

Dan, who was normally no great drinker, went down to the pub once more that evening where since the race every man in the village must have stood him a drink at least once.

"This must be the last night," he said, when he got there. "I can't go on drinking to celebrate Birthday's win for ever."

"Well then, make it a good one!" Jack Isaacs said. "Betty told me you've been drunk every night this week."

"Who knows what Betty will say or do next?" Dan said,

casting the words in an undertone between the floor and his own elbow. But the atmosphere was too busy for such an interchange to be picked up. Jack himself scarcely heard it.

Olave had brought Iris down for a pint. She was sitting in the corner with Jack's own wife. He could look at her at the same time as Margaret. He was annoyed with himself for having mentioned Betty. What a fool he was. Besides, something else distracted him. He was aware of tiny runnels of feeling that were draining away from his inner image of Betty, like sand and water draining away from underneath a building that was going to collapse. But he didn't turn against the women he was finished with. He just eventually developed a tendency akin to Bethan's; a little edge of blindness and deafness. This process had begun in relation to Dan's sister. So the sound of her name snagged on his mind. He raised his tankard to take a long pull on it, and saw Iris's hair over the brim, and the colour of it carry on down the glass. A lovely tawny wave.

There was a group of men by the bar who were trying to persuade Servini to play his violin. He only had it with him because he had come back from an orchestral practice in town. He said he'd had enough of playing for one day. "Oh, go on, mun. Just one. Look, Jack's here. He can whistle."

"What's that?"

"Come on Jack. Do that duet with Servini of *Dafydd y Gareg Wen.*"

In the end Servini took out his fiddle. He began. Isaacs, all unconscious of a few winks that were exchanged behind his back, pursed his lips and whistled. They were getting good at it. The two sounds soared and wove around each other, taking on a few more sophisticated developments. When they reached the end of it, there were shouts for more, and after a short debate Servini struck up again with a piece of Mozart he and

Jack had perfected. And damned if at that very moment there wasn't a sudden blare of noise from the basement, and the silver band practise was started.

"Tell them to be quiet!" some called out. But others argued, saying "Fair play. It's Thursday night."

"We'd better be going, Dan," Fred said. "We're on at six and you aren't going to feel at your best, mun."

"What do you mean?" Dan said. Fred put his arm under his elbow. They staggered down the hill together with Servini. In the pale gloaming of the Summer evening there was still, at ten o'clock, a patch of blue in the sky. Betty was in the kitchen.

"You're weaving around, Dan."

"That's not me, That's the walls, love," he said with a wicked smile. "Now let me get to bed and have a bit of rest, will you." And he managed the stairs like a trooper and took his boots off and almost all his clothes before he lay down.

Chapter Twenty-Two

IN THE END THEY DECIDED against entering Birthday for Niort. One long race was enough for her for the season, and for July and August Dan and Fred raced other birds and consolidated their plans for Birthday's future. They sold some eggs, let her hatch a couple more. Fred took a chick, and Jack Isaacs another. The days began to get shorter, and just when the men were beginning to be ready to talk about something else other than racing pigeons, Britain declared war on Germany.

There was actually nothing sudden about it. The news had been on the wireless for months and there were some men in the valley—Olave Richards and Servini for example—who had talked to each other constantly about European politics for the last year. But for Dan and Fred and the others, it was sudden in the sense in which a man who falls over a cliff edge is suddenly and quite differently aware of that land no matter how many times he has previously walked past or seen it.

When the word went out that there was to be an announcement on the wireless, those who had a set invited their friends and neighbours in to listen. It was a morning in September. Dan and Betty stood in the shadow-filled kitchen with Fred and Mary. They called Bethan in from the garden.

Together they listened, as Mr Chamberlain told them that there would be no more pigeon races for the foreseeable future.

Fred was the first to speak. "We should have flown Birthday from Niort," he said. His wife, sitting with a cup of tea in front of her and wearing one of her best dresses, began to cry. Fred put his hand on her shoulder, not knowing how to react. He'd have liked to say, "Well now, come on Mary. There's no need for that." But past experience had taught him that the result would be a deluge. Instead he explained to her that he would not be called up to fight because mining was a reserved occupation.

Betty's heart began to tear away at the inside of her chest. How about sheep farmers? Margaret's mother was next door. She had been widowed in the first war, and now it would happen all over again. Margaret's husband worked in the Bank. He would definitely be called up. One of the first, she wouldn't wonder. Hadn't he been in the Territorial Army when he was younger.

"Dan," she said in all innocence, "poor Margaret. John was in the Territorials with you wasn't he, just after school. They'll call him up for sure."

Then she put her hand over her mouth. There was complete silence in the room. The voice of the radio was relegated to that level of ether from which no comprehensible message gets through.

"What do they do about it?"

"I don't know. What do they do?"

"I think my grandfather got a piece of paper and he had to go to some sort of depot outside Cardiff."

"I don't mind fighting," said Dan, "but I can't leave Bethan."

"No you can't," said Betty.

"I didn't join the Territorials" said Fred. "You remember how my Aunt Glenys made such a fuss. Well, I never joined. But Owen Morgan went and so did Jack Evans. Do you remember the others, Dan?"

"No I don't," he said. He had his eye on Bethan.

Margaret came in. "Can I bring my mother?" she said. "We listened to the broadcast with Leslie in Globe Row. They've gone up into the roof space of the pub to look for flags, but Mam wanted to come down and I must get her away from those photographs."

Two more women, both with damp handkerchiefs, was more than Fred could stand.

"We should go down the Shepherd's" he said. to Dan. "There'll be more news there."

"More than on the wireless?" said Betty sarcastically, but Dan was already half way to the door.

"You never know," he said, "Olave Richards may be down, and he's been following this situation for months. He knows everything about it. We'll come back and tell you what he says."

No sooner were they out of the door than Betty stepped smartly into the front room and came back with the sherry bottle from the sideboard. "We need a drink," she said, "just as much as they do. Now girls, here are the glasses." They looked happier already, just at the thought. Perhaps, since war had now been declared, Betty, would be one of those who would rise to the occasion. She would do some vital work or keep everyone's spirits up. Already Mary, who had thought that the Germans would drop bombs on them that very day, was reassured by her and willing to talk to Margaret's mother instead of crying. Almost a party atmosphere developed. One or two other friends called in, including Jane Price who was always very kind to Bethan and sat at the table with her looking at pictures of birds.

When the men came back eventually, they were as full of news about the war and everything that had been going on, as they had previously been of pigeon racing and all things to do with the birds. Usually the end of the racing season could herald a rather flat time, when the maps and racing schedules were briefly put away and conversations lagged. But this time Hitler stepped into the gap with the sort of precision which, had he known about it, he would probably have resented. And now at last Olave Richards found that his maps of Europe and his information about foreign cities didn't automatically suffer translation into pigeon perspectives. Between an obsessive interest in birds and in the news of war, a convenient displacement was achieved within hours. Which was not to say that Dan and others like him were any less assiduous in their attention to their lofts in the days that followed. There was no change in those routines at all. As the Winter drew on and the days were short, the birds were still exercised and cleaned and fed, the difference being that Dan, for instance, if it was pleasant enough to stand outside meanwhile, would be talking to Em or Fred or Jack Isaacs or even Bethan about the German advance, or the British expeditionary force, or a hundred other possible topics related to fighting.

When the spring came round again it was hard to think what to do with the birds because racing, even from Scotland, was almost impossible. Even breeding was curtailed because some of the men who had volunteered and gone to fight left large teams of birds to be temporarily distributed among other fanciers in the valley. There was talk about call-up papers, but for a while only volunteers were contacted by the Ministry. Mining was a reserved occupation. When Dan went to work, he passed notices urging him to increase his productivity to provide coal needed for the war effort.

As the months went by and the weather got warmer he always loved working on the early shift. He would wake at five o'clock, wash, make himself a cup of tea and eat the porridge that Betty left for him, winter and summer, on the stove. He would put on his boots by the door. It was quiet. If there was a flush of pink in the sky he might wonder if, eventually, it would rain and he would step out into the egg shell freshness of the break of day.

Down the garden path he went, through the little gate in the hedge, and jumped the three steps. All he had to do now was just cross the road at a diagonal, and go down the lane past Owen Morgan's dairy, and Servini's, then about fifty yards along the edge of the stream and over the bridge to the pit head.

The wheel began to turn as he approached. It squeaked. A languid, low toned sound, as comforting to a generation of children that had been brought up in the valley as the ticking of a clock. The other men on the shift converged on the same spot. He went down in the cage with Fred. "Do you remember how exciting it was when we were boys and came down here for the first time?" "Yes," Fred said, and yawned. He yawned hugely and scratched his head, pushing back his helmet. "What made you think of that?" The cage banged its way down into the complete darkness. The smell of the upper earth in early summer gave way to another atmosphere, not without its own charm; of the dank and the dark, and the distinctive smell of cold coal. And leather, oil, wood and men's clothing.

The cage halted and the men tramped off. They worked their shift in the way you do a job that has no end in sight. No deadline to be completed, story told or house built, but just one unfathomable quantity of coal to be mined every day. They talked and thought, when they paused for breath, or to eat their sandwiches, of other things. When eventually Dan returned above ground the world had weathered in the interval of his absence. The long summer morning had dried it out, and a touch of staleness was in the air by the time the two o'clock bus bounded down on its way back from Jack Isaacs' end of the village. Dan crossed the road behind its rump and started up towards his house. Betty, returning from town on that very bus, had shopping which she would put down in the pantry and then go and make her brother's dinner. If he was not already in the kitchen when she got there, she planned to go to the back door and call him in from the garden. She was looking forward to kicking off her shoes, which were hurting her, and washing her hands under the cold tap, and putting cream on them. But when she got inside she found her brother standing by the kitchen table with a letter in his hand.

"What's that?" she said, and then stopped. There was a fresh, pleasant smell in the room from the garden and the flowers, and a breeze from the open back door through to the front. "What is it Dan?" she said.

"A letter from the Ministry."

"Oh no! What do they want with Bethan this time?"

"Not them. The War Ministry." He didn't look at her. He still kept standing there.

"So?"

"I'm being called up, Betty."

"What do you mean?" she said. She sounded as amazed as if the subject of the war and any personal involvement in it had never been mentioned.

"What I say. Look at it. I'm being called up for active service."

She was in the pantry by this time. "Let me see," she called, but she was putting something on a high shelf. She came over eventually and he handed her the paper. "You can't be called up," she said, before looking at it. She thought that perhaps this was a warning in advance for next year, or at least a long time ahead. Anything could happen. The war could be over. Hitler could have a heart attack.

"What's that then?" Dan said, pointing with his finger. "Next week. Cardiff Depot,"

She read it. "They can't mean that!"

"That's what it says. It says that I have got to report for active service. I'm to join this regiment, look. They've got it all worked out. And those are the dates when I was in the Territorial Army. The Doctor's got to sign my certificate."

"Tell him not to," Betty said. She was beginning to sound frightened. "There's Bethan. I can't look after her without you. She wouldn't do anything. She can't be without you, Dan. Doctor will have to tell the War Ministry."

Even to Betty's own ears, this sounded implausible. It wouldn't work.

"I know! Doctor Thomas can tell them that you have dust on your lungs. They sent Megan Gough's nephew back home when he tried to volunteer last month because he's had dust on his lungs."

"But I haven't got dust on my lungs," Dan said quietly. The way he said it put an end to her desperate inventions. She stood stock still for a minute, then pulled out a chair and sat on it and began to cry. She was not a crying woman, and Dan was taken aback. "I'll come back, Betty," he said. "It won't be for long..."

"I know," she said suddenly dry eyed again. "You can be a conscientious objector."

"No I can't."

"Why not. You never fight. You wouldn't even fight Geoff Matthews that time when he threatened Dad with a poker. You ARE a conscientious objector." The tears spilled out again. But for all her efforts, she knew there was no going back. She'd be left there alone with Bethan for the rest of the war. Perhaps for ever. And in from the garden at that very minute came the great girl herself, standing in the doorway with the daylight behind her, the bulk of her body holding it back like a dam holds back water, but spilling out near the top, soaking the bushy margins of her hair.

Dan saw her, and for once instead of the kindly welcome, and the smile with which he always greeted her, he seemed struck instead with something almost like anger. He was in a trap from which there was absolutely no escape, and he knew it. His daughter's unique dependence on him carried with it no rating recognisable by a recruitment Board. Every man of fighting age who had been daft enough to join the territorial army in peace time was being called up, reserved or not, in love or not, with wife pregnant, mother dying, it was all the same. He would have to go. And so he looked at Bethan with a frown of despair.

"Dad?" she said.

He pressed his bottom lip against his teeth. The instinct to protect this child was a raging passion with him. Her exceptional helplessness touched off elemental reactions that transformed a father's routine instincts to shield and guard his child into something transcendental. Above all, he had somehow succeeded in mining a little seam of happiness for her in the hard rock of the incomprehensible world, and no one else—no one—would be able to come for her if he was gone.

A minute ago he had looked at Betty's tears not really understanding this watery female sad business. But now from the very gut he felt his own salt tears tear at him. His heart ached. He couldn't speak, but he just walked to the door where Bethan was standing and put his arm around her shoulder and they went out.

Chapter Twenty-Three

IN ANY COMMUNITY IN WAR time there are plenty of tragedies working their way through the collective system like poisons in a body. And so the call-up of Dan Pugh was only another in the same vein. Although Dr Thomas did try for him, he knew that representation to the War Ministry on compassionate grounds in Bethan's case would be futile. It was. Betty was almost as desperate as she would have been to hear that Jack had been called up. When she thought of the time ahead, alone with Bethan, she was at her wits end. And others in the village sympathised with her. Everyone could well understand the unique quality of this particular tragedy, because no one was going to be able to explain what was happening to Bethan.

Dan Pugh would sit at the kitchen table with Bethan and show her photographs that had been collected from the public library, of men with guns, and groups of men running under fire, and houses exploding. But they meant nothing to her. Under the impact of her father's obvious distress she would grow sad and solemn, and on one occasion she wept. But it was because he was unhappy, and not because she understood anything that he was trying to explain to her. So he gave it up after only two days.

Then he changed tack, and started to tell her, in a cheerful voice, and with a pleasant smile, that he was going on holiday. Unfortunately, he couldn't take Bethan with him. Oh dear! That was a shame. But he would come back nice and brown and he'd bring her a present. It was similar, he said, to Birthday going to Nantes. He was going to Nantes too. But because he couldn't fly it would take him a long time to get back. Would Bethan be a good girl for Aunty Betty while he was on holiday abroad? Yes? He'd bring her back a nice present. Definitely.

He repeated all this each day until the morning when he had to leave.

When he heard the tramp of boots in the road before the morning shift, and the second siren sounding from the pit head, he couldn't really quite believe that he was no longer a part of it. There was a pane of glass in the front window that was bent with age and gave a distorted view of the bank behind the colliery. He was looking through it when Betty came down the stairs, and he held the sort of memory of it which a man would have from looking through tears.

"Oh," Betty said when she saw him. He had his clothes on ready to go away. "Well, you look a fine man, Dan," she said. "I'm proud of you anyway. And don't you worry. I'll look after Bethan. We'll have to have a lot of sweets in the house, and cake, and visits to the cinema!"

"Thank you very much, Betty love," he said. He had tears in his eyes because her spirit, and her being so brave moved him. He wished she'd be sharp, and familiar, but it couldn't be said. "I've told Emrys to look after the birds, and Fred of course. Birthday is a very valuable bird now, but there'll be no problem about that. Any chicks will be sold, and Fred has the list of takers, and the prices, which are very good, so you can use that money, Betty, to take the edge off any shortness you may otherwise experience while I'm away. It's Bethan's money, of course, but it's only right..."

"You've said all that, Dan," Betty interrupted, but gently. "You've explained it all, remember? Here's Bethan now. She's coming down the stairs." There was the click of a latch outside at the same time, and Fred came through the gate, leaving Owen in the van waiting in the road. Bethan had just appeared, looking exactly the same as every other day, and absolutely not noticing that her father was differently dressed. She looked about her at the three of them.

"Well," Dan said. "Here we are Bethan. Dad is off on his holiday now." He put on a very bright smile. "Oh, I am going to enjoy this, except of course, that I am very sorry that my lovely girl can't come with me. But we couldn't go to Nantes with Birthday either, could we. We had to send her off and wait for her to come back. So now, send your Dad off and wait for him to come back, isn't it!" And he held his arms wide, and Bethan walked into them. He kissed her. "Right, off I go now in Mr Morgan's van, just like Birthday did. Goodbye Betty." He kissed her.

And he went.

Chapter Twenty-Four

BETHAN HAD WAVED TO DAN as blithely as she did on those days when he was on the afternoon shift. Her face was unclouded. When he was gone she went immediately down to the loft with the new scraper, which was the last thing that he had given her before leaving.

After an hour or so Fred came down the path to help Bethan with settling the birds and to make sure that everything had been properly done. He found Emrys with her. They were playing in the ditch where Emrys had constructed a small scale version of a trench and a gun emplacement and he was trying to teach Bethan, without one iota of success, about modern warfare. All the chores in connection with the pigeons had been carried out, however. There was nothing more that Fred needed to do. And he realised, with a sensation of betrayal as if he had no business taking advantage of such a thing, that Bethan would go in for her supper and allow Betty to put her to bed in good time today because she thought that her father was on a night shift at the pit. Tomorrow would be another matter. He supposed that somehow or other Betty would look after the girl.

When the next day dawned Betty, with no need to time her work to fit in with Dan's shifts at the pit nor indeed to do more than half the work she was accustomed to, got up a little later than usual. To her surprise she found Bethan already up and in the kitchen in her dressing gown. At first sight she thought this was a good omen. The girl did understand, after all, that things were different now. Look, she had even put on a pair of socks, and one shoe—although where she could have found that was a mystery because, as Betty now realised, it was a sandal from the summer before last. But maybe things would not be so bad. The war would be over soon, and Dan would come home; and in the meantime Bethan might make some progress if she had just her aunt to deal with. Some vague idea like that gave Betty a momentary feeling of optimism, and she smiled at the girl and said,

"Hello, love. We'll have breakfast now. Aunty Betty didn't make any porridge last night but you can have an egg." And she reached out for the saucepan.

Bethan didn't move.

Watching her out of the corner of her eye, Betty made the tea, cut the bread, toasted it, fetched butter from the pantry and fresh milk off the doorstep. When she had put everything in its right place she said, "Come and sit down and have your breakfast now Bethan."

The girl didn't move.

"What are you waiting for, Bethan?" she asked with some beginnings of sharpness in her tone. "Sit down now." And then, when no response at all was forthcoming, "What is it?"

She was dying for a cup of tea herself, and she pulled back her chair sharply and started to pour from the pot. At least the tea came out in a good solid stream of pure, dark liquid as usual, and the sound and smell of it was the same. She filled the cup and added the milk before she realised that the sound of running liquid had outlasted the pouring from the pot. With an immediate horrified suspicion she started up again exclaiming "Bethan!" But of course it was to late. The girl was urinating where she stood.

Poor Betty felt as if that flicker of belief a moment ago in the possibility of life carrying on and not being so bad, was a flame which her niece had just crudely put out. Before she actually slapped the wretched creature she managed to persuade herself that it was not entirely Bethan's fault. After all, the girl was used to being fetched from bed every morning either by Betty or her father, and taken to the toilet before dressing and going downstairs. It was hardly her fault if this morning of all mornings Betty had forgotten. Tight lipped with the mop, after having seen off Bethan herself, changed her, washed her legs and left her with clean clothes, Betty dried the lino and swilled out the mop under the garden tap. A day like yesterday, lovely with sunlight and a fleece of white clouds was being puffed gently down the valley. She looked up at the back mountain, and out towards the watershed of the valley where Jack Isaacs would probably be already out with the sheep.

Endurance was the answer. She went back indoors and made a fresh pot of tea. She went upstairs and fetched Bethan. She successfully sat her down at the table. When the girl said, in that questioning voice, "Dad?" and then "Dad?" again, she said,

"Dad's gone to work Bethan."

She watched very closely while Bethan took in this reply. First the child's face was vacant, while the message wrote itself slowly in the mysterious texture of her brain. There was a long pause, and then a minute realignment of her features signified acceptance. She picked up her spoon.

After breakfast Bethan helped Betty with the dishes as her father had taught her to do, and then she went quite blithely off into the garden in her usual way. Betty went to the shops. She had become one of those who stepped back when they reached the front of the queue and said to the next in line, "Go before me. I'm not in a hurry." And by this means she had another five or ten minutes in which to chat. Naturally most of the talk was of whose sons, whose husband, whose brothers or nephews had gone to the war, and news of fighting. And in Betty's case there was a great deal of sympathy about Dan and questions as to how she was managing with Bethan. It relieved her to say what she could; to say that it was early days, and if Bethan could just be patient she was sure it would all come out right again.

But the loneliness she felt, and which she knew she had better not express, began already to throb like a toothache. It was not only Dan. It was Jack. She felt weighed down already as if Bethan was sitting on her head in some nightmare where she had lost the capacity to push her off and stand up like a free woman, but she might have been able to manage if it hadn't been for Jack. If only he was still there for her, she might be all right. The responsibility, day and night would not stifle her. And when lunch time came and Bethan found that her father did not return from the pit, she would know what to say.

She went home and prepared the food as if Dan would come back. She very nearly laid his place at table. She said to herself, 'Good heavens, girl, what are you afraid of?' She was afraid of the moment when Bethan would come in and look around the kitchen and say, "Dad?"

No! She would not come in and say that. She would respond when Betty went into the garden and called her. She would come down the path—yes she would—and she might be rather quiet and even sad, but she would be a good girl.

"Bethan," Betty called in the garden. Nothing. And then she got the fright of her life, because she was already standing there in the kitchen. It was true that she looked very pleasant.

It wasn't Bethan's way to be sullen exactly. Essentially she was a happy girl. She was happy now, if a bit doubtful; questioning. She said, "Dad?"

"All right," Betty said to herself. "I'll have one more go." She went right over to Bethan to be near her, and said in a coaxing voice, "Dad's not coming home just now, is he love. He told you himself. He has gone away for a little holiday. He's gone to France, just like Birthday did. And just like when Birthday went to France, we shall wait now until Dad comes back. He'll take longer than Birthday. And he said, 'Be a good girl for Aunty Betty' didn't he? Do you remember him saying that, Bethan? Yes, you do. So we'll wait until he comes home, and in the meantime we'll just do everything the same. So come and have your lunch."

She put her heart into it, Betty did. She was a nice woman, she really was. She would have loved Bethan very well if she had half a chance. She'd have made her do things her way, but a nice way. She stood up straight now, looking for the effect of her words, her red lips pursed half questioning, half smiling, her eyebrows raised. But you never saw anything so completely dull as the face of the girl in front of her in comparison with her own. Slack eyes, slack mouth, then turning her head, or rather revolving it very slowly as if it was on some sort of a gimbal, and the voice eventually coming out: "Dad?"

In a contained snap, Betty's whole form reshaped itself. Her head up, one hand on a hip, she gave the entire room one quick cursory search with her eyes as if, there being any answer around, she could snatch it up. Nothing suggested itself except the possibility of convincing Bethan that Dan was at work in the pit and would be home when the shift was over. After all, he often did an extra shift for some reason; a sick friend, or the offer of a bonus.

"Dad's awfully sorry but he's going to be late today, Bethan," she said, turning brusquely back to the oven and taking out a dish as if she was in the middle of doing ordinary things and only saying the truth. "Sit down now, and let's make sure we leave enough for him. He'll be hungry when he comes home."

Miraculously, Bethan sat down. When later on in the afternoon Fred came to see to the birds Betty told him what trouble she'd had. She looked tired already. "She can't take it in" she said. "It's no good. I can't make her understand."

"Well, he won't be gone for long," said Fred. But he was fooling himself. His words sounded doom laden in his own ears. He had found himself all day remembering the past when he and Dan were boys and talked about versions of life they found in books, and became immersed in them together, and fought other boys and fell in love with Miss Price; walking on the mountain, riding the ponies bare back, throwing stones; and then, later, always having a friend to drink with in the pub, or beside whom you were welcome to pull up a chair any time. Now what? In response to Betty's plea for help he said he'd fetch Bethan in when it was time for her tea and so he duly went down the garden. When she saw him, Bethan raised her eyes towards him and said "Dad?"

For a dreadful moment he thought she was confusing him with Dan; would insist on having him as a substitute. He said, "No!" before he could stop himself. And then—he'd known her all her life. He'd known her as a baby arriving in this world with the albatross of her mother's death around her neck. He had known her as the bewildered little creature whose late walking and stunted mental development had reanimated with the flame of compassion the heart of a man who thought he must have died with his wife. But that was Dan, not him. And now here Fred was without his friend and he found that none of those feelings which he had vicariously nurtured were in fact his own. He did not understand her as Dan had. He felt threatened and helpless as she turned her face up to him. "I'm very sorry, Bethan," he said. "But your father has gone away for a little while. He told you yesterday, didn't he. He said 'I've got to be away for a while, Bethan, but until I come back be a good girl for Aunty Betty and Uncle Fred.' Do you remember?"

His own words conveyed a great deal to him, but to her, nothing. She kept her eyes fixed on him. From her point of view the words he spoke were not linked and so she couldn't get any meaning out of them. She heard, or even saw, other things when she heard words; a synthesis of what was around her, or gaps of nothingness, or, as in the case of Betty very often and others in general, she didn't hear at all. But when her father spoke to her, several words together would combine and produce a particular meaning. This was one of the mesmeric and delightful talents of her father; the fact that he produced these tricks.

She now, fixing her gaze on Fred, tried to see if he might be amenable to a similar achievement, but it couldn't be done. He couldn't piece together the widely separated perceptions which she was holding out to him. She tried again. "Dad?" she said. He only looked more discouraged.

"You haven't had your tea yet, Bethan," he said at last. "You should come in now."

She didn't move.

Chapter Twenty-Five

Dr Thomas, who had by degrees arrived at a position unprotected by the normal confines of medical practice, was called out at nine o'clock to persuade Bethan to go to bed. Since the Pugh's house was only a step away from his own and the rain had stopped he walked there. He didn't find anything so odd about this house call. The previous morning he had operated on the eye of a Pekinese which had been torn out in a scrap with an Alsatian. And on the other hand, he had also performed, in the local hospital, an operation of plastic surgery on the hare lip of a little girl, which was destined to be written up in the medical journals. Then the constant broken heads supplied by the Irish community living in a little settlement called Brighteye, situated round the side of the back mountain; births, the whole panoply of disease, minor and also major operations still only made up about two thirds of his responsibilities. The rest were spiritual. His patients drew no line between the soul and the body.

When he arrived Bethan was nowhere to be seen. "Good evening Betty," he said as usual, but with his voice tinged with sadness.

"It's very good of you to call, doctor," she said. At the sight of him her tears had started to flow. Her friend Margaret was with her.

"Where is Bethan?"

"I can't get her to come in from the garden, Doctor. She's waiting by the pigeon loft. For her father. For Dan."

"Oh, I see," he said. He was silent for a moment, his mouth turned down, his eyebrows raised, looking softly at Betty who said miserably, "What am I to do?"

"About Dan? Nothing much I'm afraid. You must just wait for him to come home, and as long as he is safe there will eventually be an end to all this. Just remember that, Betty."

"But what am I to do in the meantime? With Bethan?"

"I'll go down now," he said, meaning down the garden. "She'll be all right once she understands I daresay. Give her time, Betty. Little by little."

He went out of the back door and along the garden path. The sky being overcast now, the valley already lay under the shadow of night's impending darkness. Four days ago Dan had stood here at this hour and seen the sky one vast evening blue, and until ten o'clock still luminous. No more. Neither the sun nor the man were still out.

"Bethan!" the Doctor called. He couldn't see her clearly—only a soft blue shadow by the shed door. When she heard his voice, she looked up at once and took a few running steps towards him before stopping. He came up to her and chucked her under the chin as he had done since she was a little girl.

"How's my little Bethan?" he said. She responded as she always did, the light going on in the face that had such an extraordinary capacity to shut down on life, so that the contrast was crudely marked when she accepted or rejected contact.

"Have you taken care of the birds?" he said. "Is Birthday on her nest ready for bed?"

She made a move towards the door. "Do you want to show her to me? Just quickly before we go in? Open the door then."

Bethan put her big little soft fingers round the handle, carefully pressed down the latch and opened it. Within the unchanged shadows of the loft the roosting birds shifted and crooned on their nests as the two figures stepped in. "And where is Birthday?" Instinctively the Doctor spoke in a hushed voice, like a man in the presence of sleeping children; or then again, there was something of the interior of a cathedral or a church in this tiny place. Bethan immediately pointed out the nest on which Birthday sat. Birthday's mate had lined it with fresh straw. She rested in it, curve to curve, with an unanswerable placidity, while turning up towards the child an eye so alert and bright.

"She knows you, doesn't she!" the Doctor said.

Bethan liked that. She made a crooning sound of her own, and smoothed the scattering of white marks across the bird's head with her finger. The bird was worth a pretty penny now. In his notebook Dan had some breeding figure written down, and the names of two studs competing for eggs.

"Well, let's be off. It's time for our bed now. Will you open the door or shall I?"

This was not the way to get out of a closed room if the door keeper had a handicap like Bethan's. She didn't move, just gazing at him with expectation. "Open the door, then." She responded at once, moving so carefully, her whole heart in it. As they stepped out into the garden once more the doctor noticed how, despite their brief time in the loft, just in those few minutes the key signature of the garden had shifted further down the minor scale. A cat, unmarked by Em, sidled past the rhubarb and into the ditch. Below the bank, in the street, the lights had come on.

The doctor walked down the path towards the kitchen and Bethan followed him. When they got in, Betty was in the pantry and the room was empty. He could see that Bethan looked around at once for Dan. He marked the sad ricochet of emptiness as her eyes searched the room and then seemed to have the capacity to return the unused space back into herself. But as soon as the doctor spoke to her the expression of emptiness was briefly replaced by the familiar look of shining expectation. He was tempted just for a moment, to sit at the table and take his torch or his stethoscope out of his coat pocket which doubled up with him as toys with which to amuse children. How many times in past years had he played in this way with Bethan, spending just a minute or two to shine the torch light through her fingers, or to let her listen to the pulse in her own wrist? But he held himself back. Instead, with a look of concern and sadness, he faced her and said,

"Well, Bethan. Where's Dad?"

She continued to gaze at him with her expression scarcely changed. "Your father," he said. "You haven't seen him for three days have you?" At that moment Betty came in and said, "Oh, thank heaven, you've got her in, Doctor. Now let's hope she'll go to bed."

"Will you go to bed now, Bethan?" he said after her, bending his face with that quizzical look, over the girl. For the first time Bethan looked uncertain. In the expectant silence that surrounded her, she sensed something that she pursued with the utmost concentration for a moment, and finally said, "Dad?"

For different reasons the doctor was almost as discouraged as Fred and Betty had been.

"Dad isn't here," he said. "He has gone away to France, Bethan, like Birthday did. And just like you waited for Birthday, and carried on with your life, and helped your Aunty Betty then until Birthday came home, so you must do the same now. Wait for Dad, and then he will come back." He waited. She was listening. "Poor Dad. We miss him, don't we. Look.

Your Aunty Betty has been crying." They were tears of frustration as well as sorrow. As for Bethan, she couldn't actually see her aunt at the moment. Betty was edited out, like a ghost, by the extraordinary workings of the child's mind. Betty's tears meant nothing to her. Absolutely nothing whatsoever. Only the inexplicable absence of her father, held at bay though it was by this visit from her friend the doctor, meant anything.

"It's no good," Betty said. "She doesn't understand." Dr Thomas sighed, and resigned the position of extreme attention with which he had been bent towards the vacant face of the child.

"Will you come upstairs to bed now, Bethan," Betty said in a more businesslike tone and going and standing at the foot of the stairs that led up from the kitchen. Once there had been a door that closed off the stairs but it had been taken away. In some of the houses it was still there, with a latch like the latch on the loft door. In fact it could have been that door that Dan had used to make an entrance for the shed. Bethan didn't move. Not a whisker.

"You see!" Betty remonstrated; but the Doctor had witnessed this scene before, and he knew what to do. He made a little gesture with his hand towards Betty, to silence her, and said to Bethan, "Go up to bed now like a good girl, with Aunty Betty."

And off she went.

As for making her understand about her father, he persuaded himself that a little time would make all the difference. He went away confident of this. He was just thinking, as he reached his own front door, that he had not had his pudding at dinner time, and it would have been kept for him. But there was a message from Globe Row. Would he call at number thirty? The old man was having great trouble breathing. So Dr Thomas went out again round to the garage, and started up his car.

Chapter Twenty-Six

SOMEHOW BETTY GOT THROUGH THREE whole months of this purgatory, and then she received a telegram from the Ministry saying that Dan was missing, believed dead, in France. For all the world, the Ministry might as well have sent someone with a gun rather than a letter and shot Betty straight through the heart.

She gave a gasp, turned as white as a sheet, and Margaret, who happened to be visiting, caught her enough to stop her injuring herself too badly as she fell. They both landed up on the kitchen floor. Betty's blouse was torn. Margaret bruised her arm. Margaret screamed as loud as she could and her mother hobbled over from next door. Together they bathed Betty's face in cold water, and then helped her onto a chair. They made tea. They wept. Others came to the house. The news seemed too cruel to be true. Whatever would become of them. Whatever would Betty do with Bethan?

Emrys was so upset that Owen could hardly make him understand English.

"Look here, Emrys. Hundreds of men have already died. Terrible though it is we have got to defend our country. By all accounts Hitler is a frightful fellow, and we'd have him here telling us what to do if men like Dan weren't willing to stand up to him."

"But he'd only just gone," sobbed Emrys.

"Well, that's because of his previous training in the Territorials. They send the territorials on active service almost at once, you see, because they know what to do. And in the chaos of Dunkirk he was just one of those who vanished. You remember when you have children of your own, don't let any of the boys join the territorial army. Now come on, Emrys. That's your third hanky. Be brave now. Stop crying. How do you think I feel?"

By the time Fred got to the house Betty was standing with the piece of paper in her hand not saying a word, dry eyed. "Oh, Betty?" he said. He took the piece of paper off her and read it himself. "I'll make you a cup of tea," said Margaret. The kettle was on, and whistling like a banshee on the hob. Strong sweet tea was listed in the First Aid Handbook that they had been studying in the ambulance classes, as the first remedy for shock. Fred had been underground when the news came. Mary had had to send Matthew to wait for him at the pit head. The shift ended after fifteen more minutes, and Fred appeared in all his dirt, the coal dust on his skin congealed in sweat lines at the base of his throat and in the crease of his wrists and elbows. The whites of his eyes looked like chalk on a blackboard. He had walked up to the threshold of the Pugh house in his boots, took them off there, and went in in his socks. Mary was waiting with the others.

He said, "Where's the letter? Let me see it."

"It's not a letter. A telegram," she said.

When he turned his eyes on the words, he said, "Well! Presumed dead doesn't mean dead. They may have made a mistake." But it wasn't very convincing. He had hoped to make something different of the words. Perhaps he would in time. But for now he stood there and two enormous tears came out of his eyes and made tracks down his cheeks. He wiped his wet face with the back of his hand, then slowly turned round and went out. He walked home in his socks, and without a word Mary walked after him carrying his boots. He never saw Bethan and neither did anyone else for hours. She was in the garden with the birds.

For the rest of that day there was as much coming and going in the house as for a party or a wedding. Many of Betty's friends strove to make much of the possibility that Dan was still alive but unconscious somewhere, or taken prisoner. But then another would say that when this particular wording was used it was because the man in question was known not to have been included in a group of soldiers taken prisoner, and the wounded had all been brought back.

Emrys wanted to know if there would be a funeral. An uncle of his had died a year ago and the body had been laid out in the kitchen for his friends to take leave of him. Emrys had been allowed to look, and with ghoulish enthusiasm he had hung around all day like a cat attracted by the smell of fish until his mother sent him packing. So now he asked this time, but his heart wasn't in it. A minute later he cried bitterly.

He went out into the garden. "Bring Bethan in," Betty's friend Margaret hissed at him, pinching the top of his arm through his coat. He found her by the loft where she had been every day. He felt almost afraid of her. What would she say if she had to be told that her father had been killed. Was dead, then. He managed to stop crying himself, so that she should not see. To anyone capable of observing it, he looked almost more shrunk than usual. The colour would not come back into his face evenly, and the hand that he had used to wipe his eyes had not been clean.

Bethan looked up at his approach, and with exactly the same demeanour as usual, came towards him. He didn't know what to say. She seemed not to notice anything amiss. She stood looking down on his grief stricken face without her expression altering one jot, and he looked up into her thick blue gaze not knowing what to think, and for once silenced by it. In the end, pulling himself together, he said, "I'm very sorry about your father, Bethan. Really I am." But then it made him sob, and the solitary sound of his own misery, apparently unshared, quelled him more than anything. She didn't even put her arm around him. If she felt nothing herself, she could have done that. That was the way he thought. He sniffed. "You've got to come in," he said, wiping his face with the back of his hand again.

Betty had had the clothes line up, of all things, and on the ground she had dropped a white pillowcase without noticing. That was how upset she was. Emrys took a hasty step forward and put his boot right in the middle of it.

"Oh Bethan," he said, "Isn't it awful!" She was crying now all of a sudden. She made no sound but huge tears, bigger, it seemed, than anyone else's, were running down her cheeks. She didn't wipe them.

He took out the handkerchief he'd been given when his mother put him in his dark suit, and reached up to dry her face. She let him. He tried to pull her over to the bench so that he could stand on it, but she wouldn't. He couldn't put his arms around her shoulders, or anything.

"Look Bethan," he said, "You've still got Birthday. We'll look after her together."

Good God he was miserable. He had wanted Bethan to feel like he did, and now that he saw her unhappiness it was only worse. Out of the corner of his eye he saw other things—a dandelion, a plastic food bowl, a peg from the line—which imprinted themselves on the matrix of his soul and when he was an old man the sight of these things still made his gorge rise. "I'm your friend, Bethan," he said. "I'll always be your friend."

She wanted to say something. He looked up at her, waiting for her to get the words out. He looked full into her face, that struggled to reflect the mystery of her mind. She said,

"Where's Dad?"

Emrys gulped. When Bethan had been carried along smoothly in the protective wake of her father, he had thought she was not that much different from himself.

He said, "He's dead, Bethan. Almost certainly he is dead. He can't come home. They made him go to the war, and now they've lost him. He's probably been shot." He touched the back of his own skull as he said it, pointing through his hair, and turning his neck round to show her. But death was a concept she simply could not understand. He was not being helpful to her, taking refuge in that sort of an explanation. She frowned at him.

"I can't help it, Bethan. I loved your Dad too. He was a wonderful friend to me. He gave me Gypsy and Scram. He let me come here and ask him questions. Do you remember our picnic on the beacons when we were training Birthday?" She smiled. She was remembering it. And then, "Where's Dad?" she managed to say again.

Chapter Twenty-Seven

FROM THAT DAY ON FRED and Emrys shared the duties of exercising and looking after the birds with Bethan. But it wasn't an arrangement that could go on for ever. Fred had his own birds, and he had his work just like Dan had had. He too did his shifts down the pit, and Emrys, who was still at school, couldn't cover for him when he was on mornings.

They were at their wits' end sometimes. It was no use asking Betty. The birds had hysterics when she went into the loft, and it was mutual because she was frightened of all those wings, and made a muddle of the feeds and wouldn't scrape the boxes. In fact it was Bethan who did most of the work. Dan had taught her well, and she had always done many of the chores in his absence, provided he told her in advance. Now she did things without him.

Emrys and Fred were not aware of how great a change this was. But neither could they rely on her without constantly worrying themselves. "There's Birthday to consider," Fred would say. "That bird is worth a load of money, Emrys."

"She's Bethan's bird," Emrys would always say.

Jack Isaacs, with an eye to buying some of those birds, weighed up the advantages and disadvantages of putting in an occasional appearance in Betty's kitchen. Just before Dan's departure he had arrived at the moment when he no longer found Betty herself really desirable. It happened with him on a regular basis, that when the flame of a sudden attraction had died down he would become acutely conscious of the risks of infidelity. Up until that moment he tended to assume that his wife was deaf and blind. But then, when he suddenly woke up to her again as a woman, simultaneously he became obsessed with the idea that she could see around every corner and hear a whisper half a mile away. This state of mind regularly gave him hell, but with Betty it was exacerbated by her sharp wits and a certain ruthless streak in her nature.

If Dan had not gone to war, it would have been even worse in one way. In her brother, Betty had lost someone she really loved, and it reduced her appetite for affection, just as a greedy man who has had some teeth out will go off his food. Consequently she didn't at first notice that falling off of Jack's attention. It was part of the greater change, which served to mask it. But after a day or so more she began to notice that he had not been to the house for a while, and she would have gone up to the other end of the village and chased him over the mountains where his wife could see him if he hadn't, in the nick of time, come knocking again at her door.

He came when he knew, from a conversation in the Shepherd's Arms the previous evening, that Fred would be attending to the birds. He went into the garden first before calling in the house. The birds were flying. He could see the pack cutting a swathe through the air. A mixture of cloud and blue patched sky emphasised the chequered pattern of light as they wheeled in formation and wings were either lit up or closed against the sun.

Down below, Fred was in the loft scraping the perches. A moment later Bethan emerged, carrying the bucket over to the vegetable patch.

"Hello," Jack called out. The man gave him a wave as he came through the door. "Bad business," Jack said, by way of greeting. He shook his head sadly. "Well, must get on with life, I suppose, for as long as we can,"

Fred replied in a gloomy voice. "You haven't been called up yet have you. But it will come perhaps, if the war drags on. I'm sorry for every man who gets his papers. Some of the young ones are all ready to go and keen as mustard, but the mothers! It breaks your heart, mun."

"What will you do with the birds? Sell them?"

Fred put down the rake, straightened his back leaning one hand on the outer wall of the loft, and gave a short dry laugh. "You too, Jack? I'll have every pigeon fancier in the valley down here before long!"

"Really!" He was taken aback. But Jack was a cool fellow. He sat down on the bench and started to roll a cigarette. "You'll have to do something, won't you? And selling the birds is just about the measure of it."

"Yes, but it's got to be done fair and square. And if, like everybody else, it's Birthday you're after, she belongs to Bethan. Registered owner." They both looked over at the girl. She was raking the manure into the soil. She had lost some weight already—an element of baby fat which until now had clung to her like the undeveloped mind of infancy. This slight change, coupled with an air of vacant puzzled sadness which had slowed her movements down, gave a better look to her appearance. In the past even the gesture of raking the soil would look over-careful and marginally uncoordinated. Odd. Now, for some reason, as the men looked at her, they could have been looking at anybody.

"Does she understand yet?" asked Jack. "Have you managed to explain to her yet." Fred just said "No."

"I thought she looked..." He searched for a word. "More

sensible you know."

"Not when it comes to that. It's as if her brain doesn't have any language for death. We've done everything. And you see, she has a life of her own. She may live a full span. And for that entire time, from what I can make out, Birthday belongs to her. Right now the chicks and eggs are selling for a lot of money and it all goes into the Post Office Savings account, like Dan said, to help pay everything while he is absent. Well, he's going to be absent a long time!"

"Hm," Jack said. "All the same. Just remember I'm interested." He struck the match on his boot and lit up.

"Have you been in to see Betty?"

"Going now," he said, and got to his feet.

"Tell her to put the kettle on."

"All right." He strolled off down the path, and in through the back door. The kitchen was empty. "Betty?" he said softly.

He heard the clatter of a plate in the pantry. He went over. She was collecting some dishes together. She had been doing something else—making biscuits; pastry. His eye took in the details only vaguely. In the open doorway he said her name again in the same tone. She stopped what she was doing, and confronted him at first with a hint of combat in her bearing, but then melted and came forward with her arms out. "Oh Jack," she said. She stopped short of his embrace for him to see the tears in her eyes, but then laid her head sadly down on his breast and let him hold her.

He did that. He smelled her unique smell that was a mixture of the kitchen, and the boudoir. Every woman, it must be said, was unique to him in some way or other. And universal. He also liked them precisely because they were all so alike.

"Oh Jack," she said. "Isn't it awful."

She was so depressed she didn't seem to want him to do

anything more than just hold her quietly. Torn between relief and waywardness he let his hand slip down to her buttocks, and pulled the firmly yielding flesh against himself. But she saw, with her eyes towards the outer door, the change in shadows which forecast the return of Fred before his frame actually appeared in the opening, and stepped smartly away.

"Come in Fred," she said brusquely, already half way across the floor. "Jack is putting the kettle on. Bethan, change your shoes, there's a good girl."

She must have said it just for educational purposes because there was no hope that Bethan would hear her, and the men could see that. They sat down at the table waiting for their tea. The girl stood by the door, not coming forward to take up her usual place, but looking instead dejectedly into the room, and then saying, "Where's Dad?"

Betty, sick and tired as she was with this refrain, said, "He's at work, Bethan. Come and sit down now."

Jack was shocked. He said, "Oh! Is that right?"

"She can't understand," Betty hissed. "I've given up. If I tell her he's at work, at least she eats and goes to bed. I can't get the doctor down here every time she needs to swallow her food, or sleep. He's the only one. She won't even do it for you, will she Fred."

"No," he said. But he cast a kindly look towards the girl, smiled, and said, "Come on, love. Sit here."

She came, her face vacant of expression like a mirror in a deserted room. Betty put a cake in front of her with icing on the top. She did it in a certain self conscious way, inviting her guests to admire the lucky girl who was so well known for liking sweet things.

"Now isn't that nice," Fred couldn't resist saying. "Aren't you going to eat it now?" Bethan picked up the cake with a forlorn glance in his direction, and bit it. He lowered his eyes before her. He felt as if the cake was stuck in his own throat.

"Well, this is very lovely," Betty said, her bitter tones cutting into the funereal silence. "My brother dies, and here I am; stuck!"

"Oh," Jack exclaimed, "Come on Betty."

"Come on Betty what?" she said, forgetting the reason not to snap at him. "There's no need to be so dainty. There's nobody listening."

"You never know," Fred remonstrated mildly, keeping his embarrassed eyes away. "These things are a mystery to us. I've heard the doctor say to Dan many times that we mustn't underestimate the possibility that more is understood than can be expressed."

"That's true," Jack said, looking very earnestly at Betty. He was essentially a kind man. It was
an accidental by-product of his way of life that he had probably caused more pain and grief than many another.

"Well then, you explain to her," Betty retaliated in an undertone, "that her father is missing presumed dead, and that this means he almost certainly is dead, and she can't have him back. Go on."

"Afterwards," Jack said. "I will. Let's enjoy this tea now, Betty." He was determined to change the subject. "Dan had Birthday entered for the Anglo Scottish Border Race. I suppose there's no chance of the Fed carrying on."

"Well, we're not absolutely sure at the moment, are we Bethan? It's the training as well. It's not fair to send Birthday without some training throws from thirty or forty miles. The club may be able to go next week; you're probably going are you Jack? But I've got my own birds, and there's a problem now about who can be at the loft to see them in."

"There are plenty of men who will help," Jack said. "I will myself. Megan and Edith can split up if you like. They both know how to work a clock."

"Oh, that's an idea. Thank you Jack. Well, we'll think about that, won't we Bethan." And so they talked until Jack stood up and said, "Well, I'll be off. Thank you for the tea, Betty." He would have gone straight out, but she wasn't forgetting his promise.

"You said you would explain to her," she said in an undertone, with significant nods in the direction of Bethan. "Go on. Let me see you try."

He bit his lip. He detected a hint of covert cruelty, or at the least, unkindness. His heart flinched; and at the same time was goaded into defiance. He looked first at Bethan, then he came back and put his chair down near her.

"Look here, Bethan," he said. "My friend Dan – your father – you know he was my friend don't you? He talked about Cwm Streak – remember? That's my bird. My best bird, like Birthday is your best bird. I saw your Dad almost every day, but I haven't seen him now for a long time." Nothing he had said so far had made any appreciable impression on her, but he went on. "Why do you think I haven't seen him? It's because he has gone to heaven. We thought he was just going into the army like he told you, but now he's gone to heaven. You see? Did your teacher tell you in school about Heaven? It's a beautiful place. He'll be very happy there. He will be living there with God. But that is why neither you nor I have seen him for quite a while now. That is why he doesn't come home. He didn't want to go without you, but he had to, and at least you can be sure that he is happy."

Now he suddenly had her attention all right. Bethan had her eyes fixed on him. Her mouth had dropped open a fraction more, and she let her face hang as it were, from the level of her gaze, as if there was a physical rope there between his mouth and her eyes, capable of taking the weight of her head. He tried not to be daunted by this.

"In heaven, you see," he repeated. "That's where people go when they die." This last sentence meant nothing to her, but it didn't matter. She had got the bit about heaven. All three adults were arrested by the moment; Betty with a caustic but attentive tilt of the head, Fred mournful, Jack slightly surprised but sticking to it. A smile of anticipation was dawning on Bethan's face. All that dull heaviness lightened, and her lips curved as she said, "Where's Heaven?"

Jack swore to himself. Damn it, what a question! "We don't know," he said, feeling a right fool. "It's a long long way away. Further than Nantes, where Birthday flew from France." But, her eyes shining and her mouth now closed tight, she looked round on them all. "Where?" she said. "I go."

This new twist on the insoluble puzzle distracted them all from the phenomenon of hearing Bethan speak.

Betty groaned. "Oh, that's it. Thank you very much, Jack."

"What have I done?"

"Only got her more muddled than ever!" she said, with eyes thrown up, and her hands putting her hair away from her face as if she had been running for a bus or bending over the stove. "Come on, Bethan. Come to bed now, or Dad will be worried when he gets back from work. Up you go."

This matter of fact attempt to close the subject of Heaven could not take away from Bethan's new discovery. She got up far more willingly than she had lately, and with a secretive, satisfied, self-contained look of anticipation, she went with Betty, up the stairs.

Chapter Twenty-Eight

IT ONLY TOOK BETHAN A day or two to find out that no one was willing to tell her the exact location of Heaven. She drew no conclusions, of course. It was just the sequence of one idea from another, or one word from another, or one observation from another, that she missed out on. The next time she saw Em she waited eagerly for him to come up the path. He shouted out "Hello Bethan," as he crossed over the steep corner between the front garden and the path across to the loft, and the local cats, who ran from him like rats running out of a burning building, made their escape. He thought he saw one, and stopped short—but it vanished. He had a stone ready in the pouch of his catapult, but he didn't use it. Instead he just twirled it round the thong a couple of times and put it back in his pocket.

When he looked towards Bethan again, he saw that she had run a few steps towards him, and she actually called out "Em." His face lit up. "Hello," he said again. She looked almost like she used to look. "We've got to put the birds out for exercise, haven't we," he said. "I'm late. That horrible Miss Price gave me detention, that's why. And I said to William – she's his aunt, remember – that I'd pay him to put ground glass in her fairy cakes when she came round to tea. I would too."

They'd reached the loft. He went straight over to the side, took the catch off the hinged wire mesh panel and let it down so that all the birds could fly out. He was watching them, making a note of which ones flew and which ones didn't. Bethan, meanwhile, like a little kettle that contained a build-up of steam on the brink of making it sing, stood beside him. When Birthday hopped onto the partition she stood as usual, near Bethan, and crooned a couple of times before rising into the sky. Then when they had all gone, Bethan burst out, first with a wild little sound which brought Emrys sharply to attention, and then the two words, "Where Heaven?"

Em was taken aback. In fact the couldn't make sense of the words, plain English though they were. Bethan didn't pronounce clearly any sounds to do with the grammar or the construct of a sentence, so that the "s" of "Where's Heaven?" was left out. For a moment he understood her to be saying "Ware Heaven." Why should he beware of Heaven? When her expression enlightened him, even then he couldn't make out how such a question could justify a look of urgent excitement, as if the answer would yield a practical result. A lot of people asked where Heaven was but they didn't ask in the same tone as one might ask "Where is Cardiff?" or "Where is Timbuktu?" That's what had confused him most.

"You mean, where is Heaven?" he reiterated, just to make sure. She nodded energetically; put her tongue against her bottom lip, smiling, silent, mouth a little open, eyes fixed on him waiting.

"Well..." he said, casting about in his mind.

"Dad!" she managed to say. So that was it. Somebody must have told her her father was there. Em said, "Well, it is a lovely place, or so I've heard. Very sunny. Lots of birds; there must be, because it's up there. They play music. And God looks after them. Very well." He emphasised that because Bethan used to love to look after Dan in certain little ways that were part of her small range of skills. For example, she used to pour his beer. So Em added for good measure, "Very well indeed. There are angels there, and they bring his slippers and pour out his beer."

She listened quite patiently to all this, but then said, with a little push against his arm, "Where?"

"Oh," he said. "You want to know where it is?" She nodded furiously.

"I don't know. No one knows exactly," he said. "It's a long way off. You can't go there Bethan."

"Where?"

"Up there," Em said, pointing at the sky. "No one knows exactly, but it's somewhere up there. None of us know where it is Bethan." But he had lost her. He could see that she had stopped hearing him, although her expression remained the same. And what was the point? At least the utterly forlorn and empty expression did not return to her face.

After that he did what he could to distract her from the idea of Heaven. It wasn't as if they had no work to do. If you don't keep a loft clean you get trouble in no time. And this was the day when the birds had to have their bath, as well. He fetched the big round tin from where it was propped up against the far wall of the loft, laid it on the grass, and he and Bethan both fetched and carried water to fill it. By the time Fred arrived the birds were all dipping in and out of the water, and a bloom had settled on the surface of it from the preening of their wings and breast feathers. Bethan was preoccupied, but that was nothing new. She usually looked most of the time, as if locked in her own thoughts. But it was some time since her preoccupation had been other than sad. Now, despite Em's disappointing ignorance of geography, she was still less sad than before. Not having heard that conversation, Fred thought to himself as he looked at her, "There you are. She will get over it. After all, people do. Even she."

Chapter Twenty-Nine

Miss Isaacs, Jack's sister, kept the shop on the opposite pavement from the Shepherd's Arms, and a little further up the hill. It is not that it was impossible to go in there, purchase something, and go out again in a few minutes, but people very rarely did, and women never. This was the place where all news came in, was sorted, and debated. It could take a really public-spirited woman half an hour to buy a box of matches.

A few days after Jack's helpful explanation to Bethan about Heaven, a particularly gripping conversation was taking place in the shop. The women involved paused briefly while the girl employed by the hairdresser next door came in for a packet of cigarettes, made her purchase, and had to hurry back to her client who was poised, a head full of wet curlers, waiting for the dryer. Miss Isaacs served her, and then the interrupted conversation in the shop was resumed.

"What did she do? How did she leave the house without Betty knowing?"

"Well, she doesn't normally have to guard the child the whole time you know. It's never been like that."

"No, it never has."

"If it had been Bethan would never have been able to stay

at home in the first place. She would have had to be Cared For." 'Cared For' in this context carried a connotation almost directly in contradiction to the words themselves in normal usage.

"Even so Betty must have been gone an awful long time. Bethan had a suitcase and everything."

"Empty though."

"Oh, love her!"

"Yes. I feel sorry for her."

"And I do."

"A girl like that needs a lot of love and it's the last thing they'll get from most."

"You're not criticising Betty are you? She's been very good, or so I always thought."

"To Bethan yes. She's good all round, yes." A very slight ripple—not a laugh, not a whisper, or even a nudge—was felt by Miss Isaac, cutting a cheese, and she looked up sharply. "Have I missed something?" she said.

"Your brother's been down there quite a lot lately."

"Has he?" Miss Isaacs responded with ready alarm. But discreet too. She kept quiet after; finished folding a measure of cheese in greaseproof paper, wrote the price on it, and looked expectantly at Meg Owen. Mrs Owen said, "A pound of sugar, please."

"Oh no, fair play. Betty's been good. But she doesn't love Bethan. Not like Dan did. Dan could do anything with that girl. She was quite easy to deal with as long as he was around."

"And so what was it that happened?"

"She caught the bus by herself." The voice went right up, expressive of the utmost astonishment, and the others all responded appropriately. "She caught the bus! No one saw her. It went a mile and a half before the conductor finished gossiping with the driver, or at least that's what I reckon, and came and asked for her fare. Of course she hadn't got any money. But she's been on the bus with her Dad, so she knows you ask for your stop, and she said 'Heaven', just like that."

"What did he say?"

"He thought it was a joke, didn't he."

"That one with the bald patch?"

"No no. He wasn't on. It was some boy who'd just started."

"Couldn't he tell that she's not quite all there?"

"Not at first apparently. He just laughed."

"And she laughed too I suppose."

"Yes, she did."

"She usually does if she sees someone else."

"Not lately though, poor girl. It makes your heart bleed just to look at her."

"So what happened. Go on."

"Apparently he just said something like, 'This bus doesn't go to Heaven, and if it did I wouldn't be on it yet, love.' The women all laughed, more or less. "So then she looked very upset. So he began to realise she meant it. And he looked a bit closer, and of course once you realise, you can easily see she's not right in the head."

"Go on."

"Well, the bus was just passing the police station, so he rang the bell. Bob was driving, and he put on the brakes, He skewed right round in the driving seat and looked behind. He could see Bethan then, so he got down and went round to the back. 'She wants us to drive her to Heaven,' the boy said to him, keeping quite a serious face now. Bob couldn't think what to say. He doesn't see much of Bethan because their house is quite far up the valley. You know. By Weekses. But he knows of her. And of course, he was very kind. He sat down beside her and said very gently that he was awfully sorry, but his bus was on another route."

The whole lot of them burst out laughing. "But poor Bethan..."

"Oh yes."

Wrapped in the thrall of gossip and compassion they fell silent for a moment. Meg Owen was going through her purse and Miss Isaacs worked the cash register.

"So she's home again now is she?"

"Yes. Of course."

"I wonder how long Betty will put up with it."

"What do you mean?"

"Well, there's no law that says she has to provide a home for Bethan."

"You mean she would send Bethan away from home? Oh, she couldn't!"

"She could. She could say she doesn't want to do it."

"She wouldn't have the heart. Don't you tell me that she could send that poor child to strangers. What would her father say?"

"Well, he's not likely to say anything, is he."

"Missing. That's what the telegram said."

"Presumed dead."

"Yes. And that means he COULD be still alive."

"Doesn't Bethan probably own the house, after her father?"

"And that bird. They say it's worth a bit!"

"Mind you, it's hard looking after someone like that. Bethan's growing up now. What about the Jackson's boy?"

"But he's a boy. That's different."

"Well, yes."

"Has Betty mentioned it to you?"

This question was aimed at Margaret who had been the lead speaker all along.

"I mustn't say anything. Betty can speak for herself. She'll give it more time, I'm sure."

"If only Bethan could understand why her father isn't coming home. If he was actually dead, perhaps she would find it easier. You can tell that a dead body is dead when you see it I suppose, however twp you are."

"And then again, perhaps not. I find it hard enough myself. It's a very peculiar idea all round, I think sometimes."

"It seems very straight forward to me."

"Yes, but you've got a more or less normal brain, Ivy."

"And I haven't!" They laughed.

"Thank you."

"Death is a peculiar idea. It's a very peculiar idea. If anyone else but God had it, it wouldn't be legal!"

And they laughed long and loud at that. Olave Richards, who had had his say on the subject that night in the Shepherd's, would have loved to hear them.

Following on this episode of the bus journey, it became clear that somebody had got to make a serious effort to communicate with Bethan. It had been hard enough getting her off the bus. It was the only time in the entire history of public transport in that area at least, that the bus had had to turn round and drive one of its passengers home to their own front door. Bob the driver told the young lad they'd have to do this. He—the conductor—sat beside Bethan to make sure she didn't have any more ideas, and Bob had to turn the whole bus round in the middle of Bethel Street. All that rattling and banging of the coachwork, and having to back onto the pavement, first waiting for a little boy to walk past pulling a rabbit on a string.

Then Betty was not at home. No one seemed to know where she might be. The truth was that she was up the back mountain with Jack Isaacs, arguing and arguing, well hidden in that part where a bigger stream flows through the wood by Baker's farm.

Jack had his arm around her in the end, and she was crying almost as bitterly as Bethan was, and from a disappointment that was not so dissimilar. She also wanted to be transported to a state that she might well have called heaven, and it was all about being with a man whose company was indispensable to her. It did not make her more understanding towards Bethan when she eventually returned home, however, her nose still reddened under the newly applied powder, to find that poor girl sobbing in the kitchen, with a bus conductor and a driver bending over her, and the town bus parked outside the door.

"What's all this then?" she demanded to know. "Are you all right, Bethan?"

"She's just a bit upset, Miss Pugh. I'm sorry; I'm Bob Douglas. I was driving the bus you see..."

Betty got the story out of them. If any one else had told her a tale like that she would have laughed, because she had a good sense of humour. But not today, and not in connection with this wretched problem to do with Bethan.

When they had gone she decided that when Emrys Morgan appeared after school, which he would do any minute and she'd keep an eye on the front path to catch him, she'd send him straight up for the doctor. With Bethan in a state she couldn't go herself. And what if the girl disappeared again? Oh Jack. Jack! All these troubles and she couldn't think of anything else but him. What a man he was. Up there, leaning against the trunk of a rowan tree, his boot in the bracken, his hand up her skirt.

With her own heart bleeding from every corner, she picked up Bethan's ridiculous suitcase. It was very light. She opened it. It was empty. There you are! The girl must have heard it said that for a long journey you take a suitcase. No one ever mentioned putting anything in it. "Oh!" She sat down at the table beside Bethan, suddenly touched. She took her hand.

"Never mind, love. Come on. Aunty Betty is unhappy too. I haven't only lost Dan. I've lost Jack Isaacs as well, damn him." She shook the lifeless fingers, and tried to smile at the girl. But Bethan had vanished. She had done that thing which she knew how to do so well, leaving the husk of herself wherever others might choose to dispose of it. There was simply no one there to share Betty's confidences, or her grief.

Someone called out from the front, and Betty recognised the voice of Emrys. She jumped up and snatched open the front door. He was there on the path, and his sister Olwyn too, who he had met on the bus.

"Emrys Owen," Betty said, "will you go up for me and ask the doctor to call and see Bethan after evening surgery? Do it now before those dratted pigeons."

"What's the matter, Miss Pugh?" he wanted to know at once. "Bethan isn't ill, is she? Can I come in and see her?"

Betty was about to say no, but thought better of it. Emrys might persuade Bethan to go down to the loft and keep busy until she forgot about catching buses to heaven. "Come in," she said, "But then go to the doctor's, all right?" Emrys wasn't allowed in Betty's kitchen very often. He took a good look round.

"What's happened to Bethan, Miss Pugh?"

"Nothing. She thought Heaven was a place she could get to by catching a bus. Someone told her Dan was there."

"Oh, that's really clever!" he exclaimed. "Fancy her working all that out."

Betty looked at him with the eyes of one starved of the company of rational people. "You can have two cakes," she snapped. "And take her out into the garden. Go on." She jerked her head in the direction of the plate that Emrys had been eyeing ever since he came in through the door. He helped himself, and said, "Come on, Bethan. We've got to go and look after Birthday. She'll be expecting us." And so Bethan got up and followed him.

Later that evening Dr Thomas faithfully responded to Betty's plea to call in the house after evening surgery, but he brought Olave Richards with him.

"He's the very man to explain things to Bethan," he said. "He's used to explaining things to children."

It was eight o'clock, and Bethan was ready for bed. They went through from the front door, all three of them, and found her there in her dressing gown and slippers, sitting at the table with a mug of cocoa. Beside her was a book containing pictures of pigeons. Dan had turned the pages for her and discussed the pigeons many times.

As soon as she saw the doctor, Bethan's face lit up almost as usual, but with a poignant remainder of the day's griefs clinging to her expression. Dr Thomas sat down beside her, smiling, and saying "How's my favourite girl, then?" She brightened up yet more at that, and something of her old radiance began to shine. Olave Richards remained standing. "You know Mr Richards, don't you, Bethan? You used to see him at school."

"Oh yes. We're old friends," Olave said. "And I haven't forgotten Bethan – look here." He took out of his pocket one of those striped peppermints like the body of a giant honey bee wrapped in a screw of cellophane. "I brought you one of your favourite sweets that you used to have from me when you had been a good girl." She took it from him, looking very pleased. He pulled out the chair opposite her and sat down.

"I'll have a glass of beer, please Betty," the doctor said, knowing she would have it for him. "Maybe Bethan can pour it for me."

"Oh yes, doctor," Betty said, going straight to the pantry. "Mr Richards, will you have one?"

Olave Richards liked a glass of Burgundy after his dinner. He declined the beer, and merely watched as Betty gave the open bottle and glass to Bethan, and very carefully tilting the rim just so, the girl poured it out.

"Very nice," Dr Thomas said, taking the glass and drinking from it with a special relish. "I always said to your father that you poured a nicer glass of beer than anyone." She beamed at him. "I hear you went to try to find Dad today." She listened very carefully to him. "Did someone tell you Dad had gone to Heaven?" She nodded vigorously. "And you thought you could catch a bus there?" She looked sulky, and then catching sight of her sweet where she had left it on the table, she surreptitiously caught the edge of the wrapper and pulled it into the palm of her hand and closed her fist around it.

"No one is saying that you did wrong, Bethan," the doctor said, noticing this manoeuvre. "But Heaven is too far away to be able to get there by bus. We say that people go there when they die, but we don't know how they go there, or exactly where it is."

Olave Richards, listening to these words, could not entirely repress his personal feelings of defiance. A bitter smile just fleetingly touched his eye. Bethan was listening to every word, but her expression was troubled.

"I think," Olave Richards said, "that Bethan must be wondering why her Dad went there without her if it was so far away; and when he will be coming back."

She turned towards him, dropping her mouth open a little further. That was exactly it.

"Now listen very carefully, Bethan, because I'm going to explain to you why your father can't come back here, even though he would like to very much." This explanation, by agreement with the Doctor and with Betty, was going to do away with the ambiguity of the message "Missing; Presumed

Dead." It was too complicated for Bethan. They had agreed to say that Dan was dead, since in all probability he certainly was. That way Bethan could be given an explanation that she had some chance of understanding. So Olave launched into his prepared explanation.

"Do you remember when Betty had a little dog called Rags? I'm sure you do. And what happened to him? He died, didn't he. Margaret took him out shopping and he had an accident in Fforest Fach and died there. He never came home. Poor Betty was very upset." Bethan looked maddeningly unimpressed. "What do I mean when I say that Rags died? I mean that he couldn't run about any more, could he? You remember that. And your Dad said at the time, I'm sure, that Rags had gone to heaven?"

Bethan moved her eyes from one of them to the other.

"It's the same now with Dad, Bethan. He went away and alas, he has died. We are all so very sorry. But there it is. And so – he has gone to heaven."

"Heaven!" she said. It was a protest? or a question?

"Yes. Anyone who dies, we say he's gone to Heaven, because it is a very very far away place that you can only go to when you are dead. God looks after you there, and it is very beautiful, so you don't have to worry about your Dad. But neither can you go there."

They all waited to see how this information would be taken. She was silent. She hung her head. "Why?" she said.

"We don't know why," Olave answered. Bethan looked at him. She wasn't sure whether she could believe that there was a thing he didn't know.

After a long pause she said, "Dada gone," in a tone so mournful it was almost too much for the school teacher. It heaped another coal on the raging fire of his rebellion against the injustice and absurdity of the human predicament. But for

Betty, on the other hand, the idea that Bethan was getting the hang of it filled her with relief. It wasn't until later on, when she herself was going to bed, that she recalled Bethan's exact words, and tears came into her eyes. Had she possessed the tiniest bit more of a capacity for communication she could have loved Bethan. She needed somebody to love, heaven knows. Before drawing her curtains, she looked out of her bedroom window. If she lifted the sash and leaned out she could look towards the left, where the cinder paths petered out into coarse grass and bracken; where the stream, that later on ran past Owen Morgan's dairy and the pit head, ran wide and shallow between rocks and in the shade of hazel trees.

Near the bus stop here burned the street lamp all night long. But up to the right at the other end of the valley, Jack would have real night around him. He would be lying in bed and hear only the occasional sound of his sheep, and the far far off tinkling of stars. Not the sound of men returning from the Shepherd's, the clump of their boots, a snatch of drunken singing in strong tuneful voices. Not the sound of the last bus driving off, with an entire orchestra of mechanical parts and body work sounding together to produce an unforgettable almost soothing harmony of its own. But Jack would have silence. She could feel it in her own heart as she looked over towards him.

Funny thing; when she had been in school she had been the prettiest girl in her class. No one had any doubt at all that she would marry. She could take her pick. So could the boys. They kept picking the other girls. Betty got a good a job in town in the Bank. And she had her triumphs; or near triumphs. She was smart and pretty enough to get someone special, without hurrying. Everyone thought so. And there was no particular moment when she turned into an unmarried woman, but that was what happened.

So what's marriage? Dan was a good deal better to live with than most husbands. And then her thoughts turned back to their beginnings. Ah, Jack! she thought. To lie in bed night after night beside him. He'd go out on the mountain every now and then with someone else. She'd have to reckon on that. But he'd come home to her. Ah! And then it was that she remembered Bethan's phrase; a two word lament capable of turning any woman's heart to water. She took hold of the edges of the curtains to draw them, and shut out the street, the dark mass of the front mountain, the sky above without its stars. "Jack gone," she said very quietly, giving herself a crooked smile in the dark.

Chapter Thirty

FOR A WEEK OR SO after the visit of the doctor and Mr Richards, things went very quietly with Bethan. She seemed to have put aside her efforts to resolve the mystery of her father's disappearance. But she still waited for him; waited, it seemed, every minute of the day. Any unexpected arrival would bring her, with her face alight, and send her away again extinguished, but inflexible. All the same, somewhere, miles inside her skull, she seemed to hear Betty when she spoke these day; enough, at least, to do as she was told. That, in Betty's opinion, would just have to do.

In Summer there was no reason why Bethan shouldn't be in the garden all day, and that was basically where she spent her time. She worked her way through all the numerous little jobs of tending the birds, with Emrys and Fred always coming and going, supervising the main routines of exercising and feeding. But there she would always be.

Sometimes when alone, she would simply stand inside the loft for hours. Goodness knows what the birds must have thought. She took up a good deal of space, but they seemed to like it. They crooned and fed and incubated their eggs, content to negotiate around her with their friendly domestic wings.

If Emrys came and didn't see her in the garden he would

know to open the loft door and look inside, and in the afterglare of bright sunlight make out the shape of the quiet girl peacefully standing there. She was always pleased to see him.

Em's sister at about this time became pregnant when she shouldn't have done. She came home one day as usual on the bus after work, but the next day she was driven home by Mr Servini. Mrs Morgan was in the dairy. She saw the car go past, and then she saw Olwyn, and she assumed it must be the half day. Olwyn living so close, her boss, Mr Servini, drove her home on half days as well as on the occasional evening when his own duties were finished early. "Good God!" Mrs Morgan exclaimed to herself, putting her hand up to her mouth, thinking it must be Wednesday and she had done all the orders as if it was Tuesday. But in the next instant she realised that was not where the mistake lay. The mistake indeed lay with Olwyn, or rather who she had lain with. This was a saleman from Pontypridd, but her mother didn't know it yet. Servini got out of the car and waited for Olwyn, who rather crawled out of her side and said, "Must we, Mr Servini?"

"Yes," he said very firmly. Olwyn had fainted at work, trying to save herself as she fell by putting one hand smack in the middle of the tray of raspberry vanilla; that very tray supplied by Booth and Co, whose young man was too handsome for his own good. She knew that she was pregnant.

"She's pregnant," Mr Servini said in a grave tone of voice to her mother, standing in his black suit next to the milk cart. "As her employer..."

"You, Mr Servini!" Mrs Morgan exclaimed. Olwyn giggled. Her mother looked at her. A trim girl, pretty as a biscuit tin lid, and plump enough to hide the first three months of anything. She bought her lipstick from Woolworth's and her shoes at the Co-op. Mr Servini blushed, and the blood made the regrowth of his beard look very black until, with his midnight blue eyes, and ink jet brows and hair, he looked like a real Mafiosi.

"Who is he then?" the mother asked. "I hope you like him, my girl, because you'll have to marry him," She wiped her hands on the wet cloth that hung from a nail. "Come into the house will you, Mr Servini. We can't talk out here."

Always a good and even a generous employer, Servini had taken Olwyn on straight from school just to be obliging to his neighbours. They had asked him, and he said yes in the simplest quiet way. Olwyn was cheeky, and ignorant. But Servini had foreseen that he would be asked to give her a job and had already discovered from Olave Richards that her arithmetic was quick and accurate and that she arrived in time for school. That said he could not be responsible for what she did when she lured the salesmen into the storage room. There among the boxes of flavourings, the sales ledgers and the various tin trays and crates of biscuits she had behaved very badly, and not only with Alan Price.

She loved it. Life was full of fun and excitement in those days. She braced her bare arm against a table and knew very well the dimple in her elbow was driving Mr Phillips mad. Or stood on one leg with the foot out of her other shoe pretending she was weary from standing, so that he could see the little toes with the nails all pained red. He went home in an absolute state and threw himself at his wife, who was very pleased and thought that the new hairdresser had done it. All that was very very delicious, and for the rest of her life she was never going to regret it, nor ever cease to do it again.

Emrys was not meant to know anything about all this, but it was useless to try to keep him out of it. Olwyn would look superior when he tried to ask her questions, and make remarks about big ears; but then she would leave coupons for free orange juice and books about pregnancy on the kitchen table, where he was bound to see them.

"She's going to have a baby next May," he told Bethan when they were sitting on the bench waiting for the birds to come back. "My Mam says she looks a disgrace, but she looks all right to me. She hasn't started to stick out. You should have seen Mrs Matthews. You know, the one in the school. She was like this." He stood up sideways and held his hands right out in front of an imaginary curve. He sat down again. "I quite like babies. When Olwyn has hers I'm going to play with it and stop it crying when everyone's working. Olwyn will have to go back to selling sweets and ice cream. Mr Servini will take her, but she'll be quite respectable. She'll be Mrs Price at least." He was silent, but only for a moment. "Good heavens, Bethan, just look at that!" He stood up, snatching his catapult out of his belt, his eye fixed on the Spencer's cat which had arrived unnoticed on its own garden wall some distance away and was either sleeping or pretending to be asleep.

"They never give up do they!" Em exclaimed with satisfaction, loosing off a stone which the cat dodged just in time. "Mr Richards was teaching us in school about government. Have you ever heard this, Bethan? 'The price of freedom is eternal vigilance.' It's a quotation. And I said to Mr Richards, "Well, what about birds?" "What do you mean?" he said. I said "Birds can't look out for themselves, or at least they are not very good at it. They need someone else to do it for them. I've seen a bird just sit there, watching a cat slinking up and not realising what is about to happen, and there's not much freedom inside the stomach of a cat! In that case I'm the one who's vigilant. I sling a shot at the cat and off it goes. But without somebody like me there, the bird can't look after itself." "Very interesting," Mr Richards said. "Plato thought of that." And he gave me this book. I don't like to disappoint him, but I'm not going to read it. It's too fat."

When it was time for the birds to come in, Em took the grain tin and the whistle, and Bethan took her special slide out of her pocket and put it in her hair. This was the compromise that had been reached with Betty. And so equipped in this way they would both stand waiting as the birds wheeled lower and lower and started to drop into the loft. Birthday would almost always land on Bethan's head just for a moment, give one or two ritualistic nudges to the cherries with her beak, and with a little brace of her claws against the girl's scalp, scramble an inch or so up in the air again, and then into the loft to join the other birds.

Then, one afternoon in September just before the end of the racing season Bethan all by herself suddenly went to see Olave Richards. Iris was returning from a visit to the shops, and as she climbed up the hill she looked up and saw Bethan walk along mountain road. Iris called out to her, "Hello Bethan. We haven't seen you up here for a very long time."

Bethan stood stock still. She said nothing while Iris climbed the hill.

"Were you coming to see us?" Iris asked kindly. "Mr Richards isn't home yet, but he won't be long." She opened the front door and Bethan followed her indoors. The narrow hallway had a floor of scrubbed stone instead of lino, and the front room where the chess set was laid out was lined with books. "Come through into the kitchen," Iris said. She put down her shopping on the table. There was a jar of chrysanthemums already on it, the colour of her hair. This room lost any direct sunlight after two or three in the afternoon. The back mountain came tumbling down only a few yards short of that side of the house. Between the windows and the sun, the soil and rocks cast a luminous shade coloured with the mix of earth and streams, thick bracken, the rowan and thorn trees. Points of reflection within the room—pieces of polished brass, or copper, or white china or linen—glinted in the deep shadow. The air was warm and smelled of soap and dust and the peppery pollen of the flowers. They had only been in there a couple of minutes when Iris heard Olave at the front door. "Guess who's come to see us," she called out.

He emerged from the narrow hallway carrying a bag of homework for correction, and seeing Bethan standing there smiled warmly, and said, "Well now, this is a nice surprise. Do we have cakes for tea, Iris?" He went to the sink in the pantry and washed his hands. The sound of his voice carried on over the cool splashing of the water. At about nine o'clock Servini would be coming up for the game of chess. It was Wednesday. Plenty of time for tea and the homework and his supper.

Iris put three cakes with pink icing on a plate. She kept sight of Bethan from the corner of her eye all the time as she boiled the kettle and fetched the cups and saucers. She would paint a portrait of her from memory afterwards. Upstairs she had canvas and paints laid out in the room that would have been occupied by children if she and Olave had had any. It always smelled of turpentine and oils. Unhung pictures were stacked twenty deep against the walls. She would lay down a base of amber and sap green for Bethan's portrait. That skin, thick and pale, but the reflective surface of which could take on the same luminescence as an egg in the nest—chrome and cadmium mixed very pale with white, and almost shaded out with a blue grey. Weren't her eyes blue grey also? Iris watched them, even as she was in the very act of pouring out the tea. The lashes were thick and blond. If the light caught them at an angle, they produced an effect as if to cross out the eye.

"Oh, you've got your painting look on," Olave said, laughing at his wife. "Would you like Mrs Richards to paint a picture of you, Bethan?" But he couldn't make Bethan smile this afternoon. She only responded with those eyes as big as saucers. She ate her cake. Perhaps she had forgotten why she came.

"Well, I'll have to resume my school work in a minute. I've forty exercise books to get through. Is there anything I can do for you, Bethan, before I start?" She put her top teeth over her bottom lip and stared straight at him. Iris had gone into the pantry. Suddenly he guessed what it was. It had to do with the letter. He had heard the story in the Shepherd's of how Bethan had been to the post office with this idea of sending a letter to her father.

As it happens, she had got the idea from Emrys. "You can send a letter anywhere," Emrys had been telling Bethan, because he had heard from his pen friend in Australia. Evidently this had made an impression on her. She had worked it out for herself. Later on she went down to the Post Office and asked Mr Bryant to write out a letter for her father, and send it to him. Perhaps the postmaster should have done what she asked, and put a stamp on it. Then she would have been satisfied. She could have waited months for an answer, and in time, on the pretext that the first one was lost in the post, send another letter. Do the whole thing again.

But as the story was recounted in The Shepherd's, Mr Bryant, a stickler for exactitude, wouldn't have any of it. He insisted on explaining to the poor girl that there was no question of the Royal Mail reaching as far as that. "Your father is with God" he was shouting at her over the counter, like someone trying to make a foreigner understand English. He always had a tendency to shout if he felt that the meaning of his words was not getting through properly. A few more decibels would, in his opinion, pierce the membrane of stupidity. It was the same if one of the pensioners made a mistake in filling out a form. Immediately Mr Bryant's voice would rise, and the words be separated one from another with hectoring gaps. “You can’t send him letters in the post if he is with God. We don’t deliver to Heaven. We don’t deliver. You see?” So Bethan apparently went away.

“Is it to do with the letter?” Olave asked her now. Still with the same expression she nodded. “Was there something you thought I could do for you?” She nodded again.

“So what would that be?”

He quite liked these conversations with Bethan when he had to think of both sides of the dialogue. It was an interesting mental exercise. As he told Iris afterwards, it closely resembled what priests had always been doing, carrying on a dialogue with someone who would never answer. In the end you made up what seemed to you a likely reply, and sometimes you probably got it right. But now Bethan started to rummage in the pocket of her dress, and brought out, very neatly folded and clean, a small piece of blank paper. She put it on the table with that almost ritualistic way of slowly moving her soft fingers, and laid it flat.

“That’s a very small piece of paper,” Olave commented. “That’s not for a letter is it?”

She nodded.

“Oh.”

She just looked at him very anxiously, in which case he added, “But it will do. It will do. Am I to write it? Very well. Now here’s my pen,” and he took his fountain pen out of his pocket and unscrewed the top. “Luckily it’s a fine nib. So...” He looked at her, poised. “Who is it to, Bethan? Your Dad? Very well. Let’s begin, Dear Dad.”

Iris had come to the door of the pantry and stood silently leaning against the door post.

“You miss your lovely father, don’t you Bethan,” Olave said. “All right. We’ll tell him that.” He wrote. “Shall I tell him you’re being a good, brave girl?” She shook her head at that.

"No? What then? There's room for a little more if I write on both sides, but what shall it be?" He paused, to give her time. "Sometimes," he said speculatively, "at the end of a letter we say, 'please write back to me as soon as you can.' But I'm not sure..."

That was exactly what she wanted. He let his voice tail off, and scratched his eyebrow with his left hand, overruled by her determination although he finished the sentence under his breath, "But I'm not sure if we can expect him to do that."

But what harm would it do? He wrote. And then later on when he was alone with Iris he said, "If that letter gets handed in through the pearly gates and God gets his hands on it, it will give the bastard something to think about."

"You want an envelope," he said to Bethan. "And a stamp. And then you can just put it in the letter box. No need to tell anyone else, you see, then." He went over to the drawer where he knew he would find what he wanted. He wrote the address and name on the envelope, stuck the stamp on, and put the little piece of paper inside without sealing it down. When he had finished, he put the lid on his pen and the pen in his pocket and Bethan, with a look of great satisfaction and care, took up the envelope.

"Well, it's been very nice to see you, Bethan. Be careful going home now. Give my love to your Aunty Betty."

Iris came forward saying, "Come on, love, I'll walk down with you." But Bethan wouldn't let her. She turned round at the door and ran away.

Chapter Thirty-One

EARLIER ON THAT SAME DAY Betty had, by the most unlucky chance, encountered Jack in town with his daughters Edith and Megan. She had faced them on the pavement, all brightness and friendliness, her heart beating unevenly under the printed cotton of her dress. But she couldn't think of anything to say. She! Betty Pugh! She made a fool of herself. She asked them all to come to tea, and of course those girls—little witches as everyone knew they were—laughed at her as soon as they had taken a pace away down the pavement.

She heard it and saw Jack turn round. He was sharing their laughter; he was sharing it! And he cast this glance over his shoulder. Just a quick glance, but he found to his dismay that her distraught gaze was fixed on him. Later on, he thought to himself, he would go down and see her. Wait until about eight o'clock. Tell his wife that he was going to the Shepherd's.

This was why, when the time came he stepped over to the Pugh's house hoping that no one would notice him, and went cautiously round the back. He didn't want the neighbours to see him calling. And if there was already anyone in the kitchen apart from Betty he would not go in. He went along the disused railway line—now nothing but a raised path that went behind the gardens—and slipped in via the ditch. It was rather like the way a fox would do it. From there he made his way quietly round to the back door. He opened it a crack. He could see nobody. He called softly. There was no answer, and in he went. There, sitting at the table was Bethan. She was staring at her pigeon magazine. There was something about her—the way she sat—that was so patient and quiet that Jack was fascinated. A man who loved animals and could do just about anything with them, it struck him forcibly at that moment how touchingly she resembled them.

She didn't answer when he said "Hello, Bethan. Is Aunty Betty in?" She just stirred in her chair slightly, as a dog might that hears a voice but no meaningful command.

Jack smiled at her. He came no further in, but made a little whistling noise through his teeth. She looked up.

"Is that a picture of Birthday?" He came over then, swivelled the book round to face himself for a moment, looked at it and said, "No. Birthday's got a scattering of little white marks over her head hasn't she. And she's a light grey. That one is dark."

Bethan's eyes were fixed on him now.

"Pigeons are wonderful," he said, in a reflective sing song tone, as if crooning to his audience as much as talking. "I have some lovely pigeons myself, if you remember. They fly up the other end, where my land is. I've got some sheep as well. Would you like to come and see them one day?" Bethan stood up.

"Not now," he said, pointing at the window. "Because it's getting dark, you see. But I'll come and fetch you later this week." He knew all about the bus and the letter. These incidents had been discussed in the Shepherd's Arms. He hadn't thought that much of it, but now that he found himself alone with the girl he knew how to deal with her; in the same way as with a dog lost on the mountain, or an injured bird.

These were his responsibilities. In fact he momentarily lost track of the fact that this had not been his reason for calling in the first place. But then he remembered.

"Betty?" he called out softly, and at that moment the front door opened, her brusque steps sounded in the passage, and she stood on the threshold, looking at him. "Well!" she said.

"I came round, Betty. You know why. I'm sorry."

"So I see."

"And I've been talking to Bethan."

"Well that's very nice for me, of course."

He was aghast. She brought him so quickly face to face with the precipice he seemed to have thrown her over.

"I'm very sorry about this morning, Betty."

She kept her distance. Even from one side of the room to the other, like magic, like scent, like particles of light in air, the essence of his being got all over her. It stung her with desire; a fierce pain, like a deep sudden cut when the severed skin springs back, momentarily bloodless, from the blade of the knife. Then the blood begins to show. Crimson beads gather on the rim, and it may be a wound that bleeds only a little, or it may pour out and be hard to staunch at all.

"Very sorry," he repeated. If he had held his arms out she would have run into then. He might have done, but for Bethan. Betty saw him glance over in that direction and desist. She thought she would die. She wished a thunderbolt would come through the ceiling and reduce the girl to dust. He took a few steps towards her, but it wasn't in order to embrace her. She drew herself up to repulse him, but he didn't come that far.

"Look, Betty," he said. "We've got to get over this somehow. I should never have done what I did but I couldn't resist you. You can't imagine how delicious you were."

"That's all right," she said in a very clipped and unexpected way. "I'm not holding it against you, Jack."

"Then can we be friends, Betty? Come on girl."

Her blood was dried to gall. He could see the effect of it in the way her lips thinned and the skin around her eyes was drawn.

"You can be what you like," she said.

"Well, I'd like to be a friend to you and Bethan."

"Me and Bethan?" Her voice rose, but not so very loud. He had never heard such fury in his life as the tone in which she repeated "Me and Bethan!" She pointed at the girl and said, even a third time, "Me and Bethan! Oh Jack. But you misunderstand me. Who am I? Who am I? I was Dan's sister; well and good. Your mistress; better still. But spare me that!" She jerked her head. She all but spat into the air in the direction of that great lump of a girl whose eyes and ears were turned inwards on some other plane of existence which included her father, and excluded all consciousness of what was going on in the kitchen.

The man couldn't take it. He reached for the latch of the door with his hand shaking. "Goodbye Betty," he muttered under his breath. He held in the frame of his eye for one moment the quiet girl in her chair, and that other one standing over her like a wolf. And shepherd though he was, he turned tail and fled.

Chapter Thirty-Two

FROM THAT MOMENT ON, BETTY was determined to get rid of Bethan.

"I'm not going to be able to manage it, Margaret," she said to her friend the very next day in a voice that was quite definite, energised after a night's sleep—of sorts. "It's not my nature. I need a job, before it's too late. A job to make use of my experience and give me something to occupy my mind. I can't – I simply cannot, I'm sorry – spend the rest of my days looking after that girl. Dan's not coming home. I know it."

"Where is Bethan now?" Margaret asked.

"Where do you think?"

And sure enough at the bottom of the garden, there was Bethan, cleaning the nest box very very slowly. When she woke in the mornings these days, she first tiptoed from her bedroom to Dan's old room to see if he had come home. The familiar taste of sadness that she woke with disappeared when she had taken a few steps outside her door in the direction of his. Although she had got out of bed full of apprehension, she then became confused between past and present. The cool lino under her feet, the middle rug, the step, were part of a pattern the next piece of which would be Dan, and breakfast, and birds. Her face lightened. Sadness left her completely. She hurried the last few steps along and opened the door with a smile on her face and said, "Dad?"

Then there was a long silence. She looked at the room, Where was he? Betty had unmade the bed, and left it heaped with folded blankets and an old sheet over the top. It wasn't the right shape to be covering a man. Nothing could compare to the stillness of that room. Even the air in it was empty. It convinced her. Bethan breathed it in like a poison, and by the time she turned away and reclosed the door it had worked its effect on her. She then went downstairs and was sent back up by Betty to dress herself. Very slowly the bewildered day inched across the unfamiliar hours. Bethan went alone down to the loft. And there she stayed.

When Fred came to exercise the birds, he almost always looked in on Betty first. On this day he found the neighbour with her, and her neighbour's husband who was retired, and Margaret. There was an atmosphere of activity in there, like washing day, only it was not clothes that were being processed. Betty, with patches of bright colour on her cheek bones and a glittering eye wielded the teapot and milk jug, cups, saucers, spoons and sugar bowl as if they were weapons.

"I'm going to have to sell the birds," she declared, confronting Fred.

"Well," he said. "Best thing, perhaps. We can't keep it going like this. And they'll be worth something."

Betty said, "I've told Mr Evans that he can come and have a look, and Gareth Swyer, Tom Price. Anyone, really, who's interested."

"You need to call in one of the big breeders," he said. "They'll be interested because of Birthday, and it might be better to send as many birds as possible to one loft." He paused, still standing there in the doorway. "Birthday, of course, is Bethan's bird."

"Well, the money we get can go towards the cost of her keep, then," Betty said tartly, "just as Dan said it should. He said the eggs and chicks should help pay for things while he was gone, and in my opinion that means the bird herself as well."

"What do you mean?"

"I mean exactly what I say," Betty repeated. "Bethan is going to have to go into Care."

He was dumbfounded.

"There's no need to look at me like that. Why should I pour my life down the drain simply because I'm here? Look at me." She certainly did look worn out. "Look at me. I'm forty-eight. You don't realise how miserable and exhausting it is looking after someone like that day after day. I've got to do everything for her now Dan is gone. And it's not as if she can say thank you, or talk back. It just one endless struggle and I do not have to spend my remaining days like this. I can be free. Like anyone else. Bethan can go into a Home, and I can live a more or less normal life. And that's the end of it."

She finished with such a flourish, but nobody contradicted her, even Fred. Indeed, Margaret said that she should do exactly what she wanted for once. She had done her duty. Fred couldn't think of any reason to gainsay Betty except that her brother, should he be able to hear what was being said, would turn in his grave.

He went thoughtfully down the narrow concrete path to the loft. Bethan was down there. She had taken the large shallow tin from its rack against the outside of the shed wall and laid it on the grass, ready for the bird's bath. She had remembered that it was their day. She was filling it with water. In so far as she ever looked happy since Dan died, she looked happy here. When her father had been alive, if she'd seen Fred coming towards her she would have looked up and smiled; maybe even come a step or two towards him. She didn't do that any more. Her mournful acknowledgement was simply to stop what she was doing for a moment and stand completely still. He made himself sound encouraging, although he himself was comprehensively discouraged by the whole thing.

"Hello, Bethan," he said with a smile. "Well, there's a good girl. You've got it all ready for us."

Perhaps he could understand Betty, at least in part. The tragedy of her father's absence sat on Bethan as a weight of dullness which homed in on her, like to like. No one could live happily with that. He himself felt strangely alienated. He never would have thought it when Dan was alive. He went to fetch the garlic and mineral powder that needed to be added to the water. They let the birds out. Birthday came to Bethan's hand before flying up to the pack. It was truly remarkable the way the bird did that. Fred stood, tall and gaunt and unnoticed, watching her. She seemed to be speaking to the bird. She made little noises. The creature preened and brushed, dropping her wings against Bethan's bare arm almost as if she were another pigeon. When Bethan laid a soft finger on her head, Birthday lifted her beak in a gesture that looked almost reciprocal, and blinked the jewel bright little eyes before finally taking wing.

Just for that moment, the child was as she had been when Dan was alive. A thread of illumination seemed to be drawn out of her, attached to the wings of the bird, until so high, and then it snapped.

So Fred would get in touch with a couple of breeding firms through the Fed. Then, of the men in the village who might buy, he personally would like to rule out Evans. He couldn't somehow stomach the idea of putting Bethan through the ordeal of seeing any birds taken by him. It might be better, on reflection, to arrange for them all to go when she herself was absent.

A few days later Betty made this precise point. There was a Home she should visit just to see it, and she would take Bethan with her. She arranged it all. She went backwards and forwards to the surgery consulting Doctor Thomas. The whole thing could be arranged quite soon, and perhaps the actual sale of the birds could wait until Bethan was well and truly out of the way.

For his part, the Doctor had never credited Betty with such resolution. In the past he had been able to bend her to his will. If she was rebellious, he had only to turn his mouth down at the corners, avoid her eye, make a certain expression compounded of sadness and disappointment and there was nothing she wouldn't do or promise to do for Bethan in order to put things right with him. But now, that was all gone. Betty was a different woman. Or at least, not a different woman, but one who was determined to go to her own way. And he was obliged to help her, more or less. He certainly couldn't put any obstacle in her path. As he said to his wife, you can't force one human being to love another, and without love you certainly can't force one relatively strong independent woman to undertake the total care of one so different. But he found himself feeling bitter about Dan Pugh's fate. The War Office had posted a confirmation that he had been killed, which Betty had received now, so there was no hope left. It was what made him ask Olave Richards the next time he stopped by for a chat with him, how his book was coming on. He was familiar with the main drift of the school master's philosophy, but interested to know exactly how he was setting it down. It was that which had him thinking now, with resentment, of the total arbitrary cut-off of death; the way the man was utterly effaced. And thinking of Betty, not for the first time he thought he could trace the corrupting effect of ignorance on those who could only witness, like helpless slaves, the unexplained brutal removal of one of their own kind.

Olave Richards had the novel idea that mankind ought to know the origin of his own arrival

in this world, and the destination and manner of his dying. Far from the self-aggrandising censorship imposed by priests, the real destiny of the human race was to know and understand all things.

"But how will we ever do it?" Servini was accustomed to ask between moves in the game. "How can we ever find out where we were before our birth, or where we will go, on dying?" "Science!" Olave would answer. He quoted Shelley, who believed that science would come to the rescue of the poor ignorant human race, currently condemned to a cruel game of blind man's buff in their manner of living out a life. Dr Thomas liked that idea, but was fond of pointing out its limitations.

"Look!" Olave would say, and he wasn't drawing attention to the fact that Servini had slipped a bishop past his castle and he would catch him out. On the contrary. "Let them just put it on the agenda. The first step towards finding out about something is to at least to put it on the agenda. Not just say, 'that's impossible,' or 'God, whoever he is, doesn't want us to know, and to find out would be disobedient and look what happened to Eve.'" He wore an expression as he said this that just might have reminded Fred of Betty, spitting her furious words across the intervening space between herself and Bethan. Olave certainly thought the traditional concept of God in all the patriarchal religions was degenerate. "Air travel was just as impossible to believe in once."

"Well," the doctor said. The conversation had made him feel somewhat better. At least Olave posited a way forward rather than the everlasting perpetuation of one of the two greatest sources of human misery.

"What. Death you mean?" Servini interjected.

"No. Only the ignorance of what it is."

"And you think if she knew what went on, Betty would behave differently?"

"Perhaps. It's difficult to walk straight when the perspective in front of you is twisted out of line by some devious interference with the horizon. Isn't it now? Even we feel that, never mind Betty." There was a very long silence. Eventually Olave's voice quietly quoting a verse he loved broke the spell. *"Fear no more the heat of the sun/ nor the furious Winter's rages. Thou thy earthly task hast done./Home art gone and ta'en thy wages."*

"Cymbeline."

Poor Dan. The doctor got up and knocked his pipe out against the side of the chimney as Servini had done. He'd only been gone half an hour, but there was no knowing what calls might have come to the house. He couldn't take the risk that someone on his list might be taken ill and have no one to take care of them.

"Wonderful poet, William Shakespeare," he said. "He'd have won the Eisteddfod, you know, if it had been going in those days!" and he walked out into the darkness.

His car was parked against the pavement, the bonnet pointing down hill at an angle of forty-five degrees. The springs gave a little lurch forward as he got in, but the handbrake was strong and he had parked in reverse gear. Handling the key and so forth with habitual delicacy his mind switched to an operation performed the previous day on a child born with a deformed hand. His attention became absorbed in speculations on what progress he would find when he visited the hospital the following day, and what the next step would be. He forgot about Betty.

Chapter Thirty-Three

WHEN EMRYS HEARD OF THE plan to sell the birds there was hell to pay.

"Bethan and I can look after them by ourselves, Miss Pugh. Really we can. You can rely on me absolutely. Is that why you're thinking of selling them?"

He dodged around her in her own kitchen. "Did you think we couldn't, Miss Pugh.?"

"Emrys Owen, I'm not telling you again. Will you please go home to your mother or out in the garden but not in here."

"But Miss Pugh..."

"Out!"

He went and stood on the other side of the open backdoor and shouted in from there.

"We'd give you all the money, Miss Pugh. If we raced well we could earn quite a lot and I wouldn't want to keep any and nor would Bethan. You can have it all."

That made no difference either. She continued to walk smartly from place to place, ignoring him. Her legs, in very pale, very thin stockings, sliced backwards and forwards like lily stalks in water.

"Well if you don't want money," he muttered, fingering his catapult," and you're not bothered about who is going to look after the pigeons, why sell them, you vicious old snake guts?"

For two pins he'd sling a nice shot at her, the old cat. But he didn't know the half of it. Even Betty couldn't bring herself to tell him that she was going to send Bethan away to a Care Home.

He went down at last to the loft. Bethan was there. She looked so nice and peaceful in her jersey and skirt. He liked the way she was so soft looking, and rounded, not sharp and silky like her aunt. Bethan's skin had a very slightly coarse sheen to it; a sort of golden grain. That's how he liked skin.

He shouted out "Hello Bethan," and she turned to face him, almost smiling as he scanned the four points of the compass for cats with a particularly sharp eye. It would have relieved his feelings to have a legitimate excuse for demonstrating just how dangerous it would be for anyone to come marauding here.

"Oh look," he said, pointing at the sky. "That's Jack Isaacs' pack coming right down over the chapel. His best bird, Cwm Streak, was killed by a hawk yesterday. I heard about it after school. What do you think of that. Bethan? He's very fed up I bet. He shot the hawk. I don't know how he was so sure it was the same one." He paused just for a second, to work it out. "Maybe it was still eating Cwm Streak."

Bethan had already let the birds out to exercise. Together she and Em scraped the nesting boxes clean, filled the water hoppers, distributed grain and fresh straw.

When everything was ready he and Bethan would sit on the bench and wait for the birds. He talked without stopping about one thing after another, but he didn't mention Betty's plans for the birds. He talked about school, about geography, about Miss Price and her unfairness. About Olwyn's baby. About Dan.

"Your father was a nice man, Bethan. I miss him a lot. Not

as much as you do, of course. Do you miss him terribly, Bethan? I feel very sorry for you. I think about you at night, when I'm lying down in bed. It's all very quiet and I do wonder how lonely you must be feeling. Are you feeling very lonely, Bethan? Never mind, Bethan. I'll look after you. Don't you take any notice of what anyone else says. She's a sharp one, that Aunt of yours. Miss Pugh. I wouldn't like to offend you, but do you know what? I don't like her. Do you like her? Is she nice to you? I bet she's nasty sometimes. Don't you mind her, Bethan. When I'm grown up, I'll look after you, not her."

But when he went down the hill, his sister Olwyn was home, and he talked to her.

"Do you know what that Miss Pugh is going to do? She's going to sell all Bethan's birds. What do you think of that?"

"Don't talk to me about that one," Olwyn said, snapping shut the door of the fridge. "Do you know what she said to me at the bus stop? I asked her if I'd missed the nine twenty, and she said that I should be careful not to run in my condition; and the Minister's wife heard her. The bitch."

"That's just like her," Em said.

"How does she know, anyway? Look at me." Olwyn stood sideways, so that her brother could get a good view of her figure. The weather was colder than it had been, so she had on a little cardigan that did up with buttons shaped like daisies. It was true that it would only just do up, but that was always the case with Olwyn. And then the same could be said for her lower down. The skirt was a bit tight, but so it always was.

"It will be months before anyone can tell, won't it."

He nodded.

"So there's no need to go putting the story about and making things awkward with the Minister. He can be very spiteful if he suspects anything has happened before the wedding. Look what he said right at the altar, with Maggie

Price."

Em had an idea. He said, "Where are you going to live after the wedding, Olwyn? Are you going to live in town with Alan? Because if you are, can Bethan and I come and live with you?"

She stood there, looking at her little brother. She hoped brain damage wasn't catching.

"No, you can't. And besides, what about the Home?"

"What home?"

"The one your Miss Pugh is going to put Bethan in."

"What?"

Olwyn realised she'd put her foot in it. She said, "Didn't you know? She's going to send her away to a Home, so that she needn't look after her any more."

"Tan Bont?"

"Or the Parks. I don't know."

His face had gone completely white. One of Olwen's friends had had a brother who died of a heart attack at the age of fourteen. She was suddenly frightened that it might happen to Em.

"Come here," she said, springing across the kitchen and taking hold of the collar of his shirt. She thrust him into a chair, ran over to the sink and poured him a glass of water.

"I hate that woman," he sobbed at the same time as she was kneeling on the floor trying to pour water into his mouth. It was sheer chance she didn't succeed in choking him.

"Let me go, Olwyn, I'm going to kill that woman. I'm going up there now with my catapult and first I'll break all her windows and then when she's screaming in the middle of the kitchen floor I'll let loose one of my best flints smack into her mouth, and it will come out the other side covered with blood and her tongue stuck on the sharp end of it."

His mother came in in the middle of all the noise.

"What on earth's going on here?"

Em sprang out of the chair.

"Mam. Can Bethan come and live with us? Please, Mam. Please. Say she can. Oh, Mam, please."

"Be quiet Emrys. What's got into you? Good heavens, what a mess. How did you get so wet?"

"It's my fault," Olwyn said.

"It would be!" her mother came back at her. "So what have you done this time?"

"Well Miss Pugh IS sending Bethan to a Home, isn't she?"

"Where did you hear that? Never mind."

She looked with a mixture of exasperation and tenderness at her youngest son, who had never stopped talking during that brief dialogue between his mother and sister, but whose voice had gone on and on, and broke through again now with practical advice about solving the problems of who could sleep where, "...so as Olwyn won't need her bedroom, Bethan could have it just so long as she can wait until next spring. Then she'll be very useful babysitting, Mam. We both will. And I'll do the milk round for nothing. Honestly. Say yes, Mam. Please."

"You'll have to speak to him!" Mrs Morgan said to Owen when he got back. "He won't listen to me. Just "Please Mam, Please Mam" until he gives me a headache."

"We can't have her living here."

"Of course not. Emrys thinks that Olwen is going to go and live in town with Alan. We'll be lucky! More likely we'll have to have Alan here."

"I'll tell Emrys that," Morgan said. "He's a clever boy, you know. He can understand anything, give him a chance."

And Emrys did understand it. "Don't you worry," he confided to Olwen. "I've got another idea. You know that typewriter Mr Servini lent you when you were doing the accounts? Can I borrow it."

"I suppose so," she said carelessly. "Don't break it, mind."

With the help of the yellow pages and also from the doctor's secretary, he quietly compiled a list of the local Homes for the disabled or mentally disadvantaged. He then very carefully composed the following letter:

"I understand that application has been made to you on behalf of Bethan Pugh. You should be informed that this patient has intervals of extreme violence and can be very difficult to handle." He then signed the letter Dr Clarke—a made-up name signifying nobody that he had ever heard of—and sent it.

This simple ruse was surprisingly effective. Two of the institutions that Betty approached sent back refusals, and the one she made an appointment with in October had every intention of turning her down, but was subtle enough to have an interview first.

Betty prepared Bethan carefully for the big day, and at the same time lined up access to the loft for those interested in looking at the birds with the object of making an offer to buy all or some of them.

Fred handled this side of the operation. He tried to keep Emrys out of the garden. Once Betty and Bethan had departed on the bus, he went up and sat on the bench, waiting, and when Emrys came he said, "Your father wants you to go down and do your homework, Emrys."

"I've already done it, Mr Potts," Emrys replied, giving him look of withering scorn. He was

shocked by such mendacity. "If you want me to stay here instead of you, I can easily show the birds."

"No thank you."

"Why not, Mr Potts."

"Because you would tell them a lot of fibs so that at the end of the day they wouldn't be interested in buying."

"Nobody says I tell fibs, Mr Potts. I'm surprised at you. Especially as you told one a minute ago."

"What do you mean?"

"My father didn't ask you to tell me to go home and do my school work. You made that up."

"How do you know?"

"Because I've already done it for one thing."

"Well, that's different."

"In what way is it different if you tell a fib rather than me Mr Potts. Because you're a grown-up? It's all right for grown-ups to tell fibs?"

"That's enough of that, Emrys. Some people are coming to look at the birds today. That's all. Only look. None of the birds will leave the loft until next week probably. Now get along. You're not wanted here."

"Mr Pugh would have wanted me here."

Silence.

"You were his best friend. I'd have thought you would want to stand up for what he loved and had to leave behind, like his birds and Bethan."

This attack, very much below the belt as it was, angered Fred who stood up and pointed towards the road and said "Are you going to leave here, or am I going to have to thrash you?"

Emrys stood his ground. He said, "You can't throw me out. I'm a buyer."

"Oh, you are are you. And which birds are you going to buy? And with what?"

"My savings. I've got a whole pig full."

"Have you indeed."

"My auntie Pat has been putting the money in for years. She said it was for a rainy day, and I asked her yesterday if this counted as raining and she says it does."

"How much have you got?"

"Three pounds exactly."

"Well –" Fred considered. "I suppose you could have a bird for that."

"Two birds," said Emrys.

"No. One, I said."

"Birthday, then."

"Birthday! Good heavens, boy, you're not getting the prize bird for that sort of money and neither is anyone else." And at that moment he spotted the motor car of one of the town fanciers parking on the road. Three men got out and looked around. Fred called out to them, and they located the gate and started along the garden path.

"Now you keep out of the way," Fred warned Emrys.

The boy turned round and scuffed his way sulkily over to the wall. From where he crouched on a low stone he could watch them all go into the loft, and then come out with various birds in their hands, and go in again. When one of the men came out of the loft for the second time and was just having a few words with Fred, he bent down suddenly with a yell of pain. "Have you got wasps here or something?" he grumbled.

"What is it?" Fred asked. "I don't think so."

The man was rubbing his ankle when he gave another yell, and this time it was his hand that had caught it. A sharp cut was already oozing blood across the nail bed of his middle finger.

"That's not a wasp sting," he was about to say, but Fred had already turned towards the wall and taking a couple of strides in that direction he shouted in a truly terrifying voice, "Emrys. Emrys Morgan. Out of this garden or I'll have the police on you."

Betty returned from the visit to the Home as smug as can be.

"It will do very well," was the verdict she confided to her friends. "Bethan liked it, didn't you Bethan."

If a stranger who didn't know her had been present, it would have looked as if Bethan acquiesced with the idea, since of course she said nothing in reply. Fred came in from the garden.

"So how did it go?" asked Betty with a significant rise of her brows and a jerk of her head in the direction of the loft. "Are we in business?"

Fred glanced at Bethan. He noted again how she gave him no special sign of recognition. When her Dad was alive, she had belonged to Fred as well in a sort of way. But now she seemed almost deliberately to refuse to acknowledge any special relationship, and to be beyond the need of any consideration of her feelings. Even so, the remarks Emrys made had cut him to the quick.

"Wait," Betty said, seeing him hesitate. "She'll go down to the loft now. The birds are all still there aren't they?" And in a louder voice, "Keep your coat on, Bethan. It's getting cold." When the girl was gone, Fred announced he'd got promises for all the birds. There were some going to local men later on in the week, but the town breeder was taking the main lot the following Monday. They'd come with their small van to remove the birds they wanted.

He sat down at the kitchen table and showed Betty the figures. There would be a nice bit out of it. The only snag was that Bethan would have to sign the transfer paper for Birthday which Mr Blake would bring with him. But that should be no problem. She could sign her name.

That night Betty went to sleep feeling as she used to feel as a child before Christmas day—as if the whole world was about to be renewed. She would have a life of her own yet. Probably there was a man out there somewhere waiting for her—not

Jack Isaacs. They might have a bit of money. She might go abroad on holiday. When day dawned once more, her mood was still the same. She was very kind to Bethan. As the child was on her way out to the loft, Betty called after her to say that there would be freshly baked cakes for tea that day, and she was leaving sandwiches on the kitchen table at lunch time, because she was having her hair done at twelve.

Bethan stepped out of the door. A sharp little wind was blowing. On the back mountain crimson rowan berries hung on the trees and the bracken had turned colour. Down here, there were sparse bitter blackberries on the brambles that grew over the wall and in the ditch. She stepped along the path. She still wore sandals that had a solid heel, but with openwork across the top of the foot, and crepe soles. They suited her ponderous but soft tread. She looked about her. The garden was empty and even the street was very quiet. No one seemed to be about. School had started again. The children, including Em, were all up at the other end of the valley.

When she reached the loft she opened the door and went straight in. The birds rustled and murmured, as if in greeting. They stirred their beautiful wings. One or two of the birds hopped down and circled near her feet. Black Rill was beside Birthday in the nest. He shifted as if to make way for Bethan, darting up at her the jewel bright glance of his little eye. His mate, quiet and soft, crooned in her throat when she felt Bethan's soft finger stroking her head; caressing the scattered white markings.

After a long while, Bethan felt in her pocket and took out the envelope Olave Richards had given her. She looked at it carefully in the dim light of the loft. After a long and simple scrutiny of the outside of the envelope she turned it over and carefully tore it open. She let the envelope drop on the ground. Holding the folded sheet of her letter in her hand, she went over to the hinged wire mesh side of the loft and looked at it by the light that was brighter there. She unfolded it. She couldn't read, but she remembered every word, and the letters each word was associated with in this one particular case. She seemed satisfied with it. When she carefully folded it again in the same creases, she looked up at the sky. She seemed to forget to detach her gaze once it was fixed. Her thoughts couldn't make their way out of the thick carapace they inhabited.

After a long while she turned again towards Birthday. Facing the bird, and concentrating with the utmost care, Bethan folded the paper up as her father had taught her to do. There was a rusting tin on a shelf containing rubber rings. She took one, and fitted the letter in it. All the while, Birthday watched her as if she knew what she was doing. The bird's eye was fixed on her, now this side, now that. When Bethan reached down to pick her up, she half stood in the nest to make way for the soft hands to wrap around her body. Bethan held her with one leg tucked between her fingers, and the other left free. Over the folded claws of the free leg she gently eased the ring. The bird murmured and struck out with one wing but was immediately pacified. Eventually, holding the bird in one hand, she opened the door of the loft and stepped out. Three hours had passed. The twelve twenty bus was just setting off for town. She sat down on the bench with Birthday in her hands, and began to talk to the bird. She held her high up so that the little head was quite near her own. Bethan's lips moved in a continuous soft soundless whisper, and the bright eyes, darkened by the lack of direct sunlight before, changed constantly their watchful and alert gaze. No creature ever appeared to listen with more attention. Every now and then, as if some particular phrase was absorbed with more emphasis, Birthday shuffled her body to reinforce the depth of her understanding of what was being said. Whatever language this was, she understood it. She felt the unfamiliar band holding the message around her leg, and her eye seemed to contain already the knowledge of her destination. The inconceivable route would unravel before her, just like the flight from Nantes to Cwm. No discouragement that ordinary people could give tongue to was capable of coming between these wings and the man whose name Bethan's spirit breathed into the soft plumage.

When the time had come, Bethan prepared to release her. It was hard to let her go. She held Birthday for a long time just in front of her mouth. The bird felt her warm breath. After many minutes Bethan lifted her a little higher, and laid her cheek against the full length of her wings. Then she let her go.

At that very moment, Emrys appeared at the bottom of the garden. He saw Bethan open her hands and the bird fly out from between her spread fingers.

"Hello, Bethan," he shouted. "It's half day in school today, so I come straight over."

He had reached her side. "Is that Birthday?" he said. "Why's she on her own?"

Bethan didn't answer. Her eyes were fixed on the bird.

"I suppose she'll come down in a minute," Em said anxiously.

"Where are the other birds, Bethan?"

He turned round. He could dimly see them through the wire mesh. Birthday circled the garden. She flew around. And flew around again. She tipped her wings as she flew over the chapel roof. Bethan watched, her soul on tiptoe to see what Birthday would do. At the same time Emrys, incredulous of the very idea of a pigeon flying away from it's own loft for any great distance and yet gripped with apprehension, watched as Birthday, all alone, flew once more over the head of Bethan and the cherry slide. Then she turned towards the front mountain and, no longer circling, aimed for the furthest gap.

"Where's she going?" he protested, seeing the unusual trajectory of her path through the air. "She is only exercising, isn't she?" he said desperately. But in the next breath he shouted "Birthday! Come back!"

He was astonished to feel Bethan's hand push him hard when he shouted. "But Bethan..." He looked down on her where she was sitting, and saw her expression. She had that look on her face as if a chord of pure light was stretched from the centre of her eye up into the clouds where the solitary bird's wings could still just be seen disappearing over the horizon. "Well," Emrys said, as the bird finally vanished from sight. "That's torn it."

Chapter Thirty-Four

FOR THE REST OF THAT afternoon Em was most unusually silent. That is to say, he talked less. He was thinking. Should he tell Fred about the episode he had witnessed? Should he tell him that he had seen Bethan send the bird up and that the bird had then flown—away? He wouldn't believe it. "Mr Potts wouldn't believe it if I told him," he said out loud to Bethan. "He'd think I was lying if I told him I had seen Birthday fly away like that. He thinks I lie anyway. That's because he lies himself. I'm sorry to say it, but he told me a fib the other day; and then the next thing, of course, is that he feels he can't trust other people. That's always the way. I don't know if you've noticed, Bethan, but people always worry most about other people doing the things to them that they know they themselves would do if they ever got the chance. It's a bit complicated."

They were scraping the nest boxes. The fact that Birthday was not there couldn't be missed. Black Rill dropped down onto the floor, pecked a few seeds, and flew up again, restless. In a few days he would start to lose weight.

"But Mr Potts is bound to notice she's missing. What did you do it for Bethan?" Em was standing with his foot on the discarded envelope. Bethan hung her head. "Well..." He made as if to sweep the floor. And then he saw the paper.

"What's this?" he said. "Heaven? What sort of an address is that? And it's stamped. Mr Richards writing that is. I should know."

He looked suspiciously at Bethan, trying to work it out. Then he got it. And then, putting together the address on the discarded envelope and the phenomenally extraordinary behaviour of the bird that had flown in the opposite direction to that dictated by Nature and instinct, he gave a low whistle. He looked at Bethan with an expression of almost superstitious admiration. "You are very clever really, Bethan," he said. "You have some wonderful ideas."

For the rest of the time while they were dealing with the birds he thought very hard about the best way of coping with the inevitable moment when the disappearance of Birthday was discovered. In some ways it gave him quite a lift to anticipate Fred's dismay and the disappointment of the breeders. Serve them right, he thought. But when it came down to it, how much should he tell Mr Potts of the real story. He'd have to say that Birthday flew away, but he definitely would not tell him anything about the bird's putative destination. He wouldn't understand, and neither would Miss Pugh.

He and Bethan had just completed all the tasks, the birds were back from exercising and the loft door was latched, when Fred appeared rather wearily walking down the garden path. He was tired after his shift. He'd been home and bathed and looked after his own birds, and now here he was with another lot to do.

"We've done everything," Emrys said as soon as he caught sight of him.

"Oh. Good." He stopped short on the path, pushed back his cap and ruffled his hair, which was still damp. "Everything all right then?"

"Well..." Emrys looked up at him, going almost cross eyed with the effort to think of how to put this.

"Well what?"

"You might not think so."

"I might not think everything's all right?"

"No. I don't think you will."

Fred narrowed his eyes and pulled his mouth into a really mean shape.

"Look here, Emrys Morgan, I'm tired. Bob Roberts missed his shift today and I had to stand in for him as well as doing my own. Otherwise the manager might have sacked him, you see. One friend looking after another. But I haven't had much sleep. So here are you, looking after the pigeons. One friend looking after another again, I hope. You are not going to say you've let me down now? What is it? You've broken the scraper again?" He took one huge stride towards the loft door, with his hand out.

"They cost money, you know."

"It's not the scraper, Mr Potts."

He had the door open. He was looking around. "What is it then?"

"Birthday's missing, Mr Potts."

"What!" he said, seeing at once the empty nesting box. "Is this your doing, Emrys Morgan. What have you done with her?"

"Me? Nothing. I didn't do anything. She simply flew away."

"Now I know you're lying, boy!" The infuriated man took hold of the back of Em's collar, slammed the loft door behind him, and marched off down the garden path dragging him along regardless of his legs or any other bit of him. "It's getting cold out here and you can come and give us your explanation in Miss Pugh's kitchen where it will be more convenient for her to boil you alive if you've done anything to that bird."

Once inside the back door he called out, "Betty!" in a tone of voice that brought her running, and at the same time not letting go of Em.

"What's the matter?"

"I'll tell you what's the matter. Birthday is missing from the loft, and I think Emrys Morgan here has taken her."

"He wouldn't," Betty exclaimed. "The breeders won't give us that price for the birds if Birthday is not among them."

"No. They won't. But Birthday will be among them. Won't she Emrys. Now you tell me exactly what you've done with her." After an instant's silence he could see that in all fairness Em couldn't tell him anything when he was in that position, and Fred let go of his collar. The boy disentangled himself. He was furious.

"Look what you've done to my clothes!" he said. "I hope you're willing to explain to my Mam that it's your fault."

"Oh, indeed. And what is your mother going to say when she hears that you've run off with the prize pigeon from Miss Pugh's loft."

It was the first time Emrys had ever heard it described like that and, typically, he allowed himself to be distracted.

"It's not her loft," he said. "Who says it's Miss Pugh's loft? She's never been interested in birds, have you Miss Pugh?"

"Never mind about that. Where's the bird? Where's Birthday."

"I'll tell you," Emrys said, standing his ground and glaring up into the face of the man who had his hand lifted to hit him. Fred stood back grimly and waited.

"I came into the garden just as Bethan released her," Emrys said. "On her own. And she circled twice, and then flew right over the front mountain. She's gone."

The fist that had been withdrawn reappeared, opened out,

and slammed very hard against the side of Em's face, nearly knocking him off his feet. The boy recovered in an instant. He came at the man in a rage, although he was nearly three times his size, and with his school boots working like hammers he launched an attack at his shins and ankles.

"I'll have you," Fred shouted, and got him once more by the neck.

At that point the neighbour, who could usually hear what was going on through the wall, came running in.

"Go across the road and get Owen Morgan," shouted Betty, "or his mother." She meant Emrys' mother.

"You will tell me the truth, Emrys Morgan, or I'll beat it out of you," Fred fulminated, having to hold the writhing boy with the full strength of his arm, and he was the one who was tired out after a double shift and had thought to spend an hour in the Shepherd's and then go straight to bed.

"Look out," Betty said. "He's going a funny colour. Put him on the chair and hold him down." She pushed forward the wooden chair with arms that Dan used to sit in. They'd just got him into it when not only Owen Morgan but the boy's mother came in as well.

"Emrys," Owen thundered. "What have you been up to?" But before Em could answer, his mother saw his face.

"Have you hit him?" she said to Fred Potts. "Have you hit my boy?"

"Yes, he has Mam."

"You be quiet," she said, rounding on him. "Well?"

This wasn't exactly what Fred had anticipated. "Leave it to us," he said. "This is a man's job." "Then what's she doing here?" She pointed at Betty. Considering it was the woman's own kitchen this was a bit rich.

"Be reasonable, Meg," Owen pleaded with her. "Give us a chance to find out what's been going on."

"I know what's been going on. They've hit my boy."

"Yes he did, Mam," Emrys said.

"You be quiet!" Quick as a flash she gave him a stinging flip on the other side of the face. "What are you saying he's done?"

"Birthday has gone missing."

"Well, what's that to do with him?"

"I think he's done it. He's taken the bird. Put her somewhere."

"And what does he say?"

"He says," Fred thundered, as if he was a priest in pulpit addressing everybody; "He says that he saw the bird fly away, all by herself, over the mountain."

"Is that right, Emrys?" Owen's mild and reasonable tone worried his son far more than all the shouting.

"Honestly, Dad," he said. "I saw her. "

"But Emrys; homing pigeons don't do that."

"I know Dad. But honestly it's not my fault if Birthday is a freak bird. I had nothing to do with it. I came into the garden and Bethan just that minute let her go."

"With the other birds."

"No. Alone."

There was a silence.

"Maybe that's it, then," Owen said after a while. "Maybe the bird, being released alone like that, was confused."

"Oh yes?" said Betty. "And that's it then. I'm left trying to settle this whole thing without the prize bird."

"Well I don't see why you're complaining that much," Meg put in. "She's not yours anyway." She had her own opinion of wandering birds, feathered and otherwise. With a daughter like Olwyn she couldn't afford to be too censorious, but she knew where Betty had been this last year wandering about on the mountains and elsewhere.

"If Emrys says he didn't take her, he didn't. He's a truthful boy, whatever else he may be."

"I'll have the police on him," Fred shouted. "You see if I don't. Dan trusted me. Birthday was a very valuable bird."

"Well if he trusted you that much, Fred Potts, what are you doing aiding and abetting Miss Pugh who wants to sell a prizee racing pigeon belonging to Bethan and keep the money herself. Why are you so worried about it, I'd like to know."

And with that, Mrs Morgan grabbed Em's hand and walked out of the door.

Later that night Emrys showed his father the envelope which he had found on the loft floor. Owen was dumbfounded. He showed it to Meg.

"I knew you weren't lying, Em," he said to his son, "but you'll have a hard job convincing the men in this valley that a racing pigeon could be persuaded to fly from her own nest and go to France. Or Germany is it?" He looked at the envelope again."Oh, yes, of course. Heaven." He looked up at the ceiling for emphasis, but then got distracted by a patch of distemper peeling off. "Not again!" he muttered under his breath, getting up from his chair and making for the door. "Megan? Megan..." He was gone.

So the matter of Birthday's disappearance was held in abeyance. It was hard on Emrys because the men of the village decided at first that he was a liar. But his father stood up for him, and showed them the envelope. Olave vouched for it, and admitted that he had penned the letter for Bethan. That letter was certainly missing, so one could assume that Bethan had inserted into the ring before releasing Birthday. What had been in the letter? Olave wouldn't say. Was it to her father (they guessed it was of course), but Olave turned round to the bar and asked Glyn for half a pint. So a girl like Bethan sends a letter via pigeon to her father who has been killed on the continent and is already dead. The village men scratched their heads and said that they would be expected to believe in fairies next. And Fred Potts sent to Birthday's previous owner to make sure she had not gone there, and he also posted a notice with the Fed. The buyers came from town, and very disappointed they were. But they took away some of the birds and other men in the valley bought some. In the end they were all gone.

Bethan watched them go. As long as Mr Evans didn't come into the garden she made no fuss, but neither was she absent. Several of the men slunk past her feeling like thieves when they took their birds. Jack Isaacs bought Black Rill. He didn't even look into the kitchen to say so much as a hello to Betty, but he stopped to talk to Bethan. He found her standing behind the loft, against the blind wall on the other side to the door. "Well, Bethan," he said. "I've bought Black Rill, you see. Do you want to look at him?" He opened the top of the wicker basket a crack. "Now, I'm going to look after him very well, and any time you want to see him, tell Emrys and he can bring you up to have a look. And if Birthday comes back, you can have him again, because she would need him. We can always come to some arrangement. And my girls Megan and Edith will always be pleased to see you, and my wife makes cakes as good as your Aunty Betty." These words of encouragement seemed to wash over her, but she did stretch out her hand and tenderly stroke Black Rill on the head. The bird crooned and settled.

"What will that poor girl do, with no birds to look after?" he said to his wife when he got home. He would have liked to say a thing or two about Betty and what she was doing, but in the circumstances he rightly felt he'd better not.

Chapter Thirty-Five

WITH THE LOFT EMPTY, BETTY was even more anxious to be rid of Bethan but word did not come from the Home. Betty did not know what to make of the delay. It was awkward from every point of view. At one time she had dreaded Bethan's reaction to the loss of all the birds, and dreaded having the child even more on her hands when, the loft being empty, she thought she would no longer go down the garden. What was there for her to do down there? So surely she wouldn't go.

But she was wrong. Bethan's routine remained exactly the same. In the morning after breakfast she went down to the loft and stayed there. The first morning that she stepped out of the back door as usual and went plodding slowly down the path, Betty tip toed after her a second or two later, to take a look. There she was, going towards the empty loft like some sort of ghost. Betty watched to see if she would go in. Or perhaps there would be some terrible reaction to the empty nestboxes. She'd come howling back down the path.

Nothing. Bethan stopped at the door; opened it; went in. After a few minutes she came out again, took up a brush and returned inside. Then nothing.

Aware that her heart was beating fast, Betty returned to the kitchen and closed the door. For a minute she wondered what to do, but then cast all thought of Bethan away. Let the girl be. She would carry on herself as if nothing was amiss, and with luck she would hear from the Home soon.

Bethan spent all day down at the loft. At first to Betty's surprise and relief, this was clearly to remain the pattern of her behaviour. In the morning as soon as she had eaten her breakfast the girl would go softly over to the back door as usual and down the garden path.

If Betty had looked for it, she would have seen that an expression of hope lightened Bethan's face at that hour every day. She would almost hurry to her place where the empty shed stood. She would open the door. The dim shadow was as void of that familiar music—the crooning and rustling of birds, the snap of wings, the scratch of claws on the wooden floor—as the day had been empty when Dan no longer sat down in the kitchen or walked along the garden path with Bethan just behind him, talking about what they were going to do next. Nevertheless she liked it. It still smelled of dust and feathers and that curious touch of spice. And outside, enveloping it, hanging over it and stretching far on every side, somewhere in those enormous spaces of sky, she knew that Birthday even now, was flying. If it rained, Bethan stood in the loft, looking out through the wire mesh at the front mountain. Otherwise she sat on the bench, or stood on the grass. But above all, she kept watch during the hours of daylight with tireless fidelity.

"What on earth's she doing down there?" Betty exclaimed over cups of tea with her many visitors. She was developing her new life already, with her reputation for good baking and ready wit and now time to welcome anyone in for a chat whenever they felt like it.

Occasionally someone would go down the garden to take a look at what the girl was up to. Bethan wouldn't notice them. If she was outside the inquirer could just spy her from half way down the path and return to the kitchen. Or if she was not to be seen, they knew she was inside the loft itself since the time that Margaret had such a fright looking for her and suddenly saw her eyes through the wire mesh.

After nearly three whole weeks a letter came from the Home to say that they were sorry, but they did not have a vacancy. They had thought they would have one, but things turned out differently, and they apologised for keeping Miss Pugh waiting. Betty was dismayed. Time was going on. It would be Christmas at this rate before she resolved the situation. Her friends in the kitchen came up with other names; other Homes nearby. Betty decided to do letters to several at once and dispense with going to see them all. It was such a job to get Bethan into her visiting clothes and onto the bus, and then another bus, and all the time no one to talk to with that silent girl as a companion and the gloomy business of seeing one of those Homes at the end of it. So she sent off three more letters and included copies of Dr Thomas's report on Bethan this time, which described her particular medical condition and case.

Two wrote back with refusals and one made veiled references to certain objections.

"Let her stay," one of the gossips ventured to suggest. "Look, she's no trouble."

But Betty remembered, above all, that last meeting with Jack; the covert glance over towards Bethan which stayed him, when he would have opened his arms to Betty to embrace her, and above all the coupling of her name with Bethan's. She was determined not to go into battle to win a new life for herself with that great lump of a girl hanging on to her.

When Emrys came to the loft these days, which he still did just as often as when there were birds to look after, he sat on the bench with Bethan, or sometimes persuaded her to walk just a little way up the back mountain. She would do this because, as he explained to her, you got a longer view over the front mountain, and therefore the approach of any bird. Because, of course, Bethan was waiting for the return of Birthday and Emrys knew it.

There were times when he longed to be able to talk to other people more about what Bethan was trying to do. It would have been good to have somebody to discuss it with in a rational way; somebody who might listen properly to his account of things. Since Mr Richards had written the message for Bethan, it put the school master in a special category in Em's mind. He wondered if he could risk asking him once again if there had really been a letter in that envelope, and what it had said. Because he hadn't quite had time, himself, to see Birthday's ring, so amazed had he been to see her fly and so taken up with the surprise of it all.

Olave Richards was skilled at being in the place where his pupils would happen to find him alone when they needed someone to talk to. Emrys found him checking the railway distances between Berlin and Frankfurt in preparation for the six o'clock news, and since there was no one else around he took the plunge, and said "Mr Richards."

"Yes Emrys," Olave said, staring at the small print and rubbing his chin.

"Mr Richards."

He looked up. Deep in his eye, as unobtrusive as a glint of metal in the shade, a spark of humour sprung to life.

"I am giving you all my attention, Emrys," he said. "What's the matter?"

"Well, I don't know, Mr Richards," he said. "Perhaps nothing is the matter."

"But if something was the matter?"

"Well, it might be to do with that letter you wrote for

Bethan. The message to her father."

"Oh, you know about that, do you," he said. "Did she post it?"

"In a manner of speaking."

"How do you post something like that?" Olave said.

Emrys gave him a suspicious look. "Are you laughing at me, Mr Richards."

"No, no, Emrys. Just tell me, now. What did she do with the letter."

"Well, you know you can send a message on a pigeon," Emrys said. "There are these rubber rings, and you put it in like that," and he mimicked the movement of putting the finely rolled paper in the ring. "Mr Pugh had them. We all do. And he had shown Bethan how they worked, you see. Well, she threw away the envelope you gave her. I saw it torn up on the floor and I kept the stamp. I hope you don't mind. Bethan said I could have it."

Olave Richards made an appropriate response.

"Well, you see, Bethan could have put the message in the ring on Birthday's leg."

"So I heard some of the men say."

"There was a letter then?"

"Yes. I'm telling you in confidence, Emrys. There was a letter. On a very very small bit of paper which Bethan brought herself to my house."

"Then she could have somehow told Birthday to fly to heaven with it, and then Mr Pugh can send her back an answer. If he's there. But I didn't actually see her do it. I didn't actually see any letter."

"Yes?"

"Well most people would say that's a bit daft."

"Can't fault your logic there, Emrys."

"You don't think she can possibly fly to heaven and come

back do you, Mr Richards."

"Well, I suppose not," the man said.

"Neither do I. But that bird has already done something so unusual that I feel mixed up about it. She flew away, you see, all alone and right off over the front mountain. That's something pigeons never do. I saw Bethan send her up into the sky. They NEVER do that, Mr Richards. I know. I've been in trouble because Mr Potts thinks I did something. He probably thinks I stole Birthday and I'm keeping her hidden. He came and looked in Scram's rabbit hutch yesterday. He said it was to check on her seed, but he was telling a fib. Again. I'm sorry to say this, Mr Richards, but not all grown ups tell the truth."

He paused for a reaction, but wisely, Olave gave him none.

"Anyway, I took my chance to tell him again: I saw Birthday FLY AWAY. And she hasn't come back either. Not for Black Rill or anyone. Mr Potts is in a bad position as far as being able to believe other people is concerned, for reasons which I won't mention because you might think I was being uncomplimentary to a grown up. But the fact is, I'm not telling any fibs. I saw her."

"I see" Olave Richards said. A difference had come into his tone of voice. He had picked up enough knowledge of pigeons to be aware that Emrys was describing an extraordinary event. And one extraordinary event may be the precursor of another. *Un train peut cacher un autre*, as they used to have written up at level crossings in France in his days there with Iris. He had always remembered that foreign tag as somehow containing a philosophical truth. As for Birthday's putative destination: he himself—Olave—he railed, he inveighed, he rampaged on the subject of mortality. He saw no reason to treat the subject with the sort of reverent fatalism which others considered to be respectable. He wasn't against divinity. He used the style of an intellectual clown because the irony of history provoked a kind of malice in him. But when it boiled down to it, he was the gentlest of believers. Jesus would never have had to curb an impulse to scepticism in him. He dreamed of a new age when man would make contact with his own origins, and who knew how it would happen. He favoured some exquisitely elegant scientific realignment himself; but a natural intervention would do. "That really is extraordinary." he said. There was a long silence.

"If she comes back, Mr Richards, where do you think she will have been."

"Well – I don't know. I suppose we must try to be realistic and say that she could fly to France. You could argue she knows the way. And Dan Pugh went missing in France, you see. That sort of thing has happened with dogs. They can find their masters anywhere."

"She's not a dog. She's a bird."

"Well Emrys, let's see what happens. I must go home to Mrs Richards now, and your mother will want you. I'll have tidier homework from you for the rest of this week, please, in return for this conversation."

And with Emrys' acceptance of the bargain, they parted.

Chapter Thirty-Six

IT WAS NOT LONG AFTER this that Miss Pugh at last found out why none of the Homes had accepted Bethan. She found out about the letters that Emrys had sent.

As you would expect in such a serious situation, Dr Thomas was asked to call in and see Miss Pugh, and Betty made sure that Emrys would be with her at the time by the simple device of making cakes for him and Bethan on that day. Emrys didn't notice anything odd about her as she gave him a loaded paper plate to take down to the end of the garden. He was always hungry, and if there was a Grecian glint in Miss Pugh's eye, he missed it.

As promised, just before evening surgery, the doctor came in and Miss Pugh showed him the letter a copy of which had been sent her by one of the Homes. His first reaction was surprise of another sort.

"Extraordinarily well written letter," he said. "Are you sure Emrys wrote this?"

"Yes, Doctor. I had my suspicions and I got hold of that sister of his, and managed to get it out of her. She lent him her typewriter."

"Still..." He turned the paper round in his hand. It was signed illegibly, and then typed underneath the signature, "Dr Clarke"

"There's no Dr Clarke that I know of."

"Of course there isn't," snapped Betty.

The doctor made no comment on her tone. He knew its cause.

"You realise why he's done this, don't you Betty," he said gently, with some return of his old manner. She ignored the appeal in his look as he bent his eyes on her. She wasn't having any.

"I presume," she said, sharp as vinegar, "that he doesn't want Bethan to go and live away from here. Well, that's just too bad, I'm afraid."

"Is it?" he said sadly.

In spite of herself a lump rose in Betty's throat. But she was determined not to give in. "Nobody thinks of me!" she exclaimed, her voice rising. "I know what you said to the Moffats because they put their dog in that cage. Well what about me? I'm not a dog, and I've been in a cage for the last fifteen years. I want to get out. I want to live, doctor."

"Well..." he said sadly.

"Margaret, call Emrys in." Betty told her friend who had been silent all this time, listening with an expression of the most intent and solemn enjoyment. Margaret hurried out and a moment later her voice could be heard calling from one end of the garden to the other, "Emrys. Emrys Morgan. You're wanted."

Whenever anyone said they wanted him, Emrys assumed that the opposite was the case, but at the same time they wished to tell him about it. He half-ran half-dawdled down the garden. He didn't dream that they could have found out about his letters to the Homes.

But when he got to the door and saw the doctor in the kitchen, his heart misgave him.

"Come in here," Betty said grimly. "We want a word with you."

He came a few steps into the room. "What is it, Doctor?" he said.

Dr Thomas rested his elbow on the table and held the sheet of paper loosely in his long thin clean fingers. He liked this boy. He looked at him kindly—the dark straight hair sticking up wildly, the lively eyes, the tough independent little legs in their short trousers, the clothes that always looked as if more ingenuity than normal had been used to put them on.

"I've got a letter here, Emrys," he said. "Did you write it?"

Em's eyes grew rounder with the effort of trying to think of a way out. Playing for time he said, "Can I have a look at it?"

"Yes. Here you are."

He crossed the floor, casting a huge look up at Betty as he passed under her bows. When he got alongside the doctor he looked at the paper and said nothing.

"Did you send this?"

"Yes." He nodded.

"Wrote it too?" The Doctor couldn't keep an expression of humorous approbation out of his voice. The boy nodded.

"Well, I must say it does credit to your school teacher, Emrys. But I'm afraid it's a bit lacking in some other respects." Emrys remained silent, just shifting his eyes and wondering what was coming next.

"Miss Pugh says that Olwen helped you."

"No she didn't. She only lent me her typewriter."

"Oh, you can type as well can you."

"It's easy," Em said, immediately entering into the new subject. "You get it like this, you see, with the lid off. And then you hit two keys at once to get a capital letter, and you have to really think before you hit any other key to make sure it's the correct one."

"I see," he said.

"Well, there you are! He's admitted it," said Betty in

triumph. "You wicked boy."

The Doctor made a gesture of silence to her, and then said, "Miss Pugh's right, Emrys. It was a wicked thing to do. Look what you say here." He picked up the letter and read out a sentence. "She appears docile as a general rule, but has intervals of violence." Now that isn't true is it?"

"No, but..."

"No buts about it, Emrys. It isn't true."

"No."

"You were just making sure that nobody would take her, so that she could remain here at home with her aunt."

"Yes."

"Oh well..." The Doctor stood up. "I want you to know, Emrys, that if you get punished for this you're not being punished for what you wanted to achieve, but for the way you did it. People aren't allowed to forge letters. Come on now. We'll go down the hill and have a word with your parents."

He made for the door, followed by Em casting backward glances at Miss Pugh.

"Shall I see you afterwards, Doctor?" she said, coming along behind.

"Not tonight, Betty. Come to the surgery tomorrow. I'll get my secretary to sort this out. She'll have a word with the various Homes on the 'phone and I'll send confirming letters," he said.

"You'll have your chance again. Once they've heard from me, one of these Homes will find a place all right; if that's what you really want."

And out he went.

Emrys scuttled alongside him. When they had got out of earshot of Miss Pugh he said, "Doctor," and gave a pull to the side of his coat. Dr Thomas stopped politely, and looked down on him.

"Excuse me please, but do we have to go and tell my Mam? I promise I won't do it again."

"I think we'd better," the Doctor said. "You see, if we don't, Miss Pugh will. She's very angry with you, Emrys."

Emrys trudged forward again. "My Mam will beat me," he said.

"You're not afraid of that, are you?"

"I don't like it."

"Well. She loves you. She won't beat you hard," he said. He forgot for the moment that Mrs Morgan could lift a full milk churn off a cart. They got to the house, and the Doctor followed Em into the house where Mrs Morgan was just giving Olwen her tea and Owen was doing his paperwork.

"What's this then, Doctor?" Mrs Morgan said. "Is he all right?"

"Nothing wrong with him that a spell in prison won't put right, I'll be bound," said Olwen, full of cheek.

"What's that, my girl?"

Olwen had an open copy of Woman's Own on the table beside her. There was a photograph of a pretty young girl in her wedding dress on the cover, with a little white fur headband holding down a cloud of tulle on her hair. The banner headline beside it said, in red print, A CHRISTMAS BRIDE.

"Emrys has got something to tell you," said the doctor.

"Will you tell her please, Dr Thomas," Emrys whispered, looking up very anxiously. "You can make it sound better."

His mother started to go red with anxiety.

"What is it?" she said. "You can tell me yourself, Emrys Morgan. Do your own dirty work."

"It's Miss Pugh," he said.

"What's Miss Pugh?" she said, slapping down a dish cloth as if there was some connection. "If you've done anything to annoy Miss Pugh, Emrys, I forgive you."

"It's a little more serious than that I'm afraid," the doctor said. "He's been forging letters." And he explained how Emrys had written a pack of lies to various Homes to stop them taking Bethan.

Mrs Morgan began to cry. She was a dramatic woman. "He's turning into a professional criminal," she said. "What are we going to do?"

"Come on Meg, it's not as bad as that," Owen remonstrated. "He's only twelve."

"I'm nearly thirteen, Dad."

"Quiet!"

Olwyn laughed.

"And that's enough from you," her mother said, and snatched up the Woman's Own. "What were you doing letting him use Mr Servini's typewriter?"

The Doctor turned towards the door. "I'll be off now," he said. "I don't want to be late for surgery."

When he was gone, Owen said, "You can go upstairs, Emrys. I don't think you've done your homework yet. Go and do it."

Em couldn't believe his luck. He said, "Where's my satchel, Mam?"

"On the chair in the front room. Do your work in there." He left.

"Shut the door after you." He shut it.

After a moment's silence, Owen said, "What about him going to stay with your sister?"

"You mean now? What about school?"

"What I'm thinking of is, if we can get him out of the way we can see if there's anything we can do to help. With Bethan, you know. But while he's around having one mad idea after another, he's more likely to end in reform school than anything."

"In what way do you think we can help with Bethan?"

"Well, there's the little room we used when Emrys had chicken pox."

"But I've got my sewing in there, and its only a big cupboard really. And besides, Owen, it's a very serious idea to take her on living with us. She won't ever go, you know."

Owen was silent. Amazingly enough, Olwen didn't say anything either. Eventually her father added, "They never used to send girls like that out of the village. Not in the old days."

"It would be one in the eye for Miss Pugh" Olwen said, and her mother's face brightened noticeably. "And Bethan can be quite useful, Mam. I've seen her doing the loft with Em, and she's really neat and all that. Perhaps she could help in the dairy."

They were silent again.

"We'd have to have Betty Pugh's consent. She's next of kin."

Mrs Morgan bunched her lips together as she gave a necessary stir to a pan she had on the stove. "I know a thing or two about her."

"Are you thinking of blackmailing her, Mam?" Olwen chimed in with glee. "Something's got to be a secret before you can use it to blackmail a person, and everyone – everyone – knows about Betty Pugh and Jack Isaacs."

"SHE doesn't know that. She THINKS it's a secret and that's enough. But won't it seem odd, though, in the eyes of everyone else, if after all this talk of a Home Bethan comes here, only just across the road?"

"I don't know. We can make out that we need help in the dairy and everyone agreed to try her out, Betty Pugh included." Olwen said, "Are you going to tell Em this?"

"Better not."

"I don't know. Perhaps we can hint at something, and then he'll stop trying to think of a solution of his own."

"If you tell him too much he'll go and tell Bethan. And then if we can't arrange it for some reason it'll be worse for the poor girl."

When the discussion had more or less wound its way to a conclusion for the time being and Mrs Morgan had gone out to the pantry to fetch something, Olwen suddenly said, "Do you think he was telling the truth about Birthday, Dad?"

Owen bit his lip and shook his head and looked like a man thoroughly puzzled. He got up and quietly went through to the other room. Emrys was still sitting at the table, up to his elbows in school books.

"Have you been listening at the keyhole just now?" he asked him.

"Yes, Dad."

"Oh!" Mr Morgan raised his eyebrows mildly, and said nothing for a moment. Then, after a pause, "And did you tell me the truth about Birthday?"

Emrys said again, "Yes Dad."

He nodded, accepting the answer. "Get on with your work now."

And he closed the door.

Chapter Thirty-Seven

Wild though she was with Emrys Morgan, Betty Pugh was happy again now that she could anticipate no further problems in finding a home for Bethan. Once the girl was gone she was planning to redecorate the house. First she was going to take the old range out of the kitchen and have a modern stove, and then there were various soft furnishings and paint colours all to be considered. While these plans were under discussion among the band of friends in the kitchen, Bethan continued to live on the very edge of Betty's life, like some object floating on the verge of the water which is never drawn out to sea but comes and goes repeatedly in the shallows.

"Where is she now?" someone would always ask. In the month before Christmas the weather had become so cold that nobody in their right mind would stay out in it for long. But Bethan spent every minute of the livelong day in the pigeon loft or on the bench outside it. Other people who had to be out of doors for some sensible reason would hurry by in the street below, muffled in Winter clothes and their minds on getting back inside in the warm. Some of them would glance up, and see Bethan there. She never stirred from the bench except to stand, or go into the loft. She only went indoors when it got dark.

As the days got yet colder and shorter, even Betty began to

be a little worried about her. What if the girl got ill so that the Home wouldn't take her? Or so that the Welfare got to hear of it and started to make a fuss about her being out all day in such weather? It hardly helped that the girl would sometimes stand inside the loft if it was raining. It was still very cold.

"What on earth is she DOING out there? The birds are all gone aren't they?" someone would ask again, accepting another cup of tea. Betty refused to worry over much. She had the offer of a job in a smart shop in town. She had already accepted. Cross fingers, Bethan would be gone in time.

Another week went by. Betty remonstrated with Emrys Morgan, saying "What can she want to spend all day every day either sitting on a bench or standing in an empty pigeon loft for? Look how cold it is. We haven't had these temperatures in December for five years according to Mr Bryant in the Post Office."

As Bethan could be seen from the road she naturally attracted some attention. There was discussion about it in the pub. One evening when Olave Richards was there, he mentioned the possibility that Bethan was waiting for Birthday to fly back in the expectation that she might bring a message from her father. No one laughed outright, out of respect for a poor half-wit whose plight was sad enough already.

"If that bird did fly back, and if the message that it flew out with had been replaced by another, what would you say then?" Olave Richards persisted.

"What message?" they asked.

He told them.

"Well, I suppose," Owen said, wanting to make something of it to please everyone, "if Birthday did come back with a message – which is impossible now; she's been gone two months – but if she did, well there's your answer."

"Or the bird may have flown to another loft, and that owner

may feed her up and then release her with another message to say what had happened," suggested Glyn. "Yes. You see."

And in the meantime day after day went by, without any change in Bethan's routine.

"Get her in," Margaret advised Betty. "She's been out there far too long now." But it was impossible. Bethan seemed simply not to hear when she was asked to go in, and she was a big girl. She couldn't be physically dragged back into the house.

"Well, I hope nobody thinks it's my fault," Betty would say with challenging tartness.

She had just received the first intimation that the Morgans would have Bethan down there if she was willing. And she had refused point blank. No one else had been told about it, and Dr Thomas had not yet been called on to adjudicate. But the sight of the lonely girl served to soften Meg Morgan's heart towards her, and she had taken on the mission of adopting her with as much feeling as if it had been her own idea in the first place. So one day she walked straight into Betty's kitchen and said, "I'd like a word with you, Betty Pugh."

There was only one other there at that moment beside Miss Pugh: Margaret.

"In private," Mrs Morgan added.

"Oh dear," Betty said with a sarcastic intonation. "That's not very convenient. Margaret and I were just going into town when we've drunk this tea. You can have some if you like."

"Thank you. I'll talk in front of Margaret, then. If you don't mind I don't mind."

She sat down. "About our offer to have Bethan to live with us."

Margaret's eyes grew round with interest. She hadn't known about this.

"It's nothing," Betty said dismissively to her friend. "Now don't you go talking about it Margaret. What would people think of me if my niece was taken in by another family, and one living so close as well. They'd think that there was something wrong with me, and that is not the case."

There was an uncomfortable silence which Mrs Morgan forbore to break, and Betty was so unnerved that her finger slipped on the handle of her cup, and a gob of tea slopped over the side, partly onto the saucer and partly onto the table. "Now look!" she scolded, wiping it up.

"They mightn't think so if it was known that we wanted her help in the dairy," Mrs Morgan said. "I could do with another hand, and I don't at all mind seeing if I can train her. Her father got her to learn all about those pigeons, and that is much more complicated."

"I don't care what you say," Betty snapped at her. "She's not going. They'll train her in the Home to do a proper job. That's my last word."

Meg just looked at her.

"Come on, Margaret," Betty said, getting to her feet. "We'll miss the bus."

"Just a minute."

"No. I haven't got the time just now. Please would you mind going."

"I had something else I wanted to discuss with you."

"Another time."

But Meg Owen came close to her and said, in a whispered voice, as if referring to a matter of deadly embarrassment, "Jack Isaacs. I would like to talk to you, Betty Pugh, about Jack Isaacs."

"Oh!"

Betty's cheeks flamed immediately. She darted a look towards Margaret, who must have been too far away to hear. "Be quiet, you!" she hissed to Meg. And then, "Margaret," she said. "I've just remembered. I promised to take Janet's shoes in for her. Can you fetch them, love? Then I can take just one last look at Bethan and perhaps Mrs Owen can get her in."

Margaret went out knowing very well that something was up. "Now what do you mean?"

"I mean this," said Meg. "I know what you've been up to. You've been making love with Jack Isaacs on the mountain. Don't deny it. My boy has seen you. Not Emrys. His brother. What would the village say about a slut like that who let herself go in the bracken they way you do? What would the Minister say? He won't have you in the Chapel once I've told him what's been going on."

"You wouldn't do that!" said Betty.

"You agree to Bethan coming to live with us, and I'll leave you in peace," she said. "It's one or the other."

Her broken heart stirred inside her, cutting with every breath, bleeding, bleeding. It would have been such a relief to her to confide in another woman. But Meg Owen was damned if she'd put her arm around her.

"Your brother loved Bethan, and she him." she said. "And Bethan loves Birthday. There are all sorts of ways of finding out about love, my girl. If you've cut yourself, it serves you right. But I won't tell on you, if you agree to let Bethan come to us. There you are. You decide."

There was brief silence. Betty had a freshly laundered handkerchief and she blew her nose. There was a bitter silence, and then,

"You can have her," she said. "And good riddance."

"Oh really," Meg came back quick as flash. "No. I think we'd better be on good terms, you and I, Betty Pugh. Much as I dislike lying, I am going to tell everyone that you and I are friends. That I hadn't realised what a very decent sort you were really. And that is the way it had better be."

Betty struggled to absorb the shock, but it wasn't easy. She stood there. She didn't even show Meg out of her own front door. She just heard it closing, and then in came Margaret.

"What did that one want then, Betty," she asked before she'd even got her breath back. She could see that Betty had been crying. "There, there. She's a real cat. I can see she upset you."

"No, Margaret. Funnily enough..."

Betty produced a brave little smile, and dabbed at her eyes again with the hanky. "I didn't know she could be such a nice woman."

"Meg Morgan?" Margaret said in astonishment.

"Well, yes. As a matter of fact. She was very nice to me after you had gone. I don't know why she was so sharp to begin with. Embarrassment, I suppose."

"Embarrassment?"

"Yes, you see. She and Morgan have been thinking of getting help in the dairy, but they can't afford it really. I mean, it's a lot of work there, and Emrys still in school too young to help, and Olwen..."

"Oh yes. That girl."

"Anyway, they want Bethan to go and live with them, and learn the dairy work."

"No!"

"Well, it's not such a bad idea," Betty said.

"It upset you though?"

"Perhaps. I'm not made of stone, Margaret Pitts. You know what it's like – I've been a bit desperate with her since Dan went, but now... when someone like Meg... I think to myself, well... And Meg can be very kind you know. Very persuasive."

Margaret looked at her, and held her peace for about three seconds, and then she said,

"Let her go, Betty. Bethan will be alright down there!"

"We'll see. Don't mention it to anybody yet. But, probably. Oh Margaret, did you remember the Co-op coupons?" And off they went.

Chapter Thirty-Eight

WHEN BETTY LOOKED OUT OF the window the next morning and saw that girl again, going down the garden path in the bitter cold, she didn't quite know what she would say later to the cronies in the kitchen. Her own feelings hurt her as she looked out. Knowing that Bethan was, to all intents and purposes, no longer her unique problem, she felt a twinge of loss. She would have liked to be loved by Bethan. Right now, when the mystery of the girl's strange mission, watching always down there by the loft, was about to be snatched away into someone else's confidence she felt, for the first time, a real twist of sympathetic curiosity. The bitter poetry of shared unrequited love stirred her. What if...?

When the others arrived, Margaret was sworn to silence on the subject of Bethan and Meg Morgan and sat there with her lip buttoned, like a cat that's had its teeth out. A few people in the village had started to make embarrassing offers about Bethan standing there all day in the cold. On the morning after the 'agreement' with Mrs Morgan, Betty now saw Fred Potts walk into the garden with a kerosene stove, and put it down not inside the loft, but outside, where it warmed Bethan a little. He crouched to light it, and then came into the kitchen. Everyone talked about it. Betty blushed. Had Meg Morgan said something, she wondered.

Sally from Globe Row said, "You know what! She's waiting for something."

It was all Betty could do not to snap at her.

"Have another biscuit," she said.

"For her Dad to come back do you think?" said Mair.

"Love her! It's sad. She'll be better off when she is in The Parks. Is that the Home you've chosen, Betty?"

But this awareness of another world going on out there—some quite different dimension that seemed to envelop the freezing loft, the parched grass and the lonely girl who never ever complained and never seemed to feel the cold—was almost ghostly. You would be afraid to set foot beyond a certain place on the path perhaps, knowing she was there.

When Betty was safely out of the way for five minutes getting something from the pantry Margaret told her mother that it wasn't natural. She was staring out of the window to where the heavy mist that was rolling down the valley between the two mountains blurred the shape of Bethan standing in her winter coat. And she was right. Had she for a moment seriously considered it, and opened the side door and stepped out, putting one bare hand in the pocket of her apron, and wishing she had her coat on, and then noticing that the air was damp, and that the 11.15 bus was just barging down the hill breaking the silence of an otherwise so still morning, she might have got so far down the path, but no further. She wouldn't have dared.

But in a couple of day's time Betty would start talking to others about a future which excluded the Parks and instated the Morgan's house in its place.

Meanwhile nothing interrupted the placid, silent routine of Bethan. The girl would come indoors because she was hungry, or because it was dark, but the loft and the garden was where she wanted to be, and if anyone suggested otherwise she seemed not to hear them. She only maintained her placid and extraordinary vigil.

"They'll have to stop her waiting for her father like that in the end," one of the miners said to the man beside him as they tramped home after the morning shift. But it wasn't Dan that Bethan was waiting for. It was Birthday. She neither knew nor cared about the schemes of Betty and her friends or, indeed, the weather. Those who bargained over her disposal, whether out of kindness or spite, existed outside the confines of her world, which had shrunk to the moment when Birthday would appear flying back home, with a message from Dan on her leg. She was simply waiting for Birthday to come back.

As she watched the sky for hours on end, if anyone got close enough to see her face they would have said that she looked almost contented. Beyond an uncomfortable awareness of her withdrawal from himself, Fred noticed nothing when he called in occasionally. He was unnerved by her still being in her old places, but somebody as quiet as Bethan could get quieter without attracting attention.

"Why don't you go indoors, Bethan?" he would say just one more time. "It's nice and warm in the kitchen. Your Dad wouldn't want you catching cold."

But she wouldn't stir. He would go. He would look back at her, and never dream of the excitement of anticipation that kept her warm.

A couple of weeks after his mother's visit to Betty Pugh in her kitchen, Emrys came as usual after school. He had a careworn look. He had not been told about the arrangements for Bethan's future, and he was worried stiff. She would be sent to a Home any day now, and he wasn't sure what he would do about it.

He came into the garden by climbing over the wall between

the Pugh's place and the Chapel. He had no wish to go even as near to Miss Pugh as skirting round her kitchen door. He sat down on the bench beside Bethan.

"Duw, it's cold!" he said, "Look at my knees." Bethan looked at them. For a while. They were mottled blue and white.

"I've had a dreadful time lately," he said. "I told you they were talking about sending me to stay with my Auntie in Shropshire. In some ways I wouldn't have minded too much for myself, because she's got horses." He paused for a split second. "You know what horses are don't you Bethan. They have them up on Price's. When she was having her baby, Mr Price came down at three o'clock in the morning to get Dr Thomas. He brought a spare pony. Did you ever hear about this? The doctor drove his car to the end of the village, and then he got on the pony to go up the mountain. You couldn't see he was wearing his pyjamas, because he'd put his coat on over them. But when he got to the top of the mountain and the baby wouldn't come out, he had to take his coat off and they were all laughing apparently, including Mrs Price." He stopped for a minute, looked at Bethan, and then followed the line of her eye which was fixed on that very point over the front mountain.

"Do you really think Birthday will come back, Bethan? Mind you, I'm sure she will. But homing pigeons always do their flying FROM the point at which the message is attached to their leg, you see, and then they fly HOME with it. They're not really meant to do it the other way round." He kicked the bench for a few seconds with his boots, and then said, "Well – just look! It's snowing now. Come on, Bethan, we'd better go in. It will be dark in less than an hour. It's started getting dark already."

He got up and stood in front of her. She wouldn't move, but she did look up at him. There was something extremely nice in her face. Her lips were almost smiling. You could swear that she was very nearly happy again.

"Well, honestly, Bethan," he said, sitting down again, "I'm freezing. And I'm hungry. Olwen promised us a bag of toffees but she forgot. She doesn't think of anything else except weddings and babies these days. Mr Servini must have an awful time with her working in the shop." He pulled the cloth of his jacket round his chest with a screwing action and then rammed his hands in the pockets. He looked at Bethan again, and then followed the line of her eye staring up over the front mountain. She sat so quietly. He fidgeted, and looked more restlessly at the same empty wastes of sky. Not a single bird was out.

Because Christmas was approaching, they had started practising carols in the chapel. As Emrys and Bethan still sat there, the sound of voices squeezed through the gaps in the windows or the roof tiles like tiny mice of sound that ran squeaking in the cold grass around their feet. Naturally there were no birds flying. None at all. There wouldn't be. Any racing pigeons being exercised had gone back to their lofts hours ago, and there were no wild birds flying high at this time of year.

"Mind you," Emrys said, as if carrying on with a subject he had already broached, "I don't believe they know what they're talking about when they say we'll never be able to get messages from heaven. I told Mr Richards, look, three hundred years ago who would have believed that we would invent electricity?"

The scattering of snow that had been floating down began to thicken. Em didn't even mention it. "And he said, 'When you're grown up, Emrys, don't you go remembering me and causing a disturbance even there, just when I'm having a bit of peace.' But he gave me that book I told you about. I decided I'd read it after all, and..."

He stopped suddenly. There was a faint dark spot in the sky just where the left flank of the front mountain dipped. He felt his heart jump. He was sure it was the mark of wings. With her hands in her lap Bethan hadn't moved, but he could see her eyes were fixed on the same spot.

"Don't get too excited, Bethan," he said. "It is bound to be another bird." Although what bird would be daft enough to be flying over the front mountain on an evening like this? The bus from the top arrived and one of the Miss Isaacs got out. She saw the two figures sitting on the bench and she called up but she couldn't make them hear her. She was able to tell everybody about it afterwards.

A vicious little wind blew up. Emrys didn't even feel it, but it razored the air, making everything raw, and it would blow shards of ice against the labouring wing feathers. It would unleash the night that was only held back by a thread. The distant tiny bird grew very slowly.

It came closer and closer. Betty came to the kitchen door and called "Bethan! Emrys Morgan!" but to no avail and she wasn't going to go out in that. And meanwhile, through the sleet and rapidly greying sky, those wings high up over the front mountain continued laboriously toward the two figures staring at them from the bench. Bethan stood up without a sound. Emrys wanted to shout or whisper or something. Yes or No. He felt as if everything was suddenly in bits, like the fragments inside a kaleidoscope. Because he couldn't believe it was Birthday coming home.

Fred Potts, who had been on his way to have a pint in the Shepherd's Arms, was just crossing Coronation Street when he looked toward the mountain to see if the sleet was coming down any faster. He took no notice of anything else. But Dan Crow, who was up from Ponty shouted out something, so he looked up again. He saw a bird. He saw a racing pigeon. Damn silly to put a bird up today. What fool would... And then he nearly tripped on the pavement, got one boot in the gutter, swore, started to run.

When eventually the bird was within a few hundred yards, Fred Potts recognised Birthday by her wing stroke. Up by the loft in Dan's garden, Emrys stood, incredulous and even silent; with his lips clenched together and his eyes staring and his heart banging. Bethan had risen from the bench, and out of her pocket she took the cherry slide. With hands that didn't even tremble she put it in her hair. She held her lower lip softly in her teeth as she had been wont to do sometimes when concentrating on exactly what her father said. When Birthday was over the garden, the rhythm of her flight could be seen to be utterly exhausted. She collapsed on the cherry slide, her claws slipping, her weight uneven. Bethan reached up and took Birthday in her hands. She drew her down and held the beloved bird against the front of her warm coat, feeling the panting heart inside her fingers.

The bird was spent and thin. Her feathers were ragged. Her flights stacked against each other without their proper symmetry. Emrys walked beside her as Bethan took Birthday into the loft. For once in his life all the things he wanted to say were stuck in his throat. He'd already seen that there was a paper in the ring on the bird's leg. But would it be the same one as the letter she went out with? Or was it a different message, sent from some place that no human eye had ever seen; that fortress of eternity from which at last, after thousands of years of trying, one small beleaguered human being had won an answer?

Bethan had fresh food and water and straw ready in the loft. She put it out every day. As she tended to Birthday, the spent bird seemed not to notice the absence of her mate, or all the empty nest boxes. She allowed herself to be set down in the nest and fed from Bethan's hand. After a few minutes, Bethan gently took the left leg in her fingers, and slid off the rubber ring. With her eyes shining and an expression of blissful peace on her face, she unrolled the paper.

"What does it say, Bethan?" Emrys whispered. "Can I see?" He wasn't tall enough to look over her shoulder. "Hold it lower. I'll read it to you." He had to climb on the empty grain box. And then he could see that it was written in Mr Pugh's handwriting. He would have recognised it anywhere. It said "Dear Bethan, Sorry not to come home but I will wait for you here. Love from Dad."

"Dear Bethan," Emrys read out loud, his voice honed by something not unlike sheer fright so that it sounded scorched. "Sorry not to come home, but I will wait for you here. Love from Dad."

"Read it again, will you?" said Fred Potts. Emrys started at the sound of the voice and nearly fell off the grain box. He saw now the large shadow of that man crammed against the open door in the almost darkness. "Emrys Morgan" Betty was shouting sharply as she made her way down the path without a torch. She had put her coat on and here she was, because no matter what, those two had got to come in now, even if it meant ruining her new hair-do and probably catching a bad cold. "Emrys Morgan and Bethan. I am not telling you again!"

Fred Potts had that little scrap of paper in his hand when she got to the loft at last.

"What are you doing here?" she said. And transferring her attention, "Emrys Morgan, have you no sense at all? You'll come in now, and bring Bethan with you. Come on now. Don't just stand there."

Fred tried to show her the paper.

"What is it? How can I see that in the dark? I didn't bring the torch did I. What is wrong with the three of you. Come. Now!"

She was off. Fred and Emrys stumbled after her. They were half way down the path before Emrys remembered Bethan and went back to the loft.

"I'll make you some hot chocolate," said Betty when she got back to the kitchen. "You can sit down." And turning herself, to realise that Emrys and Bethan were still missing, "Well! They'll be the death of me."

Fred was just standing there holding out the paper. The expression on his face, rather than his silence, at last stopped Betty in her tracks. She put down the kettle as if it was an unexploded bomb. "What is it?" she said.

He tried to answer, but couldn't. Feeling her blood drying in her veins in the instant, Betty took a step forward. Was it to do with Jack Isaacs? It couldn't. But she hadn't seen inside the loft properly. Bethan! Bethan was dead! But why the paper? "What is it, Fred?" she asked again, coming up to him and taking what he was holding out. He tightened his grip on the other side of the paper and wouldn't let her have it.

"Birthday is back" he said.

"Birthday?"

She couldn't take it in.

"Birthday is back. And she had this message in the rubber on her leg, Betty. I saw Bethan take it off. Look."

He let go of the edge of the paper and she took it. For a moment she seemed not to know what was written there. And then she fainted.

I forget the rest. I tell a lot of people this story when they come by. I'm Olave Richards, you see. You didn't think I was talking about myself when I described how I wrote the letter for Bethan, did you? Betty's kitchen looked like the last scene in Hamlet by the time I got there on the evening when Birthday flew home.

But look how late it is now! You asked me where the chapel was. You were going to the wedding. And I was pointing it out to you, because it's just beside the Pugh's garden, you see. That's what I was showing you in the beginning. If you follow along with your eye to where I was pointing on the left, you can see it just after the dry stone wall that marks the end of the garden. In fact the chapel roof comes down onto the side there, because of the lie of the land. That's why you couldn't make it out. Did you hear them singing while we were talking here? They sing very loud, but I'm afraid I've made you miss the wedding. Once I start on the story of that bird and what she did, I can't stop myself. But wait; don't go before you've looked at the letter. I have it here. I always keep it by me. It's lucky the street lamp has just gone on. You can read it for yourself. Do you see it? Now if a pigeon flies for those two months, that's roughly 61 days, times 12 hours, times 30 miles an hour – all very rough averages, I'm no racing man, nor mathematician either for that matter – I think I made it come to thirty-six thousand three hundred and thirty miles. That's too far for a pigeon and not far enough for Heaven; or death; or God. And yet, that letter, I can tell you for a fact, was written by Dan Pugh, who was already dead at the time. Birthday flew back with the original letter missing, and that one in its place. The girl Bethan took it off. Fred Potts saw her do it, with his own eyes. And it was in Dan Pugh's own hand. They were at school together when they were boys, you see. He knew his writing. And that's not counting Emrys Morgan, who knew it just as well. I'm telling you, that bird, flew to a place where no living creature has ever been before without having to stay there. And she flew back carrying a written message from a dead man.

Do you think God, up there, looked over the side of His ship as He sailed it over Heaven and had pity at last on the mortal grubs He saw swarming down below? Do you think perhaps one day it will be Him standing here instead of me, and He'll tell us all what really happened?

Go on then.